* water dam~~age~~
ash/mrr

⌦ **W9-AFG-014**

S

LEMONADE MOUTH

PUCKERS UP

ALSO BY MARK PETER HUGHES

I Am the Wallpaper
Lemonade Mouth
A Crack in the Sky

LEMONADE MOUTH

PUCKERS UP

MARK PETER HUGHES

DELACORTE PRESS

Text copyright © 2012 by Mark Peter Hughes
Jacket art copyright © 2012 by Ericka O'Rourke

All rights reserved. Published in the United States by Delacorte Press,
an imprint of Random House Children's Books, a division of
Random House, Inc., New York.

Delacorte Press is a registered trademark and the colophon is a trademark of
Random House, Inc.

Visit us on the Web! randomhouse.com/kids

Educators and librarians, for a variety of teaching tools,
visit us at RHTeachersLibrarians.com

ISBN 978-0-385-73712-8 (hc) — ISBN 978-0-385-90647-0 (lib. bdg.)
ISBN 978-0-307-97439-6 (ebook)

The text of this book is set in 11-point Galliard.
Book design by Trish Parcell

Printed in the United States of America
10 9 8 7 6 5 4 3 2 1

First Edition

Random House Children's Books
supports the First Amendment and celebrates the right to read.

For my sisters, Carolyn and Jennifer, with love

PROLOGUE

Most Esteemed Pursuers of the Great and Wondrous,
You hold in your eager hands the second volume in the
bewildering history of the late great Lemonade Mouth.

As anyone not living under a rock can attest, much has
been said and written about the fab five and their
extraordinary rise from high school nothingness. But so much
mystery surrounds the band that a lot of what has been
reported as fact is actually based on mere rumor and
guesswork. Let me tell you, it doesn't even brush the surface of
the truth. What really took place was even more astonishing
than the rumors.

I should know. I was there.

I witnessed a lot of this stuff firsthand.

Due in part to my role as senior music editor for our school
newspaper, the Barking Clam, but mostly because of my close
friendship with the band, I remain the only reporter with
exclusive permission to tell the whole sordid tale—sour notes

and all. As in the previous go-round, getting the full details of this next part of the story from each of the band members was no walk in the park. I'm still bleary-eyed from working through the stack of photocopied letters Olivia gave me, squinting at her faint handwriting to try to decipher what she said. Wen, on the other hand, agreed to be interviewed, but despite what everyone thinks, he can be as chatty as a brick wall sometimes, especially when he's hungry. I had to keep feeding him brownies to get him to open up. Charlie was perhaps the most frustrating of all. After making me wait ages for him to complete his English Comp paper so I could include it in the previous volume, this time he got the idea of continuing his own written account. It seems he took out a library book on screenwriting and it inspired him "to get creative with the written form." When he told me this, I knew it would mean only one thing: more grammar errors.

Sigh.

But take heart, Dear Reader, because the result was worth all the trouble. Let me set the stage for where this second act of our story picks up:

With their freshman year at Opequonsett High School behind them, our five misunderstood revolutionaries—Wen, Olivia, Charlie, Stella and Mo—were starting out their summer vacation still reeling from all the local media attention they'd received after their appearance at the Catch A RI-Zing Star competition and the return of the Mel's Organic Frozen Lemonade machine to their school. A short video clip from the event became an online sensation, and for a week or two afterward they started to receive messages from all over the country in support of their crusade for the unheard.

As each of them settled into their summer activities, none had any idea that their strange rocket ride into history was just beginning.

Naomi Fishmeier
*Scene Queen & Official Biographer
of Lemonade Mouth*

*A brief note about Charlie's contributions: In the interest of authenticity I previously let Charlie's many punctuation and grammatical mistakes slide (the boy is about as careful a grammarian as a sea slug) but, Dear Reader, I confess I could stand it no longer. This time around I have liberally applied my editor's correcting pen to help the boy along. You're welcome.

CHAPTER 1

When opportunity knocks, grab it by the shirt,
. pull it the heck into the house,
and offer it something to eat.
Come on, guys! This ain't brain surgery!
–Sista Slash

OLIVIA
A Pebble Tossed into Still Water

Dear Naomi,

Looking back, I can honestly say that I felt the trouble coming before it even arrived. As you know, I sometimes get feelings about these things, and I guess a part of me realized that summer vacation was starting off too well.

Things were far too good to stay that way.

I'd just finished my chaotic freshman year at Opequonsett High School and was looking forward to two quiet, predictable months of reading in my backyard, gathering shells on the beach and relaxing with my grandmother and our thirteen cats. My only real responsibility was to help out with my grandmother's mail-order printing and graphics business, which she runs from our house, but I knew that would actually be kind of fun.

Most of all, I was looking forward to hanging out with my Lemonade Mouth friends.

For a couple of weeks the five of us had been meeting in Lyle Dwarkin's garage, trying to record some new songs Wen and I had written. Lyle is so good with that techie stuff, and his mother makes amazing orange meringue tarts. But you remember all this as well as I do, Naomi, because you were there too, hanging out with us and helping Lyle arrange the microphones and all the other gear. Remember how long it took to set up Wen's trumpet mike that first session? How Lyle kept switching the angle and trying out different effects on his laptop until it sounded just right? Stella didn't say a word, but it was obvious she was about to burst with impatience, because as she gripped the neck of her new ukulele, her jaw was clenched and her face was turning red. Mo and Charlie nearly fell over themselves trying not to laugh.

But Lyle is a perfectionist. That's part of the

reason why those recordings turned out the way they did. Even Stella finally admits it now.

I now recognize those were special days, a brief period of happy calm like the still surface of a pond just before someone throws a pebble into the water. In a way, it was my own fault that everything changed. Stella and the others had been trying to get me to agree to perform live again, but even though I'd tried to overcome my fears, the idea of singing in front of a crowd of strangers made me so anxious that I often threw up before going onstage.

If I hadn't relented, maybe everything would have turned out differently. If I'd said no and Lemonade Mouth hadn't shown up to perform an hour-long outdoor set at the Seventeenth Annual Rhode Island Chowder Fest in Cranston, my tranquil summer plans might have remained undisturbed.

But of course, that's not what happened.

As everyone knows, it was at the Chowder Fest, immediately after we played our set, that our lives were forever altered.

It was a beautiful afternoon on a June Sunday. A pretty big crowd showed up to hear us, and I remember my lunch rising at the sight of so many people. But after a discreet visit to the bathroom my stomach calmed a little, and it ended up being an especially fun show. We opened with "Monster

Maker," and right away the audience was getting into it, jumping around, dancing and singing along. During the chorus of "Bring It Back!" I was amazed at how many people joined in.

I want lemonade in my cup!
Hmmmm, hmmmm
Hold it high! Raise it up!
Hmmmm, hmmmm.

The song had kind of become the unofficial anthem of our lemonade machine rebellion at school that year, and that day I watched as an entire field full of people, most of them total strangers, saluted us by raising lemonade cups, some real and some imaginary, into the air. For our fans this had become the sign of unity and revolution. I couldn't help feeling a swell of pride. After that I was having such a good time that by our third or fourth song I forgot to be nervous. But I also remember noticing a blond lady in a bright pink business suit near the back of the crowd. She stood out because of her clothing and because she was just standing there, watching us. Every now and then she seemed to scribble something on a pad of paper as if she was taking notes.

With so much chaos going on around her, it seemed weird.

When our set ended, the five of us started breaking down our equipment. As I often did, I went over to help Charlie with his drums. He uses so many of them—a giant wall of congas and timbales and cymbals and other percussion instruments I can't even name—that it always took a while to pack it all up. Anyway, as I was helping him I noticed the pink-suited lady walk up to the edge of the stage.

"Nice show," she said to us. "The crowd really liked you."

"Thanks," Mo answered, lowering her double bass into its big gray case. We were trying to move fast since there was another act scheduled to play after us.

"No, I mean I'm truly impressed," the woman said. "Your music is wild and different, and it's not often I see a band inspire this much devotion from its fan base. They know all the words, and they follow your every move. Do you always draw such a big crowd? And do you always get fans who show up in costumes?"

I looked out at the field again. The place really was packed, and a bunch of people had shown up in funny outfits—zombies, houseplants, cats, toilets and other crazy things. I remember a bunch of burly guys dressed as rubber duckies, and one couple that looked like a cookie and a giant glass of milk.

Mo shrugged. "Yes, usually," she said, still struggling with her case. "Our first real performance was at a Halloween dance. After that it sort of became a tradition at our shows. It's just fun."

"It's impressive," the woman said again. "The vibe from your audience makes your performance feel like more than just a local show. What I just saw felt bigger—much bigger." She reached into her blazer and pulled out a business card. "My name is Jennifer Sweet. I work for Earl Decker at the Decker and Smythe talent agency. Mr. Decker is interested in Lemonade Mouth."

"Decker and Smythe?" Stella asked. Until then she didn't seem to be paying much attention to Mo's conversation, but she now moved nearer and looked over Mo's shoulder at the card. She stared at it. Wen, Charlie and I stepped closer too. I have to admit, at the time I didn't understand the significance of what was going on. I'd heard of Decker and Smythe, of course, but I didn't really know much about it.

Stella must have noticed my confused expression. "Don't you get it?" she asked. "You've got to be kidding me, Olivia. Decker and Smythe? It's only one of the most important talent agencies in the history of the music industry. They've represented some of the biggest, most successful bands ever. Devon and the Hellraisers? Monica Maybe? The

Deadbeat Fingerwaggers? Exhibit A? The Church Ladies? You've heard of them, right?"

I nodded. These were all rock-and-roll giants.

"Well, there you go. Earl Decker was there when it all began. He's like . . . well, he's a legend."

The woman nodded, but her serious expression didn't change.

"Mr. Decker saw the video clip of what happened at Catch A RI-Zing Star and he sent me down to check you out in person. You guys are on to something here. If you're interested in seeing how far you can take this, call the number on that card. We'd like to set up a time to talk." Before any of us had a chance to respond, Ms. Sweet had already left the edge of the stage and was disappearing through the crowd, hurrying toward the parking lot as if she was late for another appointment.

The five of us were left standing there staring at the little white card. It was only a piece of paper, and yet, like a pebble tossed into a pond, its effect was about to send ripples across our universe. We didn't know it yet, but things were not about to go in a direction anybody expected. Certainly not us, and not Decker and Smythe either.

Lemonade Mouth had just begun a bumpy journey to a place none of us could have predicted.

STELLA
The Most Important Phone Call Ever

My friends, the good news couldn't have come at a better time for your own Sista Stella. Up until the moment Decker and Smythe dropped out of the sky and into our lives, my summer started off looking drearier and more frustrating by the day.

There were two major reasons for this.

First, despite the brief period of commotion and media attention that our recent Catch A RI-Zing Star appearance had brought to my little band of misfits and our lemonade machine cause, very little of that attention had focused on our *music*. As a musician with lofty aspirations, this was burning me up. Mrs. Reznik, our septuagenarian music teacher and Lemonade Mouth's spiritual mentor, often said, "The music is everything. It's what matters above all else."

So of course I was frustrated.

The second reason was this: My summer, young as it was, had recently been hijacked. Against my wishes, my mother had volunteered me to spend my weekday mornings filling in as a receptionist at her biochemical research laboratory. True, I was getting paid, which meant I had a chance of going to the Take Charge Festival in August. Take Charge was a giant daylong concert event in Vermont, with a dozen big-name bands promoting worldwide youth activism. It was organized and headlined by the one and only Sista Slash, my guitar-slinging activist hero, so even though tickets were expensive, I really wanted to go.

Still, being the receptionist for a small research laboratory had to be the dullest job in the world.

Picture, if you will, your musical maverick sista, her

formerly green cropped hair now an inferno of glorious pink (a fresh color for a fresh summer), sitting at a metal desk surrounded by filing cabinets and cardboard boxes. Imagine your misused heroine parked on a chair from eight to noon, Monday through Friday, in a dark-paneled space where the phone hardly ever rings, with little to do except twiddle her thumbs, surf the Internet and occasionally write her name on an electronic pad when the package delivery guy needed a signature.

"Oh, don't exaggerate, Stella," my clueless mother said at the time, dismissing my complaints with a wave of her hand. "It's not *that* bad!"

But how would she have known?

As I suffered in bored silence, she and her team of bio-chemical trailblazers were twenty feet away doing the geeky mad-scientist things they loved most, which at the time meant searching for a way to make cheap, biodegradable plastic from vegetable cells. While my mother and her genius buddies were busy trying to create a planet-saving Franken-stein plant, I was wasting my life away. The one thing I had to look forward to was recording music with my friends. I was forever counting the hours and minutes until the next time Lemonade Mouth got together again.

As you can imagine, the surprising news that the Decker and Smythe Talent Agency, that music-industry colossus, that promoter of rock-and-roll superstars too numerous to count, wanted to talk with *us*—well, it came like an unex-pected beacon of hope in a dark sea of tedium and despair.

I remember the next morning, my palms sweating as I gripped the little business card. Out of the five of us, I'd been chosen to make the call. Looking up from the tele-phone number, I could see Beverly DeVito, one of the lab assistants, on the other side of the glass window that looked into the main lab. Plump and twentyish with short brown bangs and glasses, she was hunched over a microscope. She must have sensed me watching because she looked up, but my mind was so occupied that it took me a moment to realize she was waving at me through the glass. Finally I waved back, embarrassed that I'd been caught staring. She didn't make a big deal of it. She just smiled and went right back to her work.

I liked Beverly. She was all right.

The thing was, I was in a tizzy. It was 8:45 a.m., too early to contact Decker and Smythe. It was too early for *any* sane person to have to be up and about, especially since it was supposed to be summer vacation. It weighed on me that this might be the most important phone call I would ever make in my entire life. First impressions mattered. Call too early and Lemonade Mouth might seem overeager. Leave it too late and the agency might get the idea that we weren't serious about the band's future.

Needless to say, I'd been thinking about this all night.

The best approach, I'd decided, was to wait until later in the morning—ten o'clock or so—and then ask to speak directly to Earl Decker himself. The goal was to project confidence. I'd been imagining the conversation over and over again: *Hey, Earl,* I would say (I'd agonized about what to call him, but in the end the informal approach seemed best), *you guys said you wanted to talk, so let's talk.*

But first I would force myself to wait.

To kill time I grabbed the stack of fashion magazines Beverly had left on the coffee table for visitors—as if anybody other than me ever sat in that room long enough to look at them. I flipped through each magazine one at a time, page after page of rail-thin models in tight dresses. They looked starved, every one of them, and it occurred to me that someone ought to make a thick, healthy stew to feed these poor women.

At last it was 10:02 and I couldn't stand to wait a moment longer. I dialed the number. In my mind I pictured the office somewhere in a tall building in Boston. In some other reception area—one no doubt grander and more exciting than the one I was in—a phone started to ring.

It rang once.

Twice.

Three times.

My heart was in my throat. At the end of the fourth ring my call was sent to voice mail. Somehow I hadn't expected this. I should have just hung up. I should have given myself the time to think through what to say to a machine and then called back. But the outgoing voice prompt was surprisingly short, just the name of the agency and a quick request to leave a message. By the time it was over and I heard the beep, I was still holding the phone to my ear.

My friends, the fact is I froze.

"This is Stella . . . Stella Penn," I blurted out. "Jennifer Sweet gave us her card. She said to call this number so . . . so, that's what I'm doing." I gave the callback number and quickly hung up.

The moment I did it, I realized with a flash of panic that I'd left out something vital. I'd forgotten to mention I was from Lemonade Mouth! How were they supposed to know what I was calling about? How many pointless messages did they receive on that voice mail line every day, unknown musicians trying to sneak or charm their way into the fame machine that was the world-renowned Decker and Smythe

Talent Agency? Plenty, I guessed. Did they even know who Stella Penn was? I doubted it.

I dropped my head onto the desk and pressed my forehead to the cold metal. What an idiot! From a few feet away I heard somebody knocking on the glass partition. I looked up.

"You okay, Stella?" Beverly. She was staring at me.

"I'm fine," I lied. "Just resting."

She nodded sympathetically and went back to her work.

Sitting up straight, I tried to pull myself together. Calling back now would make it obvious that I'd screwed up, but there was no getting around it. I grabbed my phone again and hit the redial button. I hoped nobody would pick up this time. If someone did, I felt sure I'd be too embarrassed to talk. There was no need to worry, though. Voice mail, just like before.

"Stella Penn again," I said. "Uh, just in case you didn't know—which you probably don't—I'm part of Lemonade Mouth. Call back, okay?"

I hung up once more and buried my face in my hands. Ugh. *Call back, okay?*

Could I have said anything more pathetic?

WEN
Crossing My Enormous Rubber Fingers

A lot of people say Lemonade Mouth made some mistakes around that time. I can't deny it, but you have to remember what our lives were like in the early part of that summer. Sure, we were working on some new recordings,

16

but we were also living our regular lives just like any other normal teenagers, and it wasn't always easy.

Take my life, for example.

My dad had just gotten married to his much-younger girlfriend, Sydney, and suddenly his whole outlook was changing. Sydney had a new business selling antiques, and my dad got it into his head that it was time for him to start a new business too. Almost without warning he quit his job as an insurance claims adjuster—a position he'd had for twenty years—and started working on a new business idea: selling hot dogs to people on the street. No joke. In a junkyard he had found an oversized passenger van that somebody had converted into an ice cream truck, and he bought it for practically nothing. In one crazy weekend he painted it yellow, replaced the engine and fitted a gigantic plastic frankfurter onto the roof. His new business was called Wieners on Wheels.

It was clear to me that my father's midlife crisis was getting way out of hand.

George, my ten-year-old brother, loved the idea of a wiener business, but I wanted nothing to do with it. Even Sydney was skeptical at first. As the three of us stood gaping at the jalopy he'd just unveiled for us, she started to pull at a lock of her shiny black hair like she was struggling with what to say.

"Look, I've been in a rut in my old job," my dad said, adjusting his glasses and smiling proudly at his creation, "and you guys all know I've always wanted to start my own business. Well, this is it! I did the math and I really think it can work. Everybody loves hot dogs in the summer, right? And it's not like there's much overhead to worry about—mostly just the cost of gas and the food. I'm planning to offer a choice of quality toppings."

Sydney was still staring. Apart from the bright new paint, the thing looked ancient, with actual patches of rust visible here and there. It was *huge* too, which was part of what made it so impressive. People would see this monster coming from miles away.

"Yes, Norm," she said at last, glancing sideways at him. "I know we agreed to this, but now that I actually *see* the van I can't help but wonder . . . are you sure you're not taking on more than you can handle?"

"Oh, don't worry, we'll be fine. I've got this all worked out. You're the artistic one, so you can help me figure out how to advertise. George can ride with me sometimes. I'll hire somebody part-time to drive around when I can't do it myself, and for everything else, well, Wendel isn't doing much this summer. He can help out too."

That took a moment to sink in. What? *Me?*

Before I could object, my dad reached across my shoulder and pulled me in close. He held Sydney's hand. He looked so happy. "Think of this as a family project."

I could only blink at him.

And that's how I ended up with a summer job that included standing on busy street corners wearing a giant wiener suit and waving to passing traffic. Adding insult to injury, I wasn't even going to get paid. It gave new meaning to the word *humiliation*.

Worse still, my father had hired my nemesis, Scott Pickett, of all people, to be his part-time driver. I guess Scott was looking for work, and being two years older than me, he already had his license. I was livid. Scott had been a creep to me and my band during the school year. He and his friend

Ray Beech and their arrogant crowd, the Mudslide Crushers, had tried to stop Lemonade Mouth from playing at our school's Halloween Bash and had even tried to ruin our shows. Those kids acted like they owned the world. Worst of all was the way Scott had treated Mo. He'd dated her briefly and then dumped her like yesterday's garbage, only to end up crawling back to her like the slime ball he was. By then Mo saw him for what he was and rejected him—thank goodness—but still, it seemed unfair to force me to be with Scott in the summertime too.

My dad was unsympathetic. "Listen, Wen, Scott has a good driving record, he told me he can be flexible with his hours, and I need the help. Whatever you have against him, you'll just have to get over it. Besides, he seems like a nice, polite kid to me. People do change, you know."

I almost laughed. I didn't believe Scott Pickett had changed. Not for a second.

So the morning after we met the Decker and Smythe lady, there I was in front of the Wampanoag Road shopping center dressed as an enormous frankfurter, doing my best to look cheerful as I held up a WIENERS ON WHEELS sign. I could see my reflection in the storefront window across the street. Most of me was hidden under stiff plastic, but unfortunately my face was visible—including my rectangular glasses and even a few wisps of my blond hair. Occasionally people I knew would pass by and I'd feel myself turn red when they honked and waved from their cars, sometimes howling with laughter.

Miserable as I felt, it was only natural that a part of me hoped my life was about to change for the better. Stella had left her message for the Decker and Smythe people a while ago, so now I kept checking my messages to see if she'd heard back. I looked again. Nothing. I wondered what was taking them so long.

"Hello, tall and handsome. Nice bun."

I had to spin my entire costumed body around just to see who it was. Olivia. She'd come to visit me. Her pale brown hair was pulled back from her face, and it hung behind her in a ponytail. Her hand was covering her smile, barely concealing the laughter as she took in my ridiculous outfit.

"So you like the look, huh?" I said. "It's not often you see huge white rubber gloves like these babies anymore. Very retro-chic."

"Yes, but it's the accessories that are doing it for me." She nodded toward the red and yellow globs that were supposed to look like ketchup and mustard. "I like a man with good condiments."

Ha ha. Oh, the comedy potential was endless.

If the situation wasn't so real I might have enjoyed it for the jokes alone.

Thing was, I had a hard time complaining about my dad or Sydney when I was around Olivia, who had much more serious family issues than I did. Her mother abandoned her and disappeared when Olivia was barely a toddler, and her dad was in prison for accidentally killing someone during a robbery when Olivia was still a little kid, leaving Olivia to be raised by her grandmother. So no matter how bad things sometimes seemed for me, having Olivia around kept it all in perspective.

But not everything was clear when it came to Olivia.

"So, are you and her, like, a *couple* now, or what?" Charlie had recently asked me over pizza. And the funny thing was, I didn't know the answer. I knew that I really, really liked being with her, but even though she and I spent a lot of time together, we'd never really labeled our thing—whatever it was—that way. Not being sure exactly where we stood was frustrating sometimes, but what could I do? With Olivia there was always a chance that if I pressed her on this subject it might make her back off. I was just taking things a day at a time.

Now, as we stood on the sidewalk together at the corner of Wampanoag and Rumstick Roads, she grinned at me. The good news was that she'd brought her accordion, like we'd planned, and my trumpet case was waiting at my feet. Olivia and I had talked about this. Just because I had to spend my mornings dressed as a processed meat product didn't mean we couldn't also use the time to write a new song or two.

I yanked off the gloves and soon the two of us had made up a new riff, a bouncy accordion progression that sounded fantastic under a series of descending trumpet notes. We played it over and over again, with Olivia humming all kinds of different melodies over the music. There were no words yet, but we could already tell the song was going to be great. A few passing pedestrians stopped to listen, and even a couple of cars slowed down. We must have looked ridiculous, but we were having such a good time, what did it matter?

After a while Olivia asked me to check and see if we'd heard from Stella. It was no secret that Olivia had mixed feelings about the whole Decker and Smythe thing. She'd never wanted to be famous. But even though the spotlight had always made her uncomfortable, she also knew that more exposure for the band meant a lot to the rest of us.

Just looking at her face, I could see she was trying her best to be enthusiastic.

There were no new messages on my phone so I sent a text to Stella: ANYTHNG? The response came a few seconds later. NOT YT. KEEP YR FINGRS CRSSD. When Olivia read it she raised an eyebrow. I knew what she was thinking. She and I both looked down at the bulky, three-fingered rubber gloves I'd tossed on the pavement.

If I had to keep those things on, following Stella's advice wouldn't be an easy task.🐦

MOHINI
Navigating a Minefield

🐦 "Monu, will you come back here, please? Your mother and I have some news we want to share with you."

My dad is standing in the doorway of the storage room at the back of our family's store, Banerjee Grocery. I hear the voice but my mind is elsewhere. I'm unloading a case of Nirav ghee jars onto the shelves and I'm thinking about Stella and the return call she's expecting from the talent agency. It's early afternoon and we still haven't heard anything.

"I'll be there in just a moment, Baba. Just as soon as I finish with this box."

There's a tap on the front window. I look up just in time to catch a flash of cat's-eye glasses and poofy brown hair before the bell on the door jingles. It's Naomi Fishmeier, my best friend since forever, and she looks like she's in a hurry. "I'm not staying," she says, breathless. "Just checking in. Any news from Stella?"

I shake my head, and my eyes linger on her outfit. Naomi's wearing one of her best concert tees, the pink one she got during the recent Zombie Blasters tour, and matching pink low-tops with her new black jean miniskirt. Not over-the-top, but very cute. Knowing her as I do, I'm sure she must have spent some time on this.

"Looking good, Naomi. Any particular reason?"

"Shut up," she says, but she smiles and blushes just a little, and that says it all.

She and I both know what's going on here. She's on her way to Lyle Dwarkin's house to help set up for our usual afternoon recording session. She hasn't officially admitted it yet, but it's obvious she's starting to have a thing for Lyle.

She starts back through the doorway again. "Hi, Mr. and Mrs. Banerjee!" she calls to my parents, who by then have both retreated into the storage room. "Well, call when you hear, okay?" she says to me. "I'll see you in an hour."

I promise I will, and then she's gone.

It takes me another minute to finish stacking the ghee jars and put the boxes away. I'm listening to the soft Indian music my dad is playing through the stereo, when I remember that my parents are waiting for me. I wipe my hands on a cloth and head to the storage room. My mother is at her desk going through a pile of receipts with a calculator. My father is next to her, reading a letter.

"You said you have news?"

"We do," he says. "Do you remember ever hearing Maa and me talk about the Kumars? Hemant and Bhavini?"

"Vaguely. They were neighbors of ours back in India, right?"

"Neighbors and very good friends. Both were students at Calcutta University back then, and you used to play in the sand with their son, Rajeev, before you could even walk. You don't remember?"

I shrug. My family left India when I was two. Of course I don't remember.

"The Kumars are moving to Lubbock, Texas," my dad continues. "They both got teaching jobs at Texas Tech, so they'll be bringing their family out there later this summer. In the meantime, they've asked if Rajeev can stay with us for a few weeks before he joins his parents in Lubbock this August."

A few quiet seconds pass.

"And? What did you tell them?"

"We said yes, of course."

The moment feels weird. Okay, so we're going to have a visitor this summer. Fine. Why are Baba and Maa watching me like they're expecting me to start squawking like a chicken or something? There's something else going on here, something they're not saying. I'm not positive what it is, but looking at their expectant faces I have a sudden, sneaking suspicion—and it's not good.

Maa leans forward and her next words leave me with little doubt. "Monu," she says, "Rajeev is a lovely boy from a good family. He's sixteen now. We're told his grades are excellent."

For a second I just stand there. I've always known that my parents' marriage was prearranged. As conservative Hindus, their parents worked it all out for them when my mother and father were still in their early teens—years before the actual wedding took place. I respect that, of course, and I love my parents, but unlike them, I grew up here in the United States, where things are different—a fact that has been becoming more and more of a problem between us lately. Sure, I've always realized that I might have to navigate this minefield at some point or another, but I never dreamed it would be so soon.

After all, I only just turned fifteen.

"That's nice," I say, keeping my voice steady and my expression blank. "Too bad I won't be around much this summer, what with Lemonade Mouth and my volunteering job at the medical clinic and everything. Plus, Charlie and I have plans."

There. That ought to send the message.

They glance at each other. "Oh, I'm sure you can work around those things," Baba says with just a hint of a nervous smile. "You're close to his age, so when he comes it will be nice for you to show him around. Introduce him to your friends. I'm sure he'll enjoy meeting them."

"That's right," Maa says. "You can help him transition into his new country. Make him feel comfortable."

"When is he coming?"

"Next Friday. The start of the Fourth of July weekend."

"Next week?" I want to point out that they must have known about this for a while. I'm tempted to tell them how obvious it is that they put off mentioning it to me only because they knew what my reaction would be. It's no secret that despite everything, they're still uncomfortable that I'm going out with Charlie. I want to tell them that no matter what their plans are, they're just going to have to accept the fact that I'll never match their idea of the perfect Bengali daughter.

But I don't say any of these things. It would be like admitting that I know what's going on, and if I don't say it and they don't say it, then I can pretend it isn't happening.

"Keep an open mind. You might find that you like him."

"Yes, Baba," I say. My voice is calm, but inside I'm burning. I spin on my heels and head back to the front counter. I can feel my face reddening. It's not fair to have to share my world with a complete stranger against my will. It's not fair that a boy I don't even remember meeting can appear out of nowhere and shake up my life. I wonder how long this has been in the works, whether this arrangement was something my parents and the Kumars talked about years ago, back when this Rajeev and I were still playing in the sand together.

. . . *a lovely boy from a good family . . . his grades are excellent . . .*

One thing I know: I'm not going to like him. He hasn't even arrived yet, but I'm already certain of it. My whole summer was just shot to pieces in a single moment. It's going to be a complete disaster—I can already tell.

The phone rings, but I'm too shaken to pick it up, so it transfers to the back room. A few seconds later Baba steps out.

"That was for you," he says. "It was Stella. She said to tell you she finally heard from someone named Earl Decker. She says you and your friends have an appointment tomorrow in Boston."

CHARLIE
The First Step on the Road to the Big Time

FADE IN:

OPENING SHOT: A crowded elevator with mirrors for walls. The camera pans across the five anxious faces of WEN, STELLA, MO, OLIVIA and CHARLIE—the members of Lemonade Mouth. Standing behind each is a parent (okay, so in Olivia's case it's BRENDA, her grandmother), all of them looking fidgety and unsure what to expect.

MRS. REZNIK is there too—a short, elderly bulldog of a music teacher with a suspiciously wiglike mountain of chocolate brown hair. Tiny though she is, she stands protectively in front of the kids like a warrior ready for anything. (Ever see that movie *Battle Axe Trolls*? Well, the way she was gripping her handbag, it kind of reminded me of that. She came along to make sure nobody tried to take advantage of us. I remember looking at her steely-eyed expression and thinking it was a good thing she was on our side. I'm a big guy, but I'd be scared if I ever had to face her in combat.)

INTERIOR. ELEVATOR—LATE AFTERNOON

CLOSE-UP ON: A finger pressing the button for the twenty-second floor. The elevator doors shut. Nobody speaks. The lights show that the elevator is rising. Mo tugs at her long dark hair and bites her nails. Charlie taps his fingers nervously.

Finally breaking the silence is . . .

                    WEN
        So . . . this is it. We're about to meet the world-famous Earl
        Decker.

                    STELLA
            (staring straight ahead, scared stiff)
        Casual is the approach we need to take, guys. When we
        see Earl, try not to look starstruck. Pretend we have
        meetings like this every day.

                    MO
            (a sideways glance shared with Olivia)
        Uh, and how are we supposed to pretend that, Stella?

                    STELLA
        I don't know! Just . . . *relax*! All I'm saying is, everybody
        stay *calm*!

Nobody says anything else as the lit numbers continue to rise floor by floor. Finally the band arrives at the twenty-second floor. As the elevator door opens, Charlie's thoughts drift back to his recent summer activities and the ordinary existence he's been living—an ordinary existence that might just be on the brink of change . . .

Okay, flashbacks are tricky and I haven't read the chapter on how to do them right yet, so I'm just going to tell you how the summer started off for me.

I admit it. Up until the Decker and Smythe thing began, I was bored out of my skull.

Sure, making those new recordings with my friends was like a dream, but other than that my life was complete Dullsville. While everybody else had summer jobs and other stuff that kept them way busy all the time, all I had was a school paper I needed to finish typing to avoid a failing grade in English Comp. Nothing like summertime homework to start vacation off with a smile. After that I still didn't have much else to do, so I spent a lot of the early part of the summer flopping around at home. I hung out in my room playing computer games. I watched a lot of TV. I made videos where I pretended to interview my mom's plants. Stuff like that. Mostly, though, I waited around for Mo to finish her shift at the store or whatever. She always had something. On recording days I would wander over to Lyle's house early and hang out with him and Naomi while they set up around Lyle's laptop. It meant watching those two pretend not to flirt with each other, but it was better than staring at a screen.

What I'm saying is, nobody was gladder than me when Decker and Smythe added a jolt of excitement to the summer.

For weeks I'd been telling my friends that all Lemonade Mouth needed was one big break. An opening-act slot on a tour with a famous band, maybe. Some kind of national exposure. Anything that could have led to a real record contract. (Notice, Naomi, how I used "have" instead of "of." See? I was listening to you and Mr. Levesque. Not that I plan on driving myself nuts trying to get everything perfect.

I don't care what anyone says—there's no point in losing sleep over a few commas.)

And then along came this meeting at Decker and Smythe like a lucky lightning bolt out of the sky. Here it was, our big chance! True, the lady who gave us the card never made any promises. She never said Earl Decker was for sure going to give us a contract or anything, but still, he wanted to talk with us, so it seemed at least *possible*, right? I figured all we had to do was avoid blowing this meeting.

By the time we got there the five of us were all so anxious that I wondered how we were even going to get through it. We had to wait in the squishy chairs in the Decker and Smythe lobby. It was a gigantic, echoing space. The walls were plastered with enormous posters, huge black-and-white images of rock-and-roll superstars looming over us like gods gazing at ants. As we looked up at them I noticed Olivia start curling into a ball in her chair, and Stella's whole head looked like it might pop.

Fortunately Mr. Decker kept us waiting only a couple of minutes.

He came out to greet us personally. Now, I'd been expecting him to be this cranky, cigar-chomping bundle of energy, because that's how everyone thinks of him, but when we actually met him he was the nicest, most relaxed guy. He had a big smiling face with silver hair and a short, scruffy beard. He was a little shorter than I imagined, maybe, and definitely older, but this was Earl Decker, the real deal. He had a diamond earring and an expensive-looking watch, but he wore them with sandals and faded jeans. It wasn't hard to picture him hanging out with the world's most famous hippie musicians back in the day. A moment later he was leading us down a hallway into his office.

INTERIOR. MR. DECKER'S OFFICE—LATE AFTERNOON

Lemonade Mouth and their small entourage shuffle nervously behind EARL DECKER. His office is impressive and cluttered with rock-and-roll memorabilia: Gold records on the walls. A collection of signed guitars. More pictures of still more rock idols, many posing next to a younger, even hairier Earl Decker. Noticing their obvious interest, Mr. Decker takes his time showing his visitors around and answering their questions.

CLOSE-UP ON: Charlie, staring wide-eyed at a pair of gold drumsticks in a frame with the label DANNY DANGEROUS, SHEA STADIUM 1992.

> CHARLIE
> (a whisper, unsure whether it's polite to ask)
> Are these . . . real?

> MR. DECKER
> (joining Charlie in the close-up, both of
> them gazing now)
> Don't be too impressed with *things,* Charlie. It's only stuff, that's all. Danny Dangerous was still a teenager at the time, not that much older than you are now. I remember the day he first wandered into this office. A cocky kid, but a real talent, there's no denying it.
> (a regretful sigh, and then . . .)
> Hey, everyone, why don't we all take a seat?

At Mr. Decker's gesture, the group settles around a long, imposing table, still adjusting to the reality of being in the presence of this legendary rock promoter. Mr. Decker looks around at the faces. He folds his hands in front of him.

> MR. DECKER
> I can't tell you how thrilled I am to meet you kids in person. I gotta be honest, I'm a huge fan. I watched that video clip, the one from that Catch A RI-Zing Star thing, over and over again. Wow. Powerful stuff. I listened to your CD too.

30

(holds it up as evidence)
Fabulous. Freaky and fun but with a solid emotional core.
Plus, it's danceable. I'm not hearing anything else quite
like it out there right now. Do you know, when one of my
assistants first told me about you guys I actually laughed?
No kidding, I really did. I didn't think it was possible that
a bunch of kids playing oddball instruments like yours
could really work. "What do you mean?" I asked. "A
trumpet and a ukulele? A standup bass? An accordion
and set of timbales?" I couldn't imagine how those things
could possibly sound right together! But man, was I ever
wrong.

REVERSE ON: Lemonade Mouth blinking back across the table at
him. Wen, Charlie and Mo sit stiffly in their chairs. Olivia is
hunched and rocking slightly with her arms crossed. Stella looks
like she's holding her breath.

                      STELLA
                (painfully quiet)
            Th-thank you, Mr. Decker.

CLOSE-UP ON . . .

                  STELLA'S MOM
              (also uncomfortable)
I know we all appreciate your interest in Lemonade
Mouth, Mr. Decker, and I'd be lying if I said I'm not
intrigued that you've asked to see my daughter and her
friends, but I must admit I'm not at all clear what's going
on. Why exactly are we here?

                  MR. DECKER
          (long thoughtful breath, still scanning the
          faces)
I asked you here because this is what I do. Now, I'm not a
doctor or a rocket scientist. I don't know how to write
a bestselling novel or find a cure for cancer. What I do
know is the music industry. My entire job is to recognize

talented musicians and make them the biggest stars they can possibly be. And believe me, I know something special when I find it.

He rises to his feet and strolls across the room, pausing near each band member as he addresses them one by one.

> MR. DECKER (CONT'D)
> I invited you here because of Olivia's big, soulful voice, and Mohini's swooping basslines. I wanted to meet you guys because of the unbelievable note bends Wen can do with his trumpet and because of the raw power I hear when Stella attacks her uke. And Charlie—with that big percussion set you play, all the crazy wild-man stuff you do up there? I've seen it, you know. Like I said, I watched the videos over and over. Ever heard of Keith Moon? Tito Puente? Tim Spooner?

Charlie is so transfixed that when he nods, his head barely moves.

> MR. DECKER (CONT'D)
> And the biggest credit of all? Well, I gotta give that nod to you, Jeannine.
> (gestures to Mrs. Reznik)
> I've done my homework. I read how all this started, how you were the one who recognized this thing from the very beginning.

Mrs. Reznik is silent but she's obviously flattered at the recognition. Mr. Decker is right. There would never have been a Lemonade Mouth if it weren't for her.

> MR. DECKER (CONT'D)
> I've been around the musical block a couple of times, and I can tell you this: You kids are the right musicians at the right time. You have the look, the sound and even a message. Those Lemonade Mouth stories in the papers? This whole "don't stop the revolution" and "underdogs of the world unite" thing? People eat that stuff up. It's

no wonder you've already started to make a name for
yourselves. That doesn't just happen out of nowhere.
Listen to the voice of experience. I know.

> (back at his chair now, leaning on the table)

Bottom line: I invited you here because I think my agency
can do exciting things for you. You made a good start in
a small, hometown kind of way, but now that little wave
is about to crest, and if you don't get a boost it's going
to peter out and wash away. What a waste that would
be. But I can help it grow. Right now is the time to act.
Photo shoots, television exposure, an autumn tour with a
big-name lineup. Oh, and all-new recordings, of course.

WEN

> (just now remembering . . .)

Oh, uh . . . we're already on top of that. . . .

> (reaches into his pocket to pull out a freshly
> burned CD, sets it on the table in front of
> Mr. Decker)

These are still rough, but we've been working with our
friend Lyle on a whole album of new stuff.

MR. DECKER

Oh, no, no. I'm sure your friend Lyle has done some fine
work, but I'm not talking about little homemade
recordings here.

> (gently pushes the CD back toward Wen)

It's time for you guys to start thinking bigger. With me
you'll start fresh. You'll record in the best studios on the
planet with the top producers and sound engineers in
the world. But it's up to you. You're the pilots of your own
destiny. So what do you say? Are you guys ready to go for
it? Are you ready to sign with me and take that first step on
the road to becoming a musical revolution unlike any the
industry has seen in years?

> (sitting forward in his chair, hands folded
> again)

Are you ready for the big time?

A breathless silence. For a few seconds nobody speaks.

Cut to . . .

EXTERIOR. SIDEWALK OF A BUSY BOSTON STREET—
LATE AFTERNOON

With their guardians trailing behind them, the five kids exit the
revolving doors of the imposing building. Their meeting now
over, they stop to stare at one another's astonished faces as traffic
rushes nearby.

                    CHARLIE
          (stunned)
          What just happened?

Stella shakes her head, too overcome to speak. Olivia opens her
mouth to answer but closes it again. In the end it's Mo who says
what all of them can hardly believe:

                    MO
          We just signed with one of the biggest rock agents in the
          world. Lemonade Mouth is going national.

The camera slowly backs away as we hear Charlie's VOICE-
OVER. . .

                    CHARLIE (V.O.)
          As the five of us stood blinking in the sunlight on that busy
          Boston afternoon, the path to our dreams seemed clear.
          But as we now realize, in life things often go wrong, and
          the future rarely happens the way you think it will.◊

CHAPTER 2

*Those who expect moments of change
to be comfortable and free of conflict
have not learned their history.*

—Joan Wallach Scott

STELLA
A Whirlwind of Activity

As you might imagine, it was a heady time for our little band of newly minted stars-to-be. Our days with the Decker and Smythe talent agency started with a whirlwind of activity.

"First we'll need to do something about your look," Mr. Decker observed, scratching his beard as he eyed us in our scraggly jeans, shorts and T-shirts. He arranged to meet us in Boston again, this time at a chichi clothing boutique on Newbury Street, where we were fitted for new clothes—a band uniform of sorts. A skinny, leather-clad fashion consultant named Blade led the project. For three hours, while our parents looked on, Blade handed out one outfit after another, a dizzying array of hats, boots, beads, ties, ripped jeans, shirts, skirts and various other items of potential rock-and-roll attire, some more bizarre than others, instructing us to try them on.

I was hesitant at first. As a member of a band of rock-and-roll rebels, I'd always thought of our unadorned look as part of our defiant aura. This was the great Earl Decker, though, a guy known for his antiestablishment roots. He'd introduced the world to the Rebellion Hellions and Mutiny! Mutiny!, two of the most trailblazing protest rock acts ever, so it made sense to trust that he knew a thing or two about what he was doing.

"Think of the great bands of history," he explained. "The Beatles kicked off Beatlemania with their mop-top haircuts and collarless suits. The grunge bands of the nineties wore plaid flannel shirts and unkempt hair for an image that rejected corporate culture. Appearance has always been a calculated part of the road to success, and it's no less important today."

As uncertain about this as I'd been, by the end of the afternoon I was amazed at how great we looked. Blade and Mr. Decker had settled on a few different outfits, but this main one was based in black. Mo looked stunning in a pleated black blouse and a ruffled skirt, and Charlie's outfit, a white oxford, a collarless button-down trench coat and a cool-looking Middle-Eastern cap like an oversized beanie, somehow gave him a serene, monklike vibe despite his feather duster of unruly, frizzed-out hair. Wen was in a dark business suit with an orange tie and a fedora. Along with his black-framed glasses, he was like some kind of sci-fi detective from Planet Cool. And Olivia—well, she looked adorable. Blade had decked her out in a pink 1920s flapper hat with a simple drop-waist dress that ruffled at the bottom. I would never have guessed it, but it totally suited her. She blushed as all of us gaped at her reflection. I noticed that Wen, in particular, couldn't stop looking at her.

And me? I'll admit I was psyched about my new duds. Now, I never claimed to be a waif—I'm six feet tall in my socks—but I'm not a muscled warrior type either. And yet the girl grinning back at me from the mirror was somehow both intimidating and attractive in a sleek black and green GI jacket, butt-kicker boots and a wide, metallic belt that hung at an angle like something out of a futuristic western. Even my mom, who didn't always agree with my fashion taste, was impressed. The girl in the reflection looked to me like someone who might step off the dance floor at any moment just to wrestle somebody to the ground.

I was thrilled.

The five of us stood staring at ourselves in the wall-length mirror. Charlie broke the silence. "I had no idea we could look this . . . this . . ."

"Me neither," Wen said.

I knew exactly what they meant. Together we coordinated in a weird, almost dangerous way. We looked like a party—the coolest party ever.

Even more, we looked like a band.

"This works," Mr. Decker announced. "It's stylish but still a little nerdy and off-kilter, and that's a good thing. It plays to your strengths. This'll be a fine starting point for us."

In no time he had us posing for pictures. We needed promotional shots for the media, he told us. He wanted to start building buzz right away.

Imagine the scene: our five heroes blinking under the bright lights with cameras clicking from all directions. It felt bizarre at first, and Olivia seemed especially uncomfortable, but the photographer, an Italian lady named Marta, was super nice and kept everything casual. Her assistant surprised us with a tray of Mel's Lemonade from a machine she'd discovered at a funky little convenience store across the street. It felt like destiny. I guess it made all of us feel more at home too, because after that even Olivia seemed to relax a little. Marta told us where to stand and whether we should lift our chins or whatever, and after a while we started having fun with it, running around with umbrellas or striking poses around old crates or whatever props they set out for us. It was all just a big laugh. After the studio shots, Mr. Decker piled us into his stretch limousine and we drove around Boston. It was our first-ever limo ride, and I thought my heart might burst. Every now and then Mr. Decker told the driver to stop and we all piled out to pose for an outside shot.

Lemonade Mouth walking down a city street.

Lemonade Mouth leaning against a brick wall.

Lemonade Mouth trying to keep straight faces while pretending to shove lemons into our ears and up our noses. (Wen's idea. Mr. Decker bought the lemons from a Haymarket grocery stand.)

We ended up having a great time that day, goofing around in front of the camera and acting as if we were celebrities. You can see it in our faces when you look at those pictures. In a lot of them we were trying not to laugh. The whole thing felt crazy and exciting. Sometimes when the limo stopped and we all got out, small crowds would form—people who didn't have any clue who we were but who stopped to watch anyway, probably figuring from our clothes and the limo and the photographer that we must be important. Maybe some of them recognized that one of the adults waiting inside the limo was Earl Decker—I don't know. What I *do* know is that I already felt a little bit like a celebrity. We all did.

It was our first small taste of what it felt like to be famous.

Mr. Decker's plans didn't end there either. He had us working on our new recordings right away. We showed up at Z-Division Studios in Woonsocket, the place where The Deadbeat Fingerwaggers did some of their most creative stuff just before they went country. I think all of us still felt a little bad about abandoning the recordings Lyle had been working so hard on, especially since Lyle had been with us from the very start. Lyle had told us not to worry about it, though, that he was psyched for us and that we would've been crazy not to jump at the chance we'd been offered.

Lyle is a good kid and a great friend.

We were shown around Z-Division and my eyes nearly popped out of my head at all the equipment. The place was like a rock-and-roll dream, with vintage instruments hanging everywhere, gigantic rooms with hardwood floors, even two cushy lounges for hanging out between takes. We were assigned to Studio B, where a producer named Chuck Fowler, a solemn-faced guy who had done some work with the Fingerwaggers and Monica Maybe, met us in the control room. On that first day he talked with us for two whole hours about our new songs (he'd heard our demos) and his ideas for how they could sound on these new, professional recordings. The plan was to lay down the basic tracks for ten songs—our new album—as quickly as possible, hopefully in ten days, and then add effects and do the mixing after that. It was going to be a lot of work, he told us, but he was going to make sure we sounded great.

The experience of being there that day was kind of

overwhelming. The whole time he was talking, the five of us kept exchanging glances. I don't think any of us could believe this was happening.

"Oh, we're just getting started," Mr. Decker said as we left the studio.

That Thursday he made sure all of us went with him to see Run Dog and JJ Slim at the Providence Civic Center. "We need to start getting you guys seen in the right places with the right people," he told us. "In the music industry, as in life, it's where you are and who you know, kids. Never forget that." Now, it should be noted that I'd already tried to get tickets to this show but couldn't because it was sold out. And yet my mother was actually pushing back on Mr. Decker about this, with the ridiculous objection that my family was planning to get up early the next day and drive to Philadelphia for the long Fourth of July weekend. But there was no way I wanted to miss Run Dog, and fortunately Mr. Decker was persuasive enough that my mother relented. He convinced her that if I was tired in the morning, I could just sleep in the car.

The show was mind-blowing. We were front and center, and afterward Mr. Decker surprised us by escorting us backstage, past a long line of screaming fans. Before we knew it we were standing face to face with Run Dog and JJ themselves, actually shaking their hands. We found ourselves rubbing elbows with a bunch of big-shot reporters too, along with music industry executives and even a photographer from the magazine *New Music Weekly*. Just about everybody knew Mr. Decker and greeted him like an old friend.

"This is Lemonade Mouth," he kept telling everyone, grinning as he led us around. "Remember that name. You're going to hear a lot of it very soon."

My friends and I were too overwhelmed to talk much.
In fact, as I remember it, we hardly said anything at all. 🐢

CHARLIE
Nailing It in Front of a Stressed-Out Hit-Maker

INTERIOR. Z-DIVISION RECORDING STUDIOS—AFTERNOON

As Mr. Decker watches on, Mo, Wen, Stella and Charlie look over the shoulder of middle-aged record producer CHUCK FOWLER (serious expression, hair gray and slicked back, flashy earrings), who sits at an enormous old-school mixing console. On the other side of a window we see Olivia standing all alone at a microphone. She looks anxious. Through headphones she's listening to the recorded instruments of the song "Let Us Begin" as she waits for her vocals cue. She keeps glancing back into the control room while we hear Charlie's VOICE-OVER.

> CHARLIE (V.O.)
> Mr. Decker wasted no time getting us started on our new recordings. Now, I'd be lying if I said that working in a high-tech studio came naturally to us. Our new producer had his own way of doing things, and it was way different from what we were used to with Lyle. But we had to adjust fast because we were on a tight schedule. It was only our third day of recording and already we were falling behind.

Chuck silently counts out three beats with his hand and then points at Olivia to let her know she should start singing, but Olivia is flustered and misses the cue. Chuck takes a deep breath and hits a button. The music stops.

> OLIVIA
> Sorry! I can't believe I did it again! Just once more, Mr. Fowler, okay? I promise I won't mess it up this time.

Chuck flips a switch and his voice carries into the studio.

                    CHUCK
          (barely hiding his impatience)
    Okay, Olivia, one more time then. Let's do this. Get ready.

                    STELLA
          (quietly, to Chuck and Mr. Decker)
    I know what the problem is. Usually we play everything
    live—all five of us in the same room. Whether we're on a
    stage or recording in Lyle's garage, it's always been the
    same. For this song Wen and I normally start off standing
    next to her and the three of us kind of . . . I don't know . . .
    play off each other's energy.

                    MO
    It's true. I felt weird too, being all alone in there doing my
    bass part. But Olivia's going to nail this. You'll see.

From the looks on everyone's faces, nobody seems confident about
that. Chuck doesn't answer. He glances at his watch. With Mr.
Decker still looking on, Chuck takes a moment to reset the
system.

                    CHARLIE (V.O.)
    What most people don't realize is that making those
    recordings—"The Z-Division Sessions," as they eventually
    came to be known—was a huge change in the way we
    did things. Up until then we'd made all our own decisions
    and everything was a lot more relaxed. But when you're
    working with professionals with platinum records on their
    walls, it only makes sense for them to call the shots. The
    pressure was definitely on.

Ready now, Chuck presses a button and the instrumental opening
to the song starts up again. All eyes are on Olivia, who takes deep
breaths to calm herself. As the music plays, the camera pans
across the nervous faces of Wen, Mo, Stella and Charlie watching
her through the window. . . .

CHARLIE (V.O.) (CONT'D)

I remember the first song we recorded. It was "Let Us Begin," a midtempo rocker that was one of my personal favorites of this new batch from Wen and Olivia. It started with Mo playing a slow, walking bassline and then Stella chiming in with moody uke chords over my congas. As good as the song was, recording it in pieces like this turned out to be a challenge for us. We were sweating it out, every step of the way.

CUT TO: Olivia, eyes closed, standing at the microphone. On cue, she takes a deep breath and begins. At last she's found her voice. Her sound is amazing—as big and gravelly and as filled with emotion as ever.

OLIVIA (singing)

I'm a child . . .
I'm a wild naked child in a storm.
I am reborn.
Let my feet squish the mud.
Let the rain wet my skin.
Now . . . let us begin.

I'm a note . . .
I'm a full-throated note in a song.
I am sure and I'm strong.
Set my melody free.
Let the rhythm soak in
Now . . . let us begin.

Destination unknown but never alone . . .
Let us begin.
Let us begin.
Let us begin.

REVERSE ON: The relieved faces looking back from the booth. Thumbs-up signs.

As anyone who ever heard those recordings knows, we
did eventually make the adjustment to working in the
studio. "Let Us Begin," "Blastoff Castaways," "Wrecking
Ball," "Street Corner of Condiment Dreams"—gradually,
layer by layer, track by track, our new tunes took the
shape envisioned by the hit makers working with Decker
and Smythe. In the end, even our cranky new producer
was pleased.

MOHINI
A Hummingbird into a Magpie

As if things aren't already exciting enough, Mr. Decker
sets up a video link from his office in Boston to tell us he
has even more news: Too Shy to Cry, one of the hottest pop
bands in the country and, as it happens, another act represented by Mr. Decker's agency, is starting a concert tour
in late August and Mr. Decker has arranged for Lemonade
Mouth to do a short stint as their opening act.

"Get ready to end the summer with a bang," he says, taking a puff of his cigar. "You guys are going on tour."

The enormity of this news hits me in waves. Okay, so it's
only for two weeks and a total of ten shows, but it's the real
thing. My brain can hardly process it. I feel like at any moment I'm going to wake up and realize this whole strange
experience has only been a dream.

Those first days of our association with Earl Decker
are like a blur—a series of momentous messages from Mr.
Decker and his assistants, commuting back and forth to
Woonsocket as we work on our new recordings, meeting
famous and important people who could end up having a
real impact on our futures. Half of our universe feels like it's

44

transforming before our eyes, which is why it feels so strange to us when we go home and find the other half continuing as if nothing much has changed.

Whenever the five of us aren't working on the recordings, we still live pretty much the same, hanging out with our families and doing normal things. I'm still squeezing in volunteer hours at the clinic when I can, and my family still expects me to work at the store. It might sound weird, but it sort of feels like we're living double lives. Going back and forth between these two very different worlds is sometimes unnerving—even a little surreal.

Case in point: one night we're shaking hands with Run Dog and JJ Slim, and the next day I'm hiding in my bedroom waiting for the dreaded guest from India to arrive—Rajeev, my childhood sandbox buddy and would-be future husband. God forbid.

My parents and my ten-year-old sister, Madhu, have already gone to the airport to fetch him. I refused to go with them, though, so instead I'm next to my bed with my bass and bow, taking out my frustration on Eccles's Sonata in G Minor. Before she left, Maa spent the morning making none-too-subtle comments about my hair. "Don't you think you should put it up today? Don't you think it looks prettier that way?" She also kept pulling out different outfits she thought I should wear, mostly skirts or summer dresses. Just suggestions, of course. The whole time I acted like I had no idea why it should matter.

If my parents aren't admitting what's really going on here, then why should I be the one to drop the bomb?

Just before she went to the car Maa abandoned the innocent act and gave me the evil eye. "You will not be rude to him," she said. "Rajeev is our guest. You will show him *courtesy*."

"Yes, Maa," I said, unable to look at her.

Now I want to scream. For my whole life I feel like I've been forced to walk the tightrope between showing respect for my parents and pushing back on their old-world expectations. None of my friends have to deal with stuff like this. Other than me, I don't know anybody who does.

They've been gone more than an hour now, and I'm trying not to think about my parents, or Rajeev, or any of that. I'm focusing only on the Eccles piece, concentrating on nailing each rapid-fire note. This sonata is perfect for venting frustration—lots of left-finger action and quick, stabbing bow movement across the strings. It's working too. For a while I feel a little better.

It's then that I hear commotion on the front steps. Mid-phrase, I stop playing. I stand totally still, listening.

The front door opens. Baba and Maa are talking in the entryway, but I can't hear what they're saying. There's another voice too—Rajeev's, obviously. Madhu giggles.

"Monu!" Baba calls up the stairs. "We're home! Come down and say hello to your old friend!"

I don't move. I know it's silly and that there's no getting out of meeting him, but I can't bring myself to do it just yet. My pulse is racing. I can picture him down there, a prune-faced, closed-minded boy with nothing in common with me—a kid raised in a world where it's perfectly normal for parents to pick spouses for their children. He's probably expecting me to be thrilled to meet him. At this moment I can imagine him thinking he's about to be introduced to his future wife, an obedient girl who'll be happy to spend her life wrapped in saris and serving him luchi every day with his afternoon tea.

If that's what you're looking for, Rajeev Kumar, you're in the wrong house.

"Monu!" my father calls again.

I take a deep breath. Okay, time to get this over with.

Everyone is already seated in the living room. When I appear on the stairs, the conversation stops. Maa looks disappointed. I'm wearing an old T-shirt, a pair of plaid Bermudas and my favorite faded Red Sox cap. My hair is down, not up. As ridiculous as it sounds, a part of me can't help feeling bad for my parents. I don't want to hurt them. Really, I don't. But I also could never be exactly who they want me to be, so it's better for them to realize it now than to spend a lifetime trying to turn a hummingbird into a magpie.

I see Rajeev for the first time. He stands when I appear, and I'm surprised at what I see. Broad-shouldered, with thick, curly black hair and deep-set eyes, Rajeev is undeniably good-looking. He's also taller than I imagined—maybe even taller than Baba, who's six foot one. Not that it matters to me what he looks like. Still, I keep my expression blank while he and I take each other in—I'm sure he's doing the same thing I am—both of us trying not to be too obvious about it.

"Hello, Mohini," he says with a shy smile. "It is nice to meet you." He looks a little rumpled and scruffy, but then it must have been a long flight, and this introductory chat with my family can't be easy on less than a good night's sleep. But I keep my sympathy in check. I remind myself not to let pity soften my will to detest this boy.

"It's nice to meet you too, Rajeev," I say as coolly as I can get away with. My parents are still smiling, but I know that Maa, especially, is watching my every move. She sends Madhu into the kitchen to make tea, and then for a few minutes we all sit around and talk about nothing. Rajeev's flight. How his parents are doing. How he's changed since the last time Baba and Maa saw him. (No surprise there—the kid was barely out of diapers at the time.) Rajeev is polite. He smiles a lot and speaks with a thick accent, but his English is good.

I sit with my arms crossed, hardly saying a word.

After a while Baba clears some of the empty teacups and takes them back to the kitchen. Maa gets up too. "I need to attend to the tarkari," she says as she collects the rest of the cups. "You two stay here. Sit and talk. You have a lot of catching up to do. Madhu, come with me."

Madhu looks annoyed. She's hardly taken her eyes off Rajeev this entire time. "What? Why can't I stay too?"

"Because," my mother says, "I need your help."

I shoot my mother a glare. I can see what she's up to, but there's nothing much I can do to stop her. Madhu is already heading out of the room all pouty. Fighting panic, I flash Maa one last pleading look. I don't want her to go! I don't want to be left alone with him! Just before she disappears into the kitchen Maa secretly gives me the evil eye again, the one that says *You will not be rude to our guest. You will show him courtesy.*

And then she's gone. Rajeev and I are alone.

There is a long, awkward silence. We're sitting on opposite ends of the sofa and I'm staring at the coffee table. All I want is to run back up to my room and shut the door. Rajeev seems just as uneasy. His thumb keeps tapping on the arm of the sofa and his knee keeps bobbing up and down.

"So . . . ," he begins, "my parents tell me you play the classical bass, and that you are in a band. They say you are thinking of going to medical school."

Okay, so this is how he's going to play it. Cards on the

table for all to see. But two can play at that game. "Is that so?" I ask casually, pretending to pick an invisible speck of dust from my shorts. "Well, parents say a lot of things. What mine told *me* is that your grades are excellent, and that you're a lovely boy from a good family."

There. Right back at you.

For a moment he's quiet, but then he breaks into a nervous smile. "Sounds like your parents have been giving you the same kind of selling job about me that mine have been giving about you. I have been hearing for weeks about how accomplished your family is, and about how beautiful you are."

"You have? They said that?"

He nods, his face reddening a little.

His honesty surprises me. I like that he actually blushed too—it's kind of sweet. For an instant I find it hard not to like him just the tiniest bit, but then I get ahold of myself. I gather my courage. "Rajeev, let me set things straight so there's no misunderstanding." I look directly at him for the first time. "I love and respect my parents, but that doesn't mean I'm going to let them control my life. I'm not interested in an arranged marriage. Not with you or anybody else. I'm sorry if this hurts you, but when I'm ready to get married it'll be with somebody *I* choose, and that decision won't come for a long, long time. You and I are just kids."

There is yet another pause as his eyes seem to study me. After a moment, though, he leans back in the chair and it's almost as if I can see a weight lifting from his shoulders. "Oh thank goodness!" he says. "I was so worried! I thought you were going to be . . ."

I wait. He doesn't finish. "What?" I ask, confused. "What did you think I would be?"

"I don't know . . . like . . . like my parents, I guess. Oh, don't get me wrong, Mohini—I love and respect my mother and father too. They mean well. It is just that they're very old-fashioned, and sometimes it's like they keep expecting me to be just like them. They seem stuck on the idea that I will get married young and spend my life doing something academic, like they both did. They told me that when I go to college I should study the same field as them—economics. They don't seem to get it when I keep telling them I don't want any of those things."

I stare. "So . . . what *do* you want?"

"I want to dance," he answers without hesitation. "It's my passion. It's what I love. Do you know Shiamak Davar?"

I shake my head.

The next thing I know, he's reaching into one of the luggage bags near his feet and pulling out a DVD. He hands it to me. It's a Bollywood movie called *Vriksh Ghar*. On the cover a crowd of people are dancing on the roof of what looks like a gigantic tree house.

"Shiamak Davar is a famous choreographer. He's brilliant. I got to work with him two summers ago as a background dancer in this movie. It was only a couple of days, but it changed my life. When I go to college in two years I'm going to continue my dance studies. I'm going to be a choreographer."

"And your parents?" I ask slowly, still trying to take this in. "They don't want you to do that?"

He shrugs. "It's not that they don't *want* me to, exactly. They want me to do whatever makes me happy. It's just that this is not what they expected. They're still trying to warm up to the idea. I'm sure they will come around eventually, but for now I think they're still having a hard time." He looks up at me again. "Breaking from tradition is an adjustment for everybody."

I'm speechless as he tucks the DVD back into his bag. All at once I'm struck with the realization that what I was thinking before—that I don't know anyone else who has to deal with the kind of stuff I do—is no longer true. In his own way, Rajeev has obviously been balancing on a tightrope a lot like the one I've been on for years. He smiles at me again, and it's clear to me now that it's not the smile of a boy who expects me to be his wife someday. It's just the nervous smile of a kid who's far from home, a little scared and hoping to make a friend. If I were in his position I'd feel the same way.

I realize I can't make myself hate him. I just can't.

Despite everything, I smile back.

WEN
An Unforgivable Weasel

It felt like our world was on the brink of change, but for me change couldn't come fast enough. Even though we were working on our new album in a real studio, even though Mr. Decker kept telling us we were about to rocket into the pop stratosphere, my dad still needed me to wear that stupid hot dog suit for him whenever I could. "It helps get the word out," he said. "People see you on the street, a friendly frankfurter waving at them, and it makes them curious. Starting my own business is a big deal for me, Wen. I know you don't love the suit, but I want you to know how much I appreciate your help."

What was I supposed to do? How could I say no when it meant so much to him?

Of course I wanted my father's business to succeed. Everyone in my family did. After all, my dad had quit his

51

job for this. So we all pitched in. Sydney—whose original idea for the summer was to take a family vacation and see the country—was spending her time putting ads in the local papers and assisting my dad with the bookkeeping. George helped hand out the hot dogs as my dad prepared them. (George *loved* riding around in that crazy van. He'd ring the bell and talk to the customers and wave when people stared as they passed. He even came up with a name for it—Penelope—as if it were a pet or something. He and my dad had started to say things like, "Honey, we'll be back in a couple hours. George and I are just taking Penelope out for her lunchtime trip to the beach." It was weird.)

But for me the hardest thing about Wieners on Wheels wasn't that van or even that I had to wear that stupid costume. It was Scott Pickett. He was becoming a regular fixture in my summer. Whenever I saw him around my father, he was always acting sickeningly polite. "Yes, Mr. Gifford. Right away, Mr. Gifford." My dad ate it up too, which was infuriating. It was like a bad joke.

Even if my dad couldn't see through Scott's act, I sure wasn't fooled.

Scott's job was to take over the wiener van driving duties in the late afternoons, cruising Penelope along the beaches and shopping areas in search of anyone with the munchies. As it turned out, the job wasn't a bad fit for him. With his spiky blond hair and quick smile, he was something of a high school heartthrob, and even during the slower times he had a way of attracting customers. I know for a fact that girls from Opequonsett High would sometimes gather at the roadside waiting for that giant, rusting yellow van to appear just so they could flag it down and hand Scott their money.

Maybe that's part of the reason why my dad liked him. Scott was good for business.

Anyway, at the end of the day he was supposed to return the van to my house, clean it and unload any leftovers into a big freezer in our garage. The bummer was that whenever I was around, my dad insisted I had to help him. Which was torture.

"So, I hear Lemonade Mouth is full steam ahead," he said to me, all fake-casual on our first night cleaning and unloading together. "I guess you guys are big-deal recording stars now." At the time my head and arm were deep inside one of the refrigerator tubs as I scrubbed it clean. We'd both been working in a chilly silence up until then, and pretty much ignoring each other, which was fine by me. Now I only grunted. Talk about uncomfortable.

I didn't know where he was going with this, exactly, but I was sure it wasn't good. Scott's band, Mudslide Crush, had recently broken up, and I think Lemonade Mouth had something to do with that.

A few minutes later I was clearing out the van's rear seats (my dad used them for collecting empty boxes and other crap that accumulated during the day) when Scott came up to me carrying a big container of mustard packets. As he passed by, he "accidentally" knocked against me, sending me flying. "Oh, I'm so sorry, man. I tripped." He looked like he really meant his apology, but I knew better. My dad wasn't around to see this, of course. Scott had made sure of that.

"Yeah, sure you did," I said, pulling myself up off the seat.

A few days later I mentioned the situation to Mo and Charlie. "I don't get it," I said. "Why did it have to be Scott? Was there nobody else my dad could have hired to drive instead of him?"

It was the morning of the Fourth of July, Stella was away, and the rest of us had separate barbecue and fireworks plans with our families. Since we weren't going to see each other later on, Mo, Charlie, Olivia and I had decided to celebrate in our own way, by meeting for breakfast at the beach. "Don't you see enough of those guys already?" my dad had asked only half-joking as I'd left that morning with a package of cream cheese in my hand. "It's not like it'd kill you to spend one twenty-four-hour period apart from them." I'd ignored him as I headed out the door.

Olivia was late, as usual.

"Sounds like there isn't much you can do about it, Wen." Charlie was talking through a mouthful of "red-white-and-blueberry" bagel. When it came to eating, he wasn't one to wait until everybody got there. "Scott's working for your dad and that's that. Looks like you're gonna have to find a way to live with it."

"But why should I have to put up with him at all? Scott's a complete jerk. You agree with me, Mo. Right?"

Mo was leaning back on her elbows and staring across the sand at the advancing waves. Now she sat up, tossing a broken clamshell into the water. "I don't know. I'm not really bothered by Scott anymore one way or the other. I wish him well."

"It's too bad about Mudslide Crush breaking up," Charlie said, still snarfing the bagel. "They really were a good band, you know? I hear Ray Beech and Scott aren't even friends anymore. They had a big fight and now they're not talking to each other."

"They're not?"

He shrugged. "That's what I heard."

Mo looked over at me. "It's not like Scott's a bad person

or anything. He's just a kid, like all of us. Maybe you should give him a chance."

"Give him a chance? How can you be so nonchalant about him, Mo? You, of all people?"

"Time marches on, Wen. There's no point in holding on to a grudge forever."

I was speechless. I couldn't believe she was saying this.

"Look, has he actually said something hostile to you? Anything unfriendly?"

"Well, no. Not exactly. But he hardly says anything to me at all."

"Isn't he going out with Lizzie DeLucia now?" Charlie asked. "I saw them hanging out together at the library."

Mo nodded.

This was news to me—and kind of a surprise. Lizzie DeLucia was a spindly girl with flat brown hair and glasses. She was a founding member of the Quilting for Cancer Club at school—a really nice person, but definitely not Scott's usual cheerleader type.

"There you go, then," she said, letting a handful of sand cascade through her fingers. "Don't get me wrong—I'm not saying I know what's going on in Scott's head, but have you considered the possibility that your dad might be right? About people changing, I mean? Maybe Scott's feeling embarrassed about the past—who knows? Maybe he just wants to make amends now so he can move on. After all, he didn't have to take the job working with you and your father."

Again. Speechless.

"You're nuts," I said finally.

By then Charlie had cream cheese on his chin and what looked like half his second bagel stuffed in his mouth. When I turned to him he said, "Don't look at me. I have no idea."

Mo's cell pinged with a new text message. "Oh, that's my dad," she said, jumping up and brushing the sand from her legs. "Sorry, guys. Rajeev's finally awake. Gotta go." Mo had already told us about this. Rajeev was a family guest who'd just arrived from India, and he was still jet-lagged from his long flight. Mo's folks told her she could only stay here with us until he woke up, and then she had to get back home so they could all get ready to give him a tour of the area. Charlie, Olivia and I had met Rajeev briefly the night before. He seemed like a nice enough guy. Tall. Kind of quiet.

Anyway, as Mo left she gave Charlie's hand a quick squeeze. She grabbed a bagel to go before sprinting back to her bike. "Tell Olivia I'm sorry I missed her! Happy Fourth!"

I waved as she pedaled away. I was still getting over her reaction about Scott. After the way he'd treated her this past year, if anyone should have hated the guy it was Mo. Not that it mattered if she didn't. To me Scott was an unforgivable weasel and nobody was going to convince me otherwise. I looked at my watch.

"What's taking Olivia so long?"

Charlie didn't answer. When I looked up he was still watching Mo, his eyes intently following her progress as she disappeared down the street. At the time I figured he was still thinking about Scott and Lizzie, same as I was.

CHARLIE
Attack of the Girlfriend Snatcher

Olivia never showed up. She texted to say she wasn't feeling well, and after a while Wen and I called it a breakfast and went our separate ways. I didn't go straight home. I wasn't sure why, I just didn't feel like it.

Okay, maybe I did sort of know why.

Ever since this Rajeev kid arrived I'd been getting strange vibes about the whole situation. It wasn't just because of what Mo had told me—about her parents' ideas on arranged marriage and Mo's suspicions about why they were so glad Rajeev was here. Not that that wasn't enough to freak a guy out. Mo was my girlfriend, after all. But she'd explained it all to me ahead of time and she'd told me she was going to ditch the kid at every opportunity, so I wasn't all that worried.

At least, not until the kid actually showed up and things started feeling weird.

It had only been two days since Rajeev first set foot in Mo's house and already the two of them were acting like peanut butter and jelly. I'd hardly even seen her since he had arrived. Like, the night before our breakfast on the beach, Mo and I were supposed to go out to a movie, but she called at the last minute to say she couldn't because her family was taking Rajeev out to a restaurant.

I tried not to be jealous. Honest, I did.

But then later, when Olivia, Wen and I stopped by their house and I finally got to meet this Rajeev guy, my heart sank. The kid looked like a movie star. He was nice and everything too. He wanted to know all about us, and he kept asking me about our music and my drums—he really seemed interested. And that was the worst part, because I couldn't bring myself not to like the guy. He also kept laughing at Mo's jokes, even the ones that weren't that funny. The whole time we were there she didn't stop smiling. Not once.

I felt like an extra in a horror flick called *Attack of the Girlfriend Snatcher.*

But I tried to play it cool. What else could I do? I told myself I was being ridiculous and that Mo was just trying to be a good hostess, putting on a show for her mom and dad so they wouldn't be on her case. What choice did she have, right? Even now, as I pedaled my bike aimlessly on the sidewalks of Opequonsett, I kept telling myself not to worry, that Mo and I were fine. After a while I found myself at the end of Mo's street and decided since I was so close anyway, why not stop by to wish everyone a happy Fourth?

Anyway, it seemed like a good idea at the time.

EXTERIOR. MO'S STREET—MORNING

Deep in thought, Charlie pedals his bike past a few houses as we hear a rhythm solo, a slow, nervous beat played on Cajón congas. The camera follows him for a few seconds and the rhythm continues to grow and swell, spilling over into the next shot . . .

INTERIOR. CHARLIE'S BASEMENT—MORNING

A close-up of bare hands as they play the beat we've been hearing. They move from conga to conga, varying the sounds by striking different parts of the drums. We watch for a few bars before cutting back to . . .

EXTERIOR. MO'S STREET—MORNING

Charlie is closer to the camera now, and we see him slow in front of a small red colonial with white shutters: Mo's house. The beat continues. Charlie leans his bike against a tree near the end of the driveway.

INTERIOR. CHARLIE'S BASEMENT—MORNING

The hands still playing the beat.

EXTERIOR. MO'S FRONT YARD—MORNING

The camera watches over Charlie's shoulder. He leaves his bike and takes a couple of steps toward the house. Passing an overgrown bush, Charlie can now see a window that had been blocked from view. It looks into Mo's living room, and when Charlie catches sight of what's happening in there it stops him in his tracks. We see what Charlie sees: Mo and Rajeev, standing with their arms around each other.

The conga music suddenly stops.

CLOSE-UP ON: Charlie's dumbstruck face.

REVERSE ON: Mo and Rajeev again. They are dancing, and even though the music playing in the living room is muted through the window, we can hear it—it's a mambo. Rajeev seems to be teaching Mo some dance steps. They're laughing and he's nodding and she's trying to follow his instructions. They look good together.

REVERSE ON: Charlie again. An extreme close-up on his widening eyes. He takes a step back from the camera. And then another. He turns to dash away and the congas start up again, only now it's an explosion, a breakneck tidal wave of sound and unleashed emotion.

INTERIOR. CHARLIE'S BASEMENT—MORNING

Charlie's bare hands striking, slapping, smacking out the new rhythm. We don't see his face, but his arms are flying across the congas. Beads of sweat shoot from the long spirals of his hair as they whip around.

EXTERIOR. MO'S FRONT YARD—MORNING

A medium shot of Charlie spinning his bike around and getting back on it. He takes one last look in the direction of the house and then starts pedaling away as fast as he can. We hear him breathing, each breath echoing in time to the panicked music. He's going back in the direction he came from. Soon he's only a small dot in the middle of the screen. The rhythm plays on.

OLIVIA
Greetings from Nowhere

Dear Ted,

Happy Independence Day, Daddy! Just a quick note to let you know I'm thinking of you, and that Brenda and the cats and I are all doing fine. Got your letter. I think it's great that they're letting you help out in the prison library now. And no, I haven't read Fahrenheit 451 *yet, but I reserved it at the library, so I'll let you know what I think after it comes in. I'm warning you, though: you were always more into the dystopian thing than I ever was—all that darkness and broken futuristic government stuff. Kind of depressing, don't you think? Still, I promise to give it a chance.*

You asked about our recording sessions—we finished the first three songs and everybody seems excited. On Thursday Mr. Decker brought two executives from Apollo Records to the studio. It was weird having guys in suits watching us record, but I guess that's how it is when you're working with a real label. I wish I could send you the draft mixes so you can hear them, but Mr. Decker says it's not allowed. As soon as I can, I will.

Well, that's it for now. I'm heading to the beach

to meet Wen, Mo and Charlie for a Fourth of July breakfast. I'm in charge of bringing the juice.

> Your daughter in freshly squeezed readiness,
> Olivia

P.S.

It's an hour later and my hands are shaking. I'm too stunned to leave the house.

I don't know what to do or who to talk to, but an earthquake just happened in my life and I have to tell somebody about it or I'm going to burst. Maybe setting down my thoughts here will help me clarify my feelings, or at least calm me down a little. Other than Brenda (who isn't here right now, which is a good thing because I'm going to need some time before I'm ready to talk with her about this), you're the only other person in the world who can really understand.

Prepare yourself. This is going to come as much of a shock to you as it did to me.

So, I was leaving the house with this letter already sealed in an envelope when I noticed that Brenda and I must have forgotten to bring in the mail from yesterday. I grabbed the small stack, carrying it back inside to the kitchen. If I'd just left

61

it on the counter and headed out without looking through it, I'd be on the beach with my friends now, still thinking today would be a normal day. But I didn't. I looked through the letters. There was an electric bill, a phone bill, a couple of flyers from stores with summer sales, but what caught my eye was a single white envelope with my name neatly written in pink script. Something about the handwriting made me stop and pick it up. I didn't realize what it was at the time. It seems weird to say it, but the penmanship looked strangely familiar, almost like I'd written it myself.

I think I already suspected who it was from.

I opened the letter. After I read the first few words my knees went weak and I had to sit down. I must have reread it a dozen times now, but the numb feeling still hasn't gone away. The letter isn't long, so I'm going to write it all out for you, word for word, so you'll understand:

Jess Russo, July 1

Dear Olivia,

I doubt you remember me, but I sure remember you. It's been a while, I know. I'm sorry I haven't been much of a mother for you, but believe me, I had my reasons for leaving. Yesterday somebody showed me an online video of you and your band,

and it made me realize how much you've grown. Wow, kid. You're practically an adult already. The last time I saw you, you were almost two, a chubby little potato in green overalls. It's hard to believe how fast the years have gone by. Watching you, I was amazed at how much you look like my mother. Except for your eyes—those you definitely get from your dad.

Anyway, I'm writing to tell you that in all these years there has never been a day when I didn't think about my little girl. I just wanted you to know that.

Love,
Mom

There. Now you know too. There's no return address, but the postmark is from Pittsfield, Massachusetts.

So what am I supposed to think? Thirteen years of nothing and suddenly this, out of nowhere. Should I be happy? Should I be mad at her for dropping out of my life and then reappearing after all this time? I don't know. Right now all I want to do is stuff the letter in the back of my sock drawer. I don't want to think about it anymore, not until the fog in my head clears.

Everything in my life seems to be changing and I have no idea how I should feel.

CHAPTER 3

Life is what happens to you
while you're busy making other plans.

—John Lennon

MOHINI
Unfamiliar Territory

"No need to come to the store today, Monu," Baba tells me as he leaves the house for the morning.

"Are you sure? I don't have anything else planned."

He nods. "Mr. Gupta is already there"—Mr. Gupta is my parents' part-time helper—"and the holiday week is usually slow anyway. I'd rather you stay in case your mother needs you. She isn't feeling well."

It's Monday and the change in plans has thrown me off balance. Plus, it turns out that Maa isn't all that sick. She just has a cold, and she spends the first part of the morning puttering around the kitchen, telling me not to fuss over her. So I'm not sure what to do. Lemonade Mouth won't be recording again until Wednesday because another band has the studio booked. I'm not even on the volunteer list at the clinic until the weekend.

Which leaves me in unfamiliar territory: a whole day on my hands and nothing on my schedule.

So I call Charlie, thinking that maybe Rajeev and I can swing by and hang out at his house for a while. Charlie doesn't answer, so I leave a message. Then I try Naomi, but she's not around; neither is Olivia, and Wen's busy helping his dad. So now I'm wondering what the heck I'm supposed to do with Rajeev all day. The poor kid comes all the way from India just to end up with nothing to do except hang out in boring old Opequonsett.

But that's when I realize the house has become quiet. Where *is* Rajeev, anyway? Madhu and I ate breakfast with him, but he's not in the dining room or the kitchen now. I take a moment to check the other rooms. Nothing.

So where has he gone?

From somewhere outside I hear a peal of laughter—my little sister's—and then Rajeev calling out something. He's laughing too. I find them in the backyard. Rajeev is pitching tennis balls to Madhu, who's grinning like a fiend as she holds a baseball bat like a golf club. Behind her are three vertical sticks shoved into the dirt with smaller sticks balanced on top.

"Monu!" Madhu shouts when she sees me. "Rajeev's teaching me how to play cricket! I'm beating him!"

"Beginner's luck," he says with a smile. "Want to join us?"

Rajeev explains the rules. It's a little like baseball except there are only two bases, and the pitcher tries to hit the sticks (called wickets) while the batter tries to protect them. Within a few minutes I get the hang of it, and before long I'm into the game and having a great time. When Maa calls out that it's lunchtime I'm surprised. We've been playing all morning. Madhu can't stop teasing Rajeev because she and I ended up crushing him four games out of five. Rajeev acts all bitter about it, but I can tell he doesn't mean it. He's just having fun with her, and she eats it up.

I check my messages. No response from Charlie, which is strange. Since yesterday morning I've tried to reach him at least four times. I wonder what's up with him. I wonder if he's still irked at me because I canceled our movie plans. I feel bad about that, I really do. I wish he'd hurry up and call me back so we can talk about it and then I can tell him about cricket and listen to his goofy jokes.

It's stupid, I know, but after only one day I already miss him.

After lunch the three of us head into town, and as we walk Rajeev and I talk about junk food. Turns out he's a big Twinkies fan, like me. He asks about Lemonade Mouth, so I tell him about the studio and how there's a lot of pressure on us to finish quickly. Then we run into Wen and end up having a blast on the street corner with him. Madhu asks if she can try on the hot dog suit and Wen says yes. After that we each take turns in the costume, holding up the WIENERS ON WHEELS sign and waving to traffic. We jump around and dance as people honk and wave back. The suit is too small for Rajeev and his shins stick out at the bottom. Out of all of us he looks the most ridiculous. He doesn't care, though. He has a great time waving at the cars and jumping around. He's hilarious. Wen laughs so hard he can barely breathe.

Again I'm thinking about Charlie. I wish he were here. I'm sure he would love to be on the sidewalk with us, taking his turn in the suit. It's just the kind of stupid thing that makes us both crack up. But when I check my messages once again and see there's still no response from him, I can't help feeling just a little annoyed. All right, so I backed out on him the other night, but it's not like it was my fault. I don't control my family. How about a little flexibility?

I take out my phone and I'm just about to hit his speed dial when I stop myself. Four messages? That's enough. It's up to him now. I put the phone back in my pocket.

If anybody's going to make the next move it sure as heck isn't going to be me.

CHARLIE
A Mighty Explosion of Fire and Destiny

It was the worst Fourth of July ever.

My parents and I always go to this big barbecue at my uncle Kyle's place in Wickford, and usually I love it, but not this time. I spent the afternoon with my stomach in knots. I was surrounded by relatives and other smiling people who kept asking about Lemonade Mouth and telling me how proud of me they were. I know they meant well and that the problem was me, not them. Everybody was just excited about all the stuff going on, and that was great, of course. But I just didn't feel like talking or celebrating. Ever have to pretend to be in a good mood when all you really want to do is crawl off somewhere and hide? That was me.

I wanted to press my face into a pillow.

I wanted to scream.

I'll admit it—there were even moments when I was close to crying.

But I couldn't. And since I couldn't bring myself to talk

about the Mo stuff with anybody, I had to walk around with a fake smile as if everything was great. As if the whole world hadn't just fallen to pieces in one giant mambo explosion named Rajeev.

The next day wasn't much better. I stayed home and watched TV. Mo called a couple of times, but I didn't pick up. What would be the point? I saw what I saw, so what more was there to say?

By Tuesday, though, after a James Bond marathon, I started to cool down. Something about the nonstop action and over-the-top crazy bad guys calmed my nerves. The world wasn't really like that, and I guess a part of me wanted to believe I was overreacting about Mo, as if some green-skinned Jealousy Monster that fed on my insecurities had been whispering in my ear and making me nuts. Maybe I'd misinterpreted what I'd seen. Maybe if Mo and I talked this over she could clear everything up and we'd laugh about my stupid mistake. *Falling for Rajeev?* she'd ask. *Me? Ha-ha! Is that what you thought? Of course not, Charlie! That's ridiculous!*

I didn't know what the explanation might be, but there had to be one, right? Her parents had told her she needed to be nice to him, so maybe she had to pretend to have a great time dancing with him. Her arms around him. His around her.

Yeah, that was probably it.

Okay, so it was a long shot, but it was all I had.

Anyway, it was time to bite the bullet and pay her a visit. My first step was to phone Stella, who was finally back from Philadelphia, and ask if she wanted to swing by Mo's family's store to say hi with me. I didn't mention the dancing stuff or anything, I just figured that if Stella came too then it would make everything seem more casual.

Fortunately, convincing Stella wasn't hard.

"Oh man, yes!" she said. "You have no idea what it was like road-tripping with my two little monkey stepbrothers—five hours each way, trapped in a car with Thing One and Thing Two. I gotta get away or I'll explode. See you in ten minutes."

As Stella and I walked to the Banerjees' store together, I secretly kept coaching myself on how I should act when I saw Mo. I told myself I wouldn't get emotional. I was going to stay calm and we were going to talk, that was all. It was going to be okay.

Problem was, it never occurred to me that Rajeev would be there with her.

First thing I saw when we stepped into the store was the two of them sitting cross-legged on the floor together, all chummy and comfortable as they unpacked two big boxes of white rice onto the shelves. They looked like best buddies, like they belonged together. Right away my stomach turned to jelly. There weren't any other customers at the time, and at the sound of the bell jingling Mo and Rajeev both looked up. They seemed surprised to see us, and for the briefest moment I felt weird vibes again, as if we'd caught them in the middle of something. I figured maybe they'd been having some hushed conversation, maybe sharing their deepest secrets with each other. I didn't know.

All I knew was that even after all the coaching I'd given myself, the Jealousy Monster was back. Only now instead of whispering it was screaming at the top of its lungs.

"Oh, what a nice surprise!" Mo said, standing up. "How

was your Fourth, Stella?" Stella and Rajeev hadn't met yet so she introduced them, and then Mo said, all casual, "So, what's going on, Charlie? I called you a bunch of times and you never called back. What have you been up to?"

"I could ask you the same thing," I said, still gripping my half-empty lemonade.

There was another weird pause. I caught Rajeev and Mo giving each other a strange look, and all of a sudden I wanted to shrink into the floor. Something was definitely going on here. My neck was warm and my head felt like it was spinning.

"Charlie, is everything okay?"

"No. As matter of fact it isn't. Can we talk? Alone?"

Her eyebrows pulled together, but she nodded. She led me back to the storage room where her parents keep their office. For some reason neither of them was around just then—they must have stepped out. And for a while I just stood there trying to get my emotions under control. It was the weirdest feeling. Mo was my best friend in the world, my first-ever girlfriend, and I was nuts about her—and up until only a couple days earlier I'd honestly thought she felt the same way about me. And yet here we were about to break up. I was feeling so hurt and confused that I wasn't even thinking straight.

INTERIOR. STORAGE ROOM—MIDDAY

Charlie and Mo stand facing each other near the door of a small storage space cluttered with boxes and shelves.

MO
(whispering, barely hiding her frustration)
Okay, so what's going on? If this is about the movie the

other night, I'm sorry about canceling on you at the last minute, but what was I supposed to—

CHARLIE

The movie? Oh, no, it's not about the movie. It's about . . . you know, about Rajeev.

MO

Rajeev? Okay . . . What about him?

She folds her arms across her chest and waits. It takes a few uncomfortable seconds, but finally Charlie takes a deep breath and begins. . . .

CHARLIE

I, uh, I just want you to know that I get what's happening, and it's okay. If you want to be with him instead of me, I'm good with it. I understand.

MO

You understand? What the heck is that supposed to mean?

CHARLIE

(shrugs)

All I'm saying is that Rajeev obviously likes you, and hey, he's a good guy and everything. What can I say? I can totally see why you like him.

MO

(a wide-eyed pause)

Are you . . . are you *breaking up* with me?

CHARLIE

Uh . . . no. I just . . . *What?*

MO

Come on, Charlie. I don't hear from you in two whole days, I leave you a ton of messages that you never return, and now suddenly you're here telling me you're okay if I'm with somebody else. What am I supposed to think?

CHARLIE

No, that's not it at all. I just . . . Hey, I saw you and him
together. I wasn't trying to spy or anything, but I could see
you through your front window. You guys were dancing
and I thought . . . well . . .

MO

(one eyebrow raised)

You saw us dancing and . . . what? You figured it meant
Rajeev and I are now an item? That we're about to start
sending out wedding invitations? Is that it?

She glares at him. He blinks back, his face reddening.

CHARLIE (V.O.)

Funny thing was, hearing her say it out loud like that, it
really did sound kind of ridiculous. But I realized that was
more or less *exactly* what I'd been thinking.

MO

Holy crap. That is it, isn't it? You're *jealous.* Charlie Hirsh,
I don't know whether to feel bad or to be furious with you!
You can be so oblivious sometimes! Don't you get it? It's
you I like, not Rajeev. He's just a friend! And I'm pretty
sure he feels the same way about me!

CHARLIE

(mortified, trying to recover)

Yeah, well, I'm not so sure. Face it, Mo, I'm a guy, and I
can tell when another guy likes somebody. And that guy
out there, he likes you!

MO

(nose to nose with him now)

Oh yeah? Well, all right, then, maybe he does like me.
What do I know? But even if it's true, it isn't my fault, is it?
How am I supposed to help how he feels?

CHARLIE (V.O.)

But as it turned out, we were both wrong. Even as Mo and I argued in the storage room, at the other end of the store destiny was playing out in a way neither of us had seen coming. It just took until that moment for one of us to look up and notice.

Over Mo's shoulder we see what has been visible in the background and what Charlie now sees: The storage room door is ajar, revealing a long grocery aisle that goes all the way to the front of the store. There, near the big glass window, are Rajeev and Stella. They met only a few minutes ago, but already they're standing close to each other, laughing and talking like fast friends. There are obvious sparks between them. Mo says something but Charlie doesn't hear.

MO
Charlie? Charlie, are you listening to me?

REVERSE ON: Charlie staring. Mo has her back to the camera. A moment passes, and Charlie nods toward the door. Following his gaze, Mo turns to see what Charlie is looking at. Now they both stare, their stupid little argument quickly forgotten.

REVERSE ON: Stella and Rajeev, seen through the crack in the doorway again. Rajeev, looking cool and dapper and in a white short-sleeved oxford and jeans, is whispering and smiling while Stella, with her pink hair and slashed-up Deadly Rebels tee, glows. She has a small bag of gummy fish and offers it to him. He takes one. In their own opposites-attract way, they look terrific together. The camera moves slowly toward them as we hear . . .

CHARLIE (V.O.)
In all the time we'd known Stella, neither of us had ever seen her like this. She was flirting with him—and Rajeev was right there with her. If fate was like a chemistry experiment, what we were witnessing was the first spark of a mighty explosion of fire and destiny. This was the start of something huge. I remember sensing what felt like

electricity in the air, and wondering where on earth this would lead. With Stella Penn involved, it could have been just about anywhere.

STELLA
On a Cloud

That's right, cherished compatriots. Your Sista Stella, your embattled warrior of justice, rock-and-roll rebel and one time loner, found herself suddenly in love. Utterly smitten. Head over metal-spiked heels!

Rajeev and I went out for a broccoli noodle stir-fry and a walk along the water, and after that I started catching myself staring out windows and thinking of butterflies. Not only was Rajeev drop-dead gorgeous, but we had so much in common it was scary. He hated sugarless gum. He loved chili peppers and vampire stories. He owned every Sista Slash album, including a rare vinyl copy of her live benefit concert in Tibet, and he was as excited about her upcoming Take Charge concert as I was.

He was even a vegetarian!

Without warning, sappy love songs that would normally have set off my delicate musical gag reflex were drifting through my head, and I didn't mind it at all. Every now and then I'd notice my mother or my older sister, Clea, staring at me with worried expressions.

"What the heck is wrong with you, Stella?" Clea asked me more than once from one of our backyard lounge chairs. Clea had recently finished her freshman year at Brown University and now seemed content spending her entire summer alternately sunning herself and stuffing her face with ice cream. "For days you've been floating around with a stupid

74

smile on your face. Did you even realize you were just humming? Snap out of it!"

"Nothing's wrong, Clea dear," I told her. "Just enjoying the morning, that's all. Shall I fetch you another scoop of rocky road?"

"Be careful," Mo advised me after Rajeev and I had been going out for almost a week. "I know for a fact that his parents are *way* traditional—even more than mine."

"So? What are you saying? That there's something wrong with me that they should be upset about?"

"No, there's nothing wrong with you, Stella. You're great, and Rajeev's a super-lucky guy. You know I mean that. But the thing is, you're not a Hindu, and I think for his parents that might set off some red flags."

I'll admit, this gave me a moment of pause—but only a brief moment. If Rajeev had a problem with me not being a Hindu, well, *that* would have been a real concern. But he never said he did, so I figured, why worry? Besides, his parents didn't even know me. If they met me, maybe they'd change their minds.

Anyway, I would cross that bridge only if I ever came to it.

Before you could say "infatuation at first sight" Rajeev and I were spending as much of our free time together as we could and my summer had gone from merely exciting to positively electrifying. Rajeev was like a Southern gentleman from an old black-and-white movie. He opened doors for me, and despite my feminist sensibilities I have to admit it didn't bother me one little bit. He was always kind and polite, but not in a way that got on your nerves. He was interested in my opinions and ideas and wasn't shy about sharing his with me even when we disagreed, which wasn't all that often. We would talk for hours and hours about everything and nothing. We *got* each other.

And to top it all off, he was one heck of a great dancer.

So is it any wonder I was on a cloud?

OLIVIA
A Little Late for That

Dear Ted,

I know, I know. Two letters in one week—what's come over me, right?

Today was another long day of recording. We spent the whole session on one song (another new one, "Zombietown"—lots of harmonies and percussion) and by the time Charlie's mom brought us home Brenda had to reheat dinner. Now it's almost midnight and she's in bed. As I write this I'm at the kitchen table with Daisy purring on my lap. Only three months old, but already she's so big that Brenda and I are starting to wonder if she's part mountain lion. She's definitely a wild thing. Today Brenda said she caught her climbing one of the curtains and leaping from there across the room onto one of the ottomans. The other cats are skittish around her. I don't think they know what to make of such a hell-raiser.

Anyway, I'm writing to tell you that I got your letter today. It was in the mail stack when I came home tonight, and now I can't think of anything else. Yes, of course I'm planning to tell Brenda about the note from Mom. I've been waiting for the right moment, that's all. Brenda's been under a lot of stress lately, and besides, you know how emotional she gets about these things. Whenever I've brought up this stuff in the past it's been like torture for her to talk about it. It's a topic I've learned to avoid.

Not that I haven't been thinking about my mother a lot in the past few days.

Funny how there are so few pictures of her around. It's almost like when she left, everything about her kind of disappeared too. I still have the photograph you gave me, though. I've kept it hidden in my bedside cabinet all these years. You remember the one, right? The two of you are at a party on a beach and she's leaning her head on your shoulder and you're staring at the camera with this sly look like a cat that just caught a mouse. You look so young, Daddy, but I guess it makes sense, because you both must have been in high school at the time. And she's so beautiful with her long dark hair and those big eyes she had, and the way she was smiling at you like she'd decided what she wanted and you were the best thing ever. It's no wonder you fell for her.

I don't remember much of anything about her, just a few moments and feelings. A green jacket she wore, how it felt rough against my skin. Her and me singing along with the radio. I can even close my eyes and picture myself watching through our front window as she rolls her suitcase toward a yellow cab waiting at the end of the driveway. She turns to wave at me before she gets in and closes the cab door and never comes back.

I imagine these things, but I couldn't have actual memories of any of it, not really. I was too little.

Okay, so now I'm going to share yet another secret with you: I've been checking the mail every day to see if she writes again. I'm curious about her. For so many years I used to wonder what happened to her. I would imagine her living in a mansion somewhere, or sailing around the world. I used to pretend to have conversations with her, long discussions where I'd share everything about my life and she'd tell me everything about hers. If she'd written to me then, it would have been so easy for me to forgive her for leaving. Later I decided that she must have died. In a strange way that might have been better, because at least it would have given me a good reason for why she never contacted me during all those years. Not one phone call. Not one letter. Nothing. Until now.

Which I suppose is why I still haven't mentioned any of this to anyone except you. I think about it all the time, though. I keep wondering, why now? Why would she drop back into my life at this moment instead of any other? What does she expect from me? Is she trying to start a new, ongoing connection with the daughter she abandoned? If so, why didn't she give an address or a phone number? Or is it that she's looking for something else? Forgiveness, maybe?

I hope it's not forgiveness. After so many years without a mother, it feels a little late for that.

Love,
Olivia 🐾

WEN
A Terrifying Limo Ride to Reality

Even while we were still making our recordings and everything else was going on in our lives, Mr. Decker was already busy behind the scenes setting up opportunities for Lemonade Mouth. The man was a force of nature. Not only did he have incredible access to high-ranking executives and other power players in the business, but he also worked fast.

Days after the holiday weekend he set up a video link to say he'd arranged for us to try out on *American Pop Sensation*.

I was floored by the news. We all were. *APS* was the biggest reality show on TV, where unknown musicians from all over the country competed in front of three opinionated judges and a live national audience. The show was huge. Each of the winners of its ten previous seasons had been unknowns who became household names and sold millions of albums. Landing us a slot on the show, even if the only guarantee was a one-minute shot in this season's preliminaries, was an amazing feat.

But it was also nuts. I'm not going to lie—at first I wondered if Mr. Decker had lost his mind.

"But does it really make *sense* for our group?" I managed to ask as the five of us gaped at his face on the monitor. "I mean, national TV. Millions of viewers. Don't you think it's kind of a big risk?"

"Relax," he said, taking a puff on his cigar. "I have a good feeling about this."

I looked over at Olivia. At the mention of national television she looked like she'd lost half her blood supply. Charlie and Stella didn't seem sure either.

"I don't know. Those judges can be kind of rough," said Mo, biting at one of her fingernails. It was a nervous habit I knew she was trying to break. "What if we screw up and end up looking ridiculous? Lots of people do. Do you really think the odds of us winning are high enough to take that chance?"

Mr. Decker chuckled. "You're not going to screw up. I have faith in you."

The point, he explained, wasn't that Lemonade Mouth had to *win*, exactly, but that any kind of national exposure would be good exposure. He asked us to trust him. None of us felt as sure as he seemed, but he was adamant that this was a good idea, and by the time the call was over he'd gotten us all to agree to do it. That was how Mr. Decker was. Once he had an idea there was no stopping him.

So a few days later, midafternoon on a sweltering day in July, we started our drive to New York City, where the show was being filmed. Mr. Decker insisted that we ride with him in his limo. "I want you to look like a band," he told us, "and it never hurts to make a big entrance." Our parents came with us, of course, and Lyle, Naomi and Mrs. Reznik too—we couldn't let something as gigantic as this happen without having them with us.

I remember how nervous and quiet all of us were during that long ride to New York. It was supposed to take three and a half hours, but it took a lot longer because of traffic. If Mr. Decker was worried he didn't show it, but I was sweating it out the whole way.

"Keep in mind that the show isn't only about your performance on the stage," Mr. Decker said as we traveled through Connecticut. "There will also be cameras on the contestants in the waiting areas, and even on the crowds in line outside the studio building. When the cameras are on you, America is watching—don't forget that."

I kept checking on Olivia. She spent most of the ride hugging her elbows and staring out the window.

"Are you okay?" I asked.

For weeks she'd been telling everyone not to worry about her, that she had her stage fright under control, but I wasn't so sure. I knew for a fact that she'd already vomited twice that day—once in the morning and once just before the limo arrived. I glanced at the driver, Ralph, a serious-faced guy with a gray mustache and dark glasses. He was concentrating on the road.

"We can still back out of this," I whispered. "Maybe it's not worth it."

"I'm all right."

For the first time in a while, she turned to face me. When she squeezed my hand I could tell that she really *was* going to be okay, at least for now. Which was even more of a relief than it might seem. For a few days I'd been worried about her—and not just because of her anxieties about performing. She'd been acting quieter than usual, and when I asked what was going on she wouldn't admit anything was wrong. Something was up with her, though. I could tell.

It was still light when we entered Manhattan, but I knew we were late. I remember looking up at the skyscrapers and feeling their weight hanging over us as we rolled through a sea of traffic and shadows and towering buildings. Olivia squeezed my hand again. After we pulled up at a curb crowded with people, Ralph stepped out from behind the wheel so he could walk around the car and get the door for us.

"Here you go," Mr. Decker said. "Good luck."

"Wait—you're not coming?" Stella asked, alarmed.

He shook his head. "I don't want the cameras focusing on me, I want them on you guys. Remember to have fun and be yourselves—and don't forget that the show begins the moment you step out onto that sidewalk." Outside the limo a small crowd was already starting to press in toward us, which was strange. No doubt they were mistaking us for somebody famous. "Don't worry," Mr. Decker said. "America's going to love you guys."

There are different opinions about Mr. Decker and the role he played that day. Some people say he had no idea what he was doing, that what happened later proved it. Others look back at the astonishing events of that evening and conclude that Mr. Decker knew *exactly* what he was doing, that getting us an appearance on that show at all was a stroke of genius, the sort of out-of-the-box inspired move he'd become famous for during his four decades in the music business. I don't know which point of view is right, but I don't think anyone, not even the great Earl Decker, could have guessed that things were about to play out the way they did.

The five of us glanced at each other as we waited for Ralph to open the door. Whatever was about to come next was going to have repercussions in our lives, for good or for bad, and suddenly I didn't want to leave the safety of the limo. In a matter of seconds it would all begin. The door would open, and we'd climb out onto the crowded sidewalk. After that there was no predicting what might happen.

CHAPTER 4

Towering genius disdains a beaten path.
It seeks regions hitherto unexplored.
—Abraham Lincoln

RALPH BICKNELL
The Faceless Guy Behind the Wheel

I've been Mr. Decker's personal chauffeur for more than
twenty-five years, and I've driven a lot of big-name stars.
Danny Dangerous. Leroy Thrasher. Rachel and the Bob-
sickles. If limousines could talk, mine would have a few stories to tell. Most passengers don't pay any attention to the
nameless guy behind the wheel. I honestly think a lot of
them forget I'm even there.

But I'm there. And I notice everything.

Sure, I remember that ride to New York with Lemonade
Mouth. It turned out to be a big day, bigger than anyone
imagined, so of course I get asked about it a lot. And whenever I do, I tell people that I remember three things:

First, I remember how scared those kids were. When we left Rhode Island they were sitting behind me full of nervous energy, but as we got closer to Manhattan (we were running late because of a tractor trailer accident on I-95) it became like a morgue back there. Everyone was silent. Mohini Banerjee was biting her nails, Stella Penn was fidgeting as if she were getting ready to explode, and Olivia Whitehead, the singer, was staring out the window like she might jump out. The adults with them seemed just as stressed.

Second, I can still picture their amazed expressions at the reception they received when we finally reached Times Square. As we pulled up to the curb a rush of people closed in around the limo, trying to peer through the tinted glass. I didn't say anything, but of course I knew Mr. Decker had arranged this ahead of time. It was an old trick of his, planting a few ringers in the sidewalk crowd to make sure his client's arrival got noticed. And it worked. There were two cameramen by the building and both of them spun in our direction to see what all the commotion was about. When I saw the surprised look on the kids' faces I had to hide a smile.

When it came to working the media, Mr. Decker played it like a violin.

But the third thing—and this is what sticks with me most whenever I think about that day—is this: even though those Lemonade Mouth kids were under a lot of pressure and must have been scared stiff about what would happen to them next, as they each got out of the car they still took the time to thank me for driving. All five of them, one at a time. And let me tell you, I appreciated that.

Now, I'm a fan of Danny Dangerous's music, but you

want to know something? In all the hundreds of rides I gave that kid, he never thanked me. Not once. He never even remembered my name.

LYLE DWARKIN
Going All the Way

People always say how I should have been mad at Lemonade Mouth, as if following their dreams with Decker and Smythe somehow meant they were dumping me. But that's ridiculous. I can honestly say I never felt that way. They were my friends and I was happy for them. Besides, with so much extra time on my hands that summer, I ended up hanging out a lot more with Naomi Fishmeier, one of the smartest, funniest people I ever met.

Let's just put it this way: I wasn't complaining.

And Lemonade Mouth always included Naomi and me whenever they could. Like, the day of the *American Pop Sensation* debacle, we rode down to New York in the limo with them.

The way I remember it, the mob scene started the moment we all stepped out of the limo. The band was out first and somebody shouted, "It's them! It's Lemonade Mouth!" and soon a small crowd was pressing in and screaming like Lemonade Mouth was this big celebrity band or something. It was a good thing Ralph, the limo driver, was such a big guy, because he was able to stand between us and the crush like a bodyguard. Seconds later two official-looking men with clipboards appeared. They told us they were from the network and that they would be Lemonade Mouth's handlers. They'd been waiting for us, they said, and they seemed kind of annoyed we were late. They told us there was still a chance Lemonade Mouth could make it before the producers bumped us from the schedule, but only if we hurried.

We rushed to follow them, but the line for the show was incredibly long. It snaked around the side of the Lane Elliott Conference Center, where the network was filming, and went back for more than two blocks. I'm told that some of the earliest people had even camped out on the street overnight just to be sure they'd get to audition, and here were my friends and me flying past it all.

The calls of "Lemonade Mouth!" continued. I saw Olivia trying to bow her head and cover her face, but that only seemed to make the camera operators *more* interested, not less. It was so crowded that Naomi and I kept getting separated from the rest of our group. Just as Stella and the others were being led into a roped-off area ahead of us, a beefy lady with an earphone blocked our path.

"Just where do you two think you're going?" she demanded. "The line starts on Seventh Avenue."

We pointed to our friends and said we were with them, but it was obvious she didn't believe us. I started to panic. Fortunately Mo looked back and saw what was happening. "It's all right! They're with us!" One of the handlers nodded, and after a moment of hesitation, ear-monitor lady waved us through.

"Can you believe this?" I whispered. "How far do you think we're going?"

Naomi looked just as astonished as I was. As we ducked past a security guard I felt her fingers reaching out to grasp mine. My breath caught. The thing was, even though I'd had a secret crush on her for a long time, I was always too nervous to say so. In a way it's kind of fitting that the first time Naomi and I ever held hands was as we were chasing after our favorite band together—a band whose members also happened to be our closest friends.

"All the way," she said, rushing us forward and giving my fingers another squeeze. "I think Lemonade Mouth is headed for the front of the line."

NORMAN GIFFORD
My Own Little Contribution
to the Rock-and-Roll Record Books

Our escorts seemed to be on a mission, powering the kids through the crowd like offensive tackles protecting a football. I heard later that they ended up knocking a few people over, which is terrible, but I didn't see any of that. I was too busy struggling to keep up. At first I was worried about Mrs. Reznik, my son's little old music teacher, but she was doing just fine. Better than I was, in fact. I had trouble keeping up with her.

I would have laughed if I wasn't so impressed.

For the hundredth time I couldn't help thinking what a shame it was that Sydney was missing all this. Back when Wen first dropped the news to us that he was only allowed to bring one guardian along, Sydney had tried her best to be the one. She'd given me her most persuasive look, actually pleading with me at one point. See, we'd both been huge fans of the show since season one. But come on. My kid's band was auditioning on *American Pop Sensation*! No way was I going to miss that. So during the entire drive down to New York she'd been texting me for updates. WHERE R U NOW? she'd write, and I'd answered her with the truth (except every once in a while just for fun I'd made up obvious lies like BACKSTAGE WITH ELVIS. U?).

Our escorts led our little group deeper into the conference center building until at last we came to a high-ceilinged waiting area. It was like a media circus. Cameras everywhere. Costumed dancers practicing their moves. Nervous-looking kids standing in circles singing, their heads nodding in time. A red light flashed and somebody called out, "Thirty seconds! Quiet everyone!" and the noise level dropped. Monique Hirsh elbowed me and I followed her gaze toward a back corner of the room. The show's blond, curvy host, Belinda Vree, was standing in front of a camera. You could have knocked me over. Belinda Vree! Everybody who followed *APS*—which had to be just about everyone with a television—knew her. She had one of the most downloaded faces in the world and there she was, only fifty feet away.

I'd be lying if I said I wasn't just a little starstruck.

"We're back, America!" Belinda said, flashing her famous toothy grin. "We're nearing the end of day two of our New York auditions, and we're broadcasting live from the Pressure Chamber!"

One of the network guys whispered for us to stay put while he went off to tell one of the assistant directors we were here. I stood blinking at the chaos, hardly able to believe I was in the middle of all this. Belinda was interviewing a skinny preteen girl in rainbow spandex, one of the contestants for the upcoming round, and my phone vibrated. Another message from Sydney.

UPDATE?

I held up my phone, snapped a photo and sent it to her in reply. As it turned out, that shot ended up being a good one—my own little contribution to the rock-and-roll record books. I've since seen it posted on Lemonade Mouth fan sites all over the Internet. In the center of the frame you can see Belinda and the spandex girl—the same scene that Sydney and millions of television viewers were watching live on TV at that very moment. But my shot also captured what the TV audience couldn't see—the crowd of excited people behind the camera and, off to one side but clearly visible, Wen and Stella and the others all huddled together, looking pensive, like they were deep in thought. But the truth is (and I know this from talking with them later), they weren't thinking much of anything at all. They were just standing there feeling terrified and overwhelmed.

It wasn't until that moment that the immensity of the situation fully registered in my mind. This was the real thing, and it was happening to my son and his friends. I could only hope they were ready for it.

VINNY PANDIMIGLIO
Trying to Calm CJ

The day Lemonade Mouth was on *American Pop Sensation* was also supposed to be a big deal day for me and my buddies, but for reasons that had nothing to do with Lemonade Mouth. That's because we were auditioning too.

We're called CJ and the Belmar Boyz—same now as it was back then—and we're all about the harmonies. There are four of us, with CJ and me being the leaders. Back then we'd performed a few times at our high school and at small, local places around Belmar and West Belmar where we grew up in New Jersey. We were always a big hit at nursing homes.

But now, at last, after a long day of waiting, we were about to get our big chance to show the world we were somebodies.

So yeah, we had big dreams that day.

As always, *American Pop Sensation* had five acts auditioning in each round, and everything was streamed onto the Internet. But we'd lucked out, because we got picked to be in one of the four evening rounds that got shown live on prime-time TV. My guess is the show chose us because we were joking around when the camera guy talked to us in line. Some people say that wasn't it, that it was really just because they liked our Jersey accents. What do I look like, a mind reader? Anyways, it turned out we were in the same round as Lemonade Mouth. I'd never heard of them before then. In fact, I hardly even noticed when they walked into the Judgment Room with only seconds to go until the round started. I just remember a line of geeky-looking kids shuffling into the last seats at the other end of the front row.

Man, was I on edge. Me and my buds were going on third, right after a couple of burly, short-haired chicks who looked like twins, and then a blond guy with bowling pins gripped in his hands. Third was good. It meant not having the pressure of first but still getting it over with.

The three judges—Celeste, Davey Dave and Franco—were offstage somewhere. I hadn't seen them yet. But I'd been watching the vid screens all day, so I knew they were in an ornery mood. Especially that big guy, Franco. He can be funny, sure, but if he don't like you he's not exactly known for being Mr. Tactful. Mostly, though, I was worried about CJ. He was next to me all bug-eyed and sweaty like he was on the verge of a freak-out. Not a good sign. See, I always sing the harmonies with Wayne and Paulie, but CJ takes the melody, and I know from experience that when he gets too nervous it can make his voice shake.

"Relax, man," I whispered, trying to sound confident. "We worked hard for this. They're totally gonna give us a golden ticket. Believe it. We're heading to Vegas, baby!"

CJ nodded, but his knee was popping up and down like a piston.

Some lady with a clipboard came out and shouted for everybody to shut up. There was a commercial right then, but it was almost over. The judges were about to take their seats, she told us, and we were going live in ten seconds.

MONIQUE HIRSH
Of Romans and Lions

While my son, Charlie, and his Lemonade Mouth friends were practically being shoved into their seats in the front of the studio, the rest of us from our group were being herded into the last remaining chairs in the back row by a scowling stagehand with a bad haircut. Within seconds a lady with headphones and a wad of chewing gum stood up at the front and told everyone to shut our mouths—she actually said that—adding, "and if anyone makes a peep you'll be kicked out on your butts so fast you won't know what happened." Pleasant. The whole experience was like that, to tell you the truth. I used to make my living driving an eighteen-wheeler with a company of cantankerous truckers, so a certain amount of gruffness usually slides right off me, but this was ridiculous.

Whatever happened to courtesy?

From the seat on my left, Lila Penn elbowed me. An

applause sign lit up just as the three famous judges stepped into view. I admit that I was gaping as much as anybody. I'd seen them countless times on TV but now there they were, just fifty feet away. Celeste looked oddly retro with her bouffant red hairdo and a fake pelican around her shoulders—only a former supermodel like her would even attempt such a weird look. Davey Dave seemed shorter and paler in real life than he did on TV, and he looked bored as he took his seat.

But the biggest celebrity, the *real* star of the show, was Franco.

Lean and muscled, with his goatee and ever-present black beret, Franco sauntered to the judges' table looking as grumpy as ever. Of the three, he was always the judge to watch, the one whose wisecracks and blunt opinions regularly sparked controversy in schoolyards and offices everywhere. Personally, I'd always thought he was kind of a jerk. A few minutes earlier Norm Gifford and I had caught a brief glimpse of him as he'd flown past us in the hallway. He seemed to have been in a heated argument with a tired-looking woman who somebody told us was the show's director. Actually, it was just Franco who appeared to be having the argument, jabbing his finger in the air and doing all the talking. From what I saw, he didn't let the poor woman get a word in.

Suddenly the show's theme music was blasting. The camera lights changed from red to green. This was it, I realized. This was live television, and millions of viewers all across America were watching.

The first two auditions went by in a flash—and the judges were not impressed. Davey Dave told the first act—a pair of chunky, banjo-playing identical twins who called themselves Glenda and Glenda—that they had no talent. Then Franco sent this droopy-eyed teen rapper/juggler named Jeremy back to his seat with "I have to be honest, Jeremy—I was bored. If you were the last juggling rapper in the world I still couldn't recommend you to entertain at a toddler's birthday. You're that dull." Some people in the audience thought this was hilarious, but I thought it was just plain mean. Neither of those acts was *that* bad. But I suppose meanness was part of the show, in a way. Sort of like when the Romans used to send prisoners into the lions' den for entertainment. With each new brutal comment they made, the judges seemed to be in better spirits. They were enjoying this. Even as the next act, a group of teens who called themselves CJ and the Belmar Boyz, stepped up to the stage, the three judges were still elbowing each other and snickering at how hilarious they were.

Uh-oh, I thought. *This doesn't bode well.*

WAYNE BASSO
Getting Off Easy

As just about everybody knows, that audition didn't exactly go great for us. Before we even got sent up to the stage I could see CJ's hands shaking. And it wasn't just him. My palms were a slippery mess and my mouth was so dry I wondered how I was going to sing at all. Finally they called us up and the four of us stood in front of all those lights and cameras. We started off okay. Look back at the online video clip and you'll see it's true. It was only after a few seconds that CJ's voice started to crack. Too bad it was on a high note, so it was totally obvious. I think it kind of killed the last of CJ's confidence, and after that it kept happening over and over again. Oh man, it was horrible. When we finished, Celeste held her nose like we'd stunk up the room, and Franco pointed us back to our seats. "Come back when you've finished with puberty, CJ," he said, and then he added, "Better yet, don't." A bunch of people were rolling in the aisles at that one, but to us it was like a kick to the stomach. Our hopes had been so high. I honestly thought we were gonna get to go to Vegas, but now I wondered how we could even show our faces again in Belmar. I could see that CJ was taking it even harder than the rest of us, and I felt especially bad for him. Thing is, CJ has an amazing voice. Just because maybe that day wasn't his best don't mean he's not super-talented. Trust me, the kid can belt out a song.

That guy Franco don't know nothing.

But it turned out we got off easy. The next act was a nervous-looking twelve-year-old from Oswego, a scrawny girl named Ruby. She had bad skin and a rainbow leotard that looked like it came from a secondhand shop. The poor kid didn't stand a chance. As soon as she stepped onto the stage the judges started rolling their eyes, which got some of the audience laughing too. Okay, so the girl had an acne problem and wasn't exactly glam, but not everybody has to look like a movie star. Besides, the kid was only twelve! She was staring like a frightened bird up there, but when she sang, she sang her heart out. It wasn't a silky pop-star voice, the boring kind that usually wins on that show, it was a little more raw and interesting, and I'm telling you, to me it was beautiful. That girl was the best act of the round so far, and I'm including us. But when she was done, those judges just sat there curling their lips while that little big-eyed kid blinked into the lights and waited.

After a long silence, the only thing that pinhead Franco

said to her was "I'm not going to lie, Ruby—you sounded like a buzz saw in need of an oil change. And by the way, haven't you ever heard of pimple cream? Good heavens, girl. Wash your face."

RAY BEECH
Watching from Home

Do I remember my *reaction* when I heard that? Sure I do! I laughed so hard I nearly fell off my sofa. Come on, it was *funny*! And yeah, that little girl took it hard, but I remember thinking so what? Sometimes the truth hurts, kid, and you can always count on Franco to tell it like it is. That's why everybody watches the show night after night. It isn't just to catch the contestants who might eventually win, it's also because people love to see what kind of losers try out, and to hear the hilarious stuff the judges say about them. It's not like anybody forces those people to audition. Even when it's totally obvious that a kid isn't going to win, that they're only going to make fools of themselves, they show up anyway, time and time again. Whose fault is that?

If you'd asked me, I would have told you: Any freak who auditioned for the show was begging for whatever insult they got.

Lemonade Mouth was up next, and I could hardly wait.

See, I knew those kids. We went to the same school. I'd lost my band, Mudslide Crush, and even my best friend the previous school year because of them, and yet for some infuriating reason everybody seemed to think those five were like god's gift to nobodies or something. It burned me up.

All I wanted was for everything to go back to the way it used to be when Mudslide Crush ruled and all was right with the world.

But since that wasn't going to happen, at least *American Pop Sensation* was about to dish out some justice.

NAOMI FISHMEIER
Oblivion or Glory

And now, Faithful Readers, it is my privilege to describe what I, your humble reporter, witnessed at that fateful moment. It so happens that during the entire *American Pop Sensation* incident I was surprisingly near to Lemonade Mouth—so near, in fact, that I was able to see and hear things that few others could.

Before I convey what I observed, though, allow me first to back up just a few minutes.

I need to explain where I was and exactly how I got there.

Back when our little Lemonade Mouth entourage was being rushed through the building, my thoughts had been clouded in a fuzzy pink fog of happy emotion. Even apart from the excitement of the auditions, this had already turned out to be a gigantic day for me. For six incredible weeks Lyle and I had been spending most of our time together without openly admitting that we liked each other, and now here we were running hand-in-hand as we dodged through a crowded building to watch our friends appear on one of the biggest TV shows there was. I was practically floating.

But then at last we arrived at the Judgment Room.

Just when a cranky stagehand was about to lead our

group up a set of metal steps to the last available seats, my natural journalistic instincts finally switched back on again. As everyone knows, a good reporter strives to be as close to the action as possible, so it occurred to me right away that the nosebleed section wasn't going to work. I glanced around. Lyle and I were being led past a wall of green curtains that lined the side of the audience. Scanning along its folds, I spotted a narrow band of darkness where two of the curtains didn't quite meet. Whatever was behind there, the secret space was only a few steps away and very near the front row, where Lemonade Mouth was about to be seated.

I made a split-second decision.

Squeezing Lyle's hand, I yanked him along with me, and in all the confusion nobody noticed us ducking behind the curtains.

Dear friends, modesty prevents me from boasting. Suffice it to say that this wasn't the first time quick thinking and a reporter's natural intuition had come in handy for me.

Which was why Lyle and I now had a front-row view of music history.

The space turned out to be filled with crates full of wires and unknown equipment. It was cramped and uncomfortable, but the vantage point was unbeatable. If either of us had reached through the narrow slit of the curtain (which of course we didn't), we could have touched Charlie's elbow. That's how close we were. Which was the reason I was able to see so clearly the growing horror on each of Lemonade Mouth's faces as they watched the judges rip apart each of the first four acts, one by one. It wasn't simply that the famous threesome didn't like the performances. Celeste, Davey Dave and Franco gave each of those acts a verbal thrashing, a public and personal humiliation they'd never forget. Sure, I'd seen them in dangerous moods plenty of times before, but I'm ashamed to say that only now, when I was close enough to see the devastation on the faces of each of the ridiculed contestants, did it finally hit me how unfair and tragic this system could be. Those judges wielded an almost godlike power—the power to grant or deny dreams, sending people with high hopes to the heights of glory or the depths of oblivion depending on the words they chose, which in turn depended only on how they happened to feel at that moment.

And for whatever reason, the gods were showing little mercy that night.

I squeezed Lyle's arm. Lemonade Mouth was up next, and already I had the sick feeling we were about to watch our favorite band—our *friends*—get destroyed on prime-time television. I wasn't the only one with that feeling either. The instant the show finished with Ruby from Oswego and cut to a commercial, I heard Charlie whispering under his breath.

"We're gonna get creamed. If they didn't like that amazing little girl, they'll hate us too."

Olivia was taking deep gulps of air. The others appeared just as panicked. A short distance away, a team of network stagehands was leaping onto the audition platform to move Lemonade Mouth's instruments into position.

"Guys, keep it together," Wen whispered. "We can do this."

Stella was sitting slumped in her chair, her arms crossed and her jaw tight. "Keep it together? Wen, didn't you hear how they trashed everybody? Doesn't it bother you? None of those acts deserved what they just got. They're people with feelings, but the judges treated them like *jokes*."

"It's what they do, Stella," Mo said. "It's part of the show."

I leaned a tad closer, straining to hear their voices—especially Mo, who was sitting farthest away from me. I had to be careful, though. I didn't want to think about what might happen if the curtains moved and somebody noticed. Or worse. What if I were to accidentally lose my balance and fall headfirst in front of the stage?

All five of them turned their heads subtly toward Ruby, who was sitting ashen-faced with her eyes on her knees. Her mother's arm was around her shoulder as she whispered into Ruby's ear, but the girl wasn't answering. She didn't seem to hear her.

Stella shook her head. "Doesn't mean it's right."

Something in Stella's voice must have caught Wen's attention, because after a pause he said, "Stella, please don't get any wild ideas. Not now. This isn't a high school and those *APS* judges aren't a soda company. This is too big for us. We can't change it."

Stella's hardened expression remained the same. "Maybe not," she said, "but we don't have to agree to be willing *participants* in this massacre. How about if we stay in our seats? What if we refuse to go on?"

She looked around hopefully at the others but they only stared back at her. Mo's forehead wrinkled. "Um, Stella, you can't be serious. We can't do that. We made a commitment to Mr. Decker. He pulled a lot of strings to set this up for us and we can't let him down."

Wen nodded. "Besides, if refusing to play is supposed to be our way of making a statement, it wouldn't be a very clear one. People would think we only pulled out because we're scared."

"They'd be right," Charlie said without a hint of comedy. "I *am* scared. I'm petrified."

Stella's face was reddening. She still looked livid, but she couldn't disagree with Wen and Mo. They were in a bind.

"Okay, so what are we saying?" Mo said, her voice even more urgent as she glanced toward the platform. The stage-hands were almost finished setting up the last of Charlie's congas. "Are we backing out or are we doing this?"

Stella narrowed her eyes at the judges. "I say we take a stand. We should refuse to go on."

After the briefest hesitation, Charlie nodded. "And I say Mo's right. We made a commitment, so we can't back out."

Wen took a deep breath. "I agree with Stella. That's two votes that we go through with the audition, two that we don't."

"Where's Mr. Decker when we need him? If he were here we could talk with him about this."

"But he's not here, Mo," Stella said, still eyeing the judges' table. At that moment the three of them were quietly chuckling over something, a shared joke, perhaps, and looking generally pleased with themselves. "This isn't up to Mr. Decker. This is *our* decision."

Wen turned to his left. "You're the last vote, Olivia. It's all up to you. What do you say?"

Olivia looked ready to curl into a ball. She was practically shaking. But there was no time for any more discussion, because one of the stagehands, a freckled boy who looked young enough to still be in high school himself, appeared in front of them. A tag on his shirt said his name was Cliff. "You guys are up and your instruments are all set," he said, scratching the peach fuzz on his chin. "You're on in thirty seconds. Follow me."

It was a moment that felt heavy with fate. Even from behind the curtain Lyle and I could both sense it. I was watching Olivia, who glanced nervously around at her friends and then back at Cliff. Then she stood up.

"We're ready," she said, her voice barely loud enough to hear.

The others followed her lead and rose to their feet—even Stella and Wen, although they didn't look happy about it. None of them did. But it was clear they all understood what had just happened. Olivia had cast her vote.

Lemonade Mouth's destiny was now set in stone.

I watched them follow Cliff toward their instruments. One of the clipboard people shouted that everyone had to be silent again. The show was going back on the air in ten seconds. Lyle's arm brushed against mine. Even as I felt the new warm glow between us, my eyes were locked on Lemonade Mouth. This was it, the big moment. Oblivion or Glory.

Don't screw this up . . . , I silently called to them in my thoughts. *Please, please, don't blow this. . . .*

But of course I could never have guessed what was about to happen.

Nobody could.

MRS. REZNIK
A Sneaking Suspicion

I gripped the arms of my chair as I watched them take their places on the little stage. So far, every act in this round had been gleefully and, in my opinion, *unfairly* ripped to shreds by the judges, those three pompous, self-important promoters of homogenized mediocrity. Excuse my frank language.

What did those three bozos know, anyway?

By then I was secretly fuming at Mr. Decker. He should

have considered that something like this could happen. If he really cared about Lemonade Mouth, why would he set them up to risk a public shaming? It made no sense. It's no secret that over the past year I'd grown especially fond of these students—these five young *musicians*. They deserved better than this.

The commercial ended and the applause light came on again, and suddenly Mohini, Charlie, Olivia, Stella and Wen were squinting into the spotlight. In their new black outfits they looked oddly out of place.

"Our next audition," Celeste announced with a sweep of her hand, "is a high-school band called . . . uh . . . Lemonade Mouth." She paused to look more closely at the index card she was reading from. Almost under her breath she asked, "Is that right? Lemonade Mouth? Now, *that's* a weird name. . . ." Beside her, Franco and Davey Dave nodded glumly, as if the band had already offended their refined sensibilities.

I was burning up inside.

But then Charlie called out the beat. The music began, and within seconds I felt a profound change come over the room.

The song was "Humanator," one of their newest and among my favorites. It started quietly, with Mo and Charlie setting a soft, staccato rhythm underneath Olivia's voice, which began as little more than a whisper:

> *Hello . . .*
> *You don't know me.*
> *In the grand scheme of things*
> *I'm a stranger,*
> *Unimportant in your life.*

But that's all right.
Hello . . .
You may never know my name
And I may never know yours,
But we are both walking this same busy path
At the same time
On the same day,
So in that way
I'm just like you.
So what do we do?
Before we pass by
And never see each other again?
I'll smile at you
If you'll smile at me
And in that way I'll be
Just like you
Just like me.
Hello . . .

The music quickened and expanded with the addition of Stella's ukulele and Wen's trumpet. The judges leaned forward in their chairs, their gloomy expressions fading. I think they were startled by the sheer power of the instruments and by the emotion in Olivia's unusual, gravelly voice, which seems to astonish everyone the first time they hear her. I swelled with pride. From my seat at the back of the audience I saw people all across the room nodding in time to the driving beat.

In this world of disconnection
Won't you be my human correction?
For you, for me, please won't you be

My humanator . . . humanator . . .
Won't you be my humanator?

It was all going so well. I'd heard them practice this piece a few times and always it left a lump in my throat, but this performance of the song was one of the most moving I'd ever heard. The audience clearly liked them too, and even the judges looked pleasantly surprised.

So perhaps you can imagine my utter shock when, just as Olivia was about to begin the second verse, she looked around at her band mates as if she were trying to make up her mind about something. And then, with a reddening face, she stepped back from the microphone. She simply *stopped singing*.

The others appeared confused but only for a moment. Within a few beats Stella stopped strumming her ukulele, Mo set down her bow and Wen and Charlie stopped playing too.

Oh no, I thought. *What on earth are they doing?*

There was a strange moment then, an odd tension I can hardly describe. All five of them stood still, gazing toward the other contestants in the front row. Those other acts were probably looking back at them just as bewildered as I was, wondering what exactly was going on.

And then it hit me, a sneaking suspicion.

By then I'd known these kids a while, remember. They were practically family to me. Which is why an idea hit me— a crazy inkling. I wasn't certain, mind you, but it occurred to me that maybe I should have seen this coming.

I held my breath.

CLIFF NOONER
What They Deserve

Yeah, I was there. I was the stagehand who had to lead that little kid, Ruby, back to her seat after Franco got through chewing her to pieces. The girl was practically in tears.

It's funny, but whenever I tell people that just before my senior year of high school my TV-executive uncle got me a summer internship working for *American Pop Sensation,* their faces usually light up like it must have been the cushiest job ever. I'm telling you, it wasn't. Sure, I was lucky to be there, but it was two months of backbreaking labor, long hours and taking abuse from those judges. Those three were a piece of work, let me tell you. You know that whole mean act they did all the time? Well, it wasn't an act.

Especially for that windbag, Franco.

That afternoon, for example, he and the show's director— a nice lady named Helena Pang—got into this big thing. I guess Franco wanted a fruit basket for his dressing room but it didn't arrive, and somehow he figured it was Helena's fault, so he'd threatened to get her fired.

So now it was Lemonade Mouth's turn to face the firing squad—and things were getting weird fast.

When these kids first started playing I was surprised. The music wasn't like anything I'd ever heard before, as if a band of nerdy-looking Martians had just dropped from the sky. And it totally rocked. But then, right in the middle of the song when everyone was really getting into it, they just sort of stopped. It wasn't a technical glitch or anything, I was pretty certain of that. They'd just ended the song early.

Holy crap! I thought. What the heck was up with them?

"Why did you stop?" Franco asked. "I'm surprised to hear myself say it, but that was actually quite good."

Celeste and Davey Dave agreed, and the next thing you know, Lemonade Mouth had three thumbs-ups from the judges, which meant that after playing only half a song they already had their golden ticket to be included in the next competition phase in Las Vegas. But something strange was still going on, a weird tension. I didn't think any of those kids looked happy. They were just standing there looking at the judges. Kind of staring them down, actually.

That's when it happened.

The singer, the girl with the mousey hair, stepped back toward the microphone. Her face was kind of red, like she was getting emotional for some reason. "No," she said in this soft, shaky voice, "we're not interested in competing any more on this show. We're done."

I'm telling you, unless you were there in that room you can't appreciate the full weirdness of that moment. In the whole history of *American Pop Sensation* nobody had ever refused a golden ticket. The audience was supposed to stay silent, but you could hear muffled gasps as people realized that the reason these five had stopped wasn't because they were nervous—it was because they had something to say. And from their expressions, it wasn't going to be a love-fest.

I spun my head toward the control booth. If something bad was about to happen—like, maybe if they started swearing or something—Helena could easily have shut down the feed and cut to a commercial using the seven-second delay. But she didn't. She kept broadcasting, and the reason was obvious: Whatever was about to go down, it was likely to be memorable.

Which meant sky-high ratings.

"Done?" Franco repeated, raising an eyebrow. "Didn't you come here because you wanted to compete in Las Vegas?" Celeste and Davey Dave looked just as confused.

The singer nodded, but she stepped back from the microphone—I guess she really *was* done. Then the other kids in the band spoke up, starting with that boy who played the trumpet. "We don't like the way you treated these other kids," he said pointing to the front row. "The way you laughed at them and the mean things you said."

The Indian-looking girl with the double bass nodded. "It wasn't necessary to do that. It was cruel."

Behind them, that big, frizzy-haired kid with the giant wall of weird drums was gripping his sticks so hard his knuckles were turning white. "It was pointless too," he added. "Look, we know you're trying to be entertaining and everything, but that doesn't make it okay to be just plain nasty."

On the monitors I saw close-ups of Celeste's and Davey Dave's faces. Their jaws dropped. Franco tugged at his beret and squinted his eyes toward the stage. "Oh, so that's what this is then, eh? Some silly little protest?"

"That's right," said the pink-haired girl with the uku-lele. She stepped forward and gripped the microphone. Now her voice rang out even louder and clearer across the studio. "That's exactly what this is. We're speaking up for all the people who make sacrifices to come out here and do their best for you, only to be humiliated with some stupid, vicious comment. Nobody's saying you have to *like* their acts, but you should at least *respect* the people themselves, because they deserve it. They're *people,* guys. Come on, don't you get that? They're only trying to follow their dreams."

I was bug eyed. I'd never known anyone with the nerve to stand up to those three like this, especially not a bunch of kid contestants. And what they were saying was true—every word of it. I looked around at the other stagehands and noticed I wasn't the only one trying not to grin. At last somebody was giving those jerks what they deserved! Franco glared toward Helena in the control booth. It was obvious he wanted her to shut this down, but she shook her head at him and kept broadcasting, barely hiding a smirk.

There were twenty-two million viewers that night. This was going to make every morning news show in the country.

Helena wasn't shutting this down. No way.

GLENDA MAY PUTRIDGE
Stand

Until then my twin sister, Glenda Lee, and I had been feeling like two smudge marks on the floor. "Talentless and unattractive" was what the judges called us. After a comment like that, how could I help wondering if maybe it was true? But now this Lemonade Mouth thing, this bunch of kids we didn't even know, was up there speaking out for us on national television.

"Stand up for justice!" the girl with pink hair was calling out, pointing toward the audience. "Stand up for reaching for your dreams! They belong to all of us, and they're important! Nobody should be able to get away with shooting them down just for a cheap laugh!"

"That's enough, young lady!" Franco said, his face turning purple. "All of you, back to your seats!"

But those kids just ignored him. Suddenly all five were

calling out for people to stand up. My fingers gripped tight to the armrests. This was *American Pop Sensation,* after all, and nobody had ever seen anything like this before. And then a few people in the audience started doing what the kids asked, rising from their chairs. I remember one of them, a big man with a Hawaiian shirt, glaring at the judges as he stood, and then looking over at me and the other contestants to give us the thumbs-up sign. One by one, others started standing too.

It was crazy. It was the beginning of an open revolt.

RUBY HERNANDEZ-GERMAIN
Thirty-Three Seconds

"Stand up for respect!" the ukulele girl shouted. "Let the world see it means something to you, and that none of us are gonna take cruelty sitting down!"

Franco slapped his palm against the table. *"This audition is over! Get back to your seats!"*

But it wasn't stopping. More people rose from their chairs, and some of them started clapping. Others cheered. And it was all for *us,* the contestants. To my astonishment, even a few of the stagehands were getting in on it, stepping out from the shadows.

I felt something happening inside me. I don't know if I can explain it, exactly, but before that night I'd never been the kind of person who made a fuss about anything. Until a few seconds earlier, I'd been sitting slumped in my seat staring at my knees and wondering if I could ever face going to choir practices again. What was everybody going to say to me at school? I was so mortified I could hardly breathe. But then I saw those twins and some of the other contestants rising to their feet, and the next thing I knew, I was pulling myself up from my chair and standing too. As soon as I did it the whole place erupted in cheers. It was amazing, as if the air in the studio had been electrified. Not everyone in the room was standing, but most were, and suddenly I felt like a whole battalion was behind me, an army of supporters applauding and filling the room with their voices.

Thirty-three seconds. That's how much time passed from the moment Lemonade Mouth turned down the golden ticket to when the network finally cut to a commercial. I know this because since then I've watched the online video maybe a hundred times. It probably sounds weird, but something happened to me during that half-minute. It might just have been the greatest thirty-three seconds of my life.

LILA PENN
Reconsidering Earl

The show went to a commercial as my daughter Stella and her friends left the stage. I'd been terrified for them, but at the same time I was so proud of what they'd done. People were still cheering and calling out for them. I want to be clear that the crowd was energized but not out of control—things never got to the point where there was any danger. But the atmosphere in the room was charged. As the kids headed to the exit and our little group of parents and friends trailed after them, the judges scowled at us from their table. But there really wasn't anything they could do. Most of the audience was with Lemonade Mouth, not them, and the damage had already been done.

Not a lot of people know this because it was never picked up by any microphone, especially under all the shouting, but near the exit stood one of the network executives, a donut-faced man with slicked-back hair and a dark suit, and as the kids came near he spoke to them.

"You think you're funny?" he asked, narrowing his eyes. "You think you own this place?"

That got my blood boiling. I was about to say something, but the kids' response was better than any I could possibly have given. They simply marched past him through that door, with the rest of us following.

Now, I'll admit that only a few minutes earlier I'd been furious at Mr. Decker. I'd even grumbled under my breath that he was an idiot for setting the kids up for all this. We'd all known, of course, that putting them in front of those unpredictable judges while millions watched was a risk, but I didn't realize just how *big* a risk. It could have ended the band. But it didn't. As our little entourage slipped through corridors crowded with onlookers who must have seen the whole incident on the monitors, what struck me was all the wide-eyed stares and the way people kept stepping back to let Lemonade Mouth pass.

Maybe I'd been wrong about Mr. Decker. Was it possible that somehow he'd understood Lemonade Mouth better than any of us?

Maybe Earl Decker wasn't an idiot after all.

Maybe he was a genius.

CHAPTER 5

When all seems perfect and contentment
sets in, that's when to be most on guard
that disaster is waiting to leap from
its dark hiding place and eat you.

–Phineas Flynn

Charlie
On the Verge

INTERIOR. LYLE'S MESSY GARAGE—MIDDAY

Lyle, wild-haired and intense, stares at his computer monitor as the
five members of Lemonade Mouth, plus Naomi Fishmeier, watch
over his shoulder.

> CHARLIE (V.O.)
> Over the next few days the online video clip of our
> appearance on *American Pop Sensation* went viral,
> peaking on the favorites charts for a whole week.

REVERSE ON: The computer monitor. The camera closes in on
the glowing screen as we see and hear a few seconds of the clip:
Stella calling into the microphone. The furious faces of the judges.

The defiant audience members rising to their feet, applauding, cheering. Chaos in the studio.

> CHARLIE (V.O.) (CONT'D)
> (over the ongoing audio from the clip)
> In the first twenty-four hours alone it was watched and shared more than two hundred thousand times. Let me say that again: the video clip got *two hundred thousand views* in just one day.

REVERSE ON: The seven dumbfounded faces still watching the clip.

> CHARLIE (V.O.) (CONT'D)
> We were only doing what we thought was right, but I guess we must have hit some kind of a nerve out there, because there were lots of comments from all over. Not all of them supported us, but most did.

REVERSE ON: The monitor again. We pan down to the comments area. As the words fill the screen, the monitor image fades so that behind the words we can also see a series of commenters, each one speaking the words aloud as we read them. (Note to whoever directs this: I'm thinking we could use big-name actors for this part. Good idea, right? It'd be a chance to put some A-list stars in cameo roles. Just a thought.)

> COMMENTER #1: RUMPLED
> MOTHER HOLDING A BABY
> It's about time somebody stuck it to Franco. Nice job, guys!

> COMMENTER #2: CUTE TEEN
> GIRL
> OMG! Way to go, Lemon Head! Those judges had it coming!

> COMMENTER #3: MIDDLE-AGED
> DUDE IN A SUIT
> I laughed out loud the first time I saw this. Didja catch the look on Franco's face? Classic.

Thank you, Lemonade Mouth! You said exactly what I've been thinking for a long time!

COMMENTER #5: GRUMPY OLD
MAN

Who do these snot-nosed kids think they are? And that name! Lemonade Mouth? Really? What kind of twisted person makes up a crazy name like that?

COMMENTER #6: KNOW-IT-ALL
GIRL

Fake, fake, fake. Is it me or is it not totally obvious this was a publicity stunt staged by the show to get higher ratings??? Come on, people!!!! What are you, gullible?

COMMENTER #7: LITTLE KID
WITH BRACES

Lemonade Mouth for president!

CHARLIE (V.O.)

And on and on . . .

DISSOLVE INTO: A television set. The late-night talk show host CHET ANDERS (late forties, shaved head, dapper) is doing the opening monologue of his nightly show.

CHARLIE (V.O.) (CONT'D)
(over Chet's voice and the audience's reactions)

For a few days, not only was Lemonade Mouth all over the blogosphere, but the story got picked up in other places too. We even got mentioned on *After Midnight with Chet Anders,* a late-night talk show that was available on cable outlets across most of the country.

CHET
(relaxed, a pro at this)

Oh, so anyone happen to catch *American Pop Sensation*

last night? Those kids who turned down the golden ticket because they didn't like how Franco and the other judges made fun of the other contestants?

Audience laughter, applause.

                              CHET (CONT'D)
Well, uh, as I understand it, Franco's agent still isn't taking calls after the testy incident. When asked if he's planning to take the kids' advice about being a little nicer, Franco reportedly responded, "Shut up, stupid. You're ugly and you bother me."
                    (deadpan)
Which for him is gentle, so I guess that means he's taking it under consideration.

Howls of laughter from the audience. A gap-toothed grin from Chet.

INTERIOR. EARL DECKER'S STRETCH LIMOUSINE—NIGHT

CLOSE-UP ON: Mr. Decker's face. He's happily checking his messages as highway lights speed past the window behind him.

                             CHARLIE (V.O.)
As for Mr. Decker's reaction to what we did, well, he was a little hard to read. Even back then there was talk that maybe he'd known ahead of time that something like that could happen, so I asked him.

                              MR. DECKER
                    (looking up from his messages)
Did I know *exactly* how it would play out? Well, no, Charlie, of course not, but I had a feeling you kids might stir up some press, and, well . . . you sure did.

                        CHARLIE (OFF-SCREEN)
So . . . you're not mad at us?

                              MR. DECKER
                    (a half-smile)
What can I say? You took a chance and veered off the traditional map a little and it worked out . . . this time.

> (a pause, smile suddenly vanishes)
> But we can't push our luck again, guys. From now on, we
> stick to the map.

Dissolve to . . .

EXTERIOR. OLIVIA'S BACKYARD—LATE AFTERNOON

Lemonade Mouth, plus Lyle and Naomi, having an epic water fight
in Mo's backyard with hoses blasting and huge plastic water guns
firing away. Everybody's soaked and laughing.

> CHARLIE (V.O.)
> Those were crazy days for us. It all seems kind of
> dreamlike now. It might seem hard to believe but while all
> this stuff was going on, to us it felt as if it was happening
> sort of in the background. We were regular kids, right?
> That didn't change. That never changed.

Rajeev and Mo's little sister, Madhu, sneak like ninjas around the
side of the house carrying a huge bucket of water balloons. They
crouch behind a bush and peek commando-style over it, waiting
for just the right moment to attack. The moment comes. They
start hurling the balloons, dousing Mo and Wen—a nice barrage.
Mo shrieks. But Stella has the hose and is quick to fire back.
Soon Rajeev and Madhu are surrounded and dripping wet, with
everybody cheering and whooping.

Dissolve to . . .

EXTERIOR. RECORDING STUDIO—DAY

Lemonade Mouth stands around a microphone at Z-Division
Studios, all five of them with headphones on. They're adding a
group vocal track—the humming part of their song "No Words
Can Say It."

> CHARLIE (V.O.)
> (over the music)
> We completed the recordings for Mr. Decker. One last
> session of finishing touches, and after that it felt like we

had time on our hands again. You know, time for *normal* things like summer jobs, hanging out at home, stuff like that.

Music continues over a montage of shots:

A. Stella answering the phone in the lobby of her mom's lab, with Rajeev flipping through a magazine beside her.

B. Olivia helping out with her grandmother's printing business, both of them stuffing envelopes at the kitchen table.

C. Charlie helping Mo's dad pack a shelf with rice sacks at Banerjee Grocery while, nearby, Mo talks with a customer.

D. Wen and Olivia writing music together in Olivia's backyard.

E. Stella walking hand-in-hand on the beach with Rajeev with the sun setting and waves rolling gently over their bare feet.

F. Wen in the wiener suit on a busy street corner. He's playing his trumpet while Stella, grinning beside him, attacks her uke with some killer riffs. Charlie, hair flying, slaps an all-out merengue odyssey on a garbage can. They're jamming out and having an amazing time. Rajeev is there too, popping and sliding and flipping like a mad dog to the music. (I'm telling you, he could dance like nobody else, as if he could defy space and time and gravity. The kid was unbelievable to watch.)

INTERIOR. STELLA'S FAMILY'S STUFFY LIVING ROOM—EARLY EVENING

Lemonade Mouth are back at a computer monitor again, only this is a different day and a different place. On the screen is Earl Decker, puffing on his cigar as he listens to Stella talking, asking him questions. Her words are indistinct to us as Charlie narrates:

CHARLIE (V.O.)
In retrospect everything was happening incredibly fast, but at the time it seemed to us like things were taking forever. We had the Too Shy to Cry shows to look

forward to at the end of August, but most of us couldn't wait that long to play another gig—a real gig, wherever it was going to be. Mr. Decker kept telling us we needed to wait it out.

> MR. DECKER
> (Zen-like, a rock guru giving sage advice
> from the screen)
> Patience, kids. It takes time for the tide to shift. The winds of opportunity are about to fill your sails, but first there's work still to do in preparing the ship for the voyage.

REVERSE ON: The five faces taking this in, foreheads wrinkling.

> CHARLIE (V.O.)
> Mr. Decker had a way with words. In a parallel universe, maybe he could have been a sailor.

Dissolve to . . .

EXTERIOR. A QUIET BEACH—EARLY MORNING, THREE YEARS FROM NOW

Dressed in his favorite lambswool parka and Hawaiian shorts, Charlie, older and more mature, is looking pensive as he walks barefoot in the sand. Beside him, the ocean drifts in and out in gentle waves. Other than Charlie, the beach is empty. (Note to whoever directs this: I'm thinking this is kind of a documentary-style part here, where a future me is strolling along the edge of the water, hands in my pockets, talking to the camera.)

> CHARLIE
> But as for me, even with all the excitement, underneath it I was going through a personal crisis. I guess it started with the realization of my own stupid jealousy when it came to Mo and Rajeev, and the total disaster it might have caused for Lemonade Mouth. For me it was an important reminder that Lemonade Mouth was a delicate balance, just like everything else in the Universe—and my own

balance seemed to be out of whack. My whole life was changing, and I realized that something was missing, something I needed to find even though I didn't know exactly what it was. I can't explain it better than that.

Picks up a pebble and tosses it into the waves.

CHARLIE (CONT'D)
I didn't understand it myself at the time, but I felt it, believe me.

Dissolve to . . .

EXTERIOR. SLEEPY SUBURBAN STREET NEAR STELLA'S HOUSE—PRESENT DAY

A long shot of the road. Lemonade Mouth gets smaller on the screen as they run laughing down the street, away from the camera. The sun is setting and the kids' shadows stretch long behind them.

CHARLIE (V.O.)
Not to say that it wasn't a happy time, or that I didn't get caught up in the thrill of the moment just like everybody else. I did. In fact, maybe that was the problem. Looking back, sometimes you see the past in a different light. For a short while things seemed to be going so crazy good for us that it was like we were living in a dream. And maybe that explains why we made the mistakes we did. Maybe our recent taste of success somehow ended up throwing our judgment out of whack. Who can say? The fact is, even though none of us knew it yet, things were about to take an unexpected turn. The universal balance was about to shift, and Lemonade Mouth was on the verge of screwing up big-time.🔋

OLIVIA
Secrets at the Kitchen Sink

Dear Ted,

Got your letter. Let me get this out of the way so we can both move on, okay? No, I still haven't told Brenda about the note from Mom yet. She's stressed enough already, I can tell. In fact, I've been thinking maybe I'll hold off on telling her until things calm down. It's not just her either. Every time I think about Mom it makes me upset. Plus, my life is already going nuts, as you know, so adding even more chaos doesn't seem like the best idea—not for Brenda or for me. Please understand. My mother made her decision long ago. Why should I let her shake up my world just because she decides all of a sudden to parachute back into my life after all these years?

That's it. I'm done with that subject now. I love you, but I'm asking you to please stop pushing me about this.

Moving on from the bizarre to the surreal . . .

Yes, the <u>American Pop Sensation</u> thing was a total fluke. Even now I find it hard to believe it actually happened. And no, we didn't plan any of that ahead of time. Before we went into the studio my only goal was to stop myself from barfing on national television. I barely made it, and afterward my hands shook for almost an hour. I've been doing what you suggested, trying to pretend that the people just aren't there, but it's not working. (I can almost hear your next suggestion, but no, I don't want to quit doing this because I love making music with my friends, and, besides, I don't want to let everybody down. I'll figure this out somehow, Dad. I have to.)

Anyway, I'm glad to hear that the other inmates are treating you like a celebrity now. As long as you're enjoying that, I'm happy for you.

You asked for an update on Daisy: she's the same—a complete mystery to me. This morning she dug a giant hole in the middle of the yard, dropped one of Brenda's orthopedic shoes into it and then hissed whenever Brenda or I came near it. I never had a cat like that before. Good thing she's cute, because I think she might also be certifiably bonkers.

That's it for now. Wen just stopped by with a new riff he wants us to work on.

     Love,
     Olivia

P.S.

Wen just left. You might not know it, but you and he are quite a team. He keeps pushing too.

Again and again he's been asking me what's the matter. I don't know how he picks up on it so easily. I don't want to be a burden on anyone, so I've been doing my best to act like everything's normal—or at least as normal as anything could be right now. Which is why I still didn't tell him about Mom's letter. I haven't told anybody but you.

Daddy, please understand what I said about this. I'm trying to balance a lot of things at once here. I'm doing my best.

Dear Ted,

I want to scream. I feel like jumping up and down and pounding my fists against the walls but I won't because it'd only make Brenda come check on me. I don't want to talk to her right now. I don't want to talk to anyone. I'm just sitting here on my bed fuming.

So I caved in and took your advice about talking with Brenda. But guess what? It turned out you were wrong—it didn't make things better at all. Just like I thought it would, it made things worse.

Much, much worse.

Let me set the scene for you: Brenda was washing the dishes when I walked in and showed her the letter. She took a minute to read it silently. When she was finished she didn't say a word; she just handed it right back without looking at me.

The weirdest thing was that she didn't even seem surprised. She'd just found out that her long-lost daughter had reappeared out of nowhere after more than a decade, and yet she didn't even bat an eye.

"So . . . what do you think?" I asked her quietly.

"Oh, honey," she said after another long silence, "you don't want to get involved in this."

My mouth went dry. All at once it hit me that Brenda didn't seem surprised because she wasn't surprised. "You . . . already knew about her, didn't you?" I asked, still trying to take it in. "You knew she was in Massachusetts."

Brenda nodded. Her hands were gripping the counter now, and she had this empty expression. She still wouldn't look at me. "She wrote me two months ago," she said. "Olivia, your mother's got . . . problems. Real problems. Health issues, among other things."

"What health issues?"

"Well, for one thing, her kidneys aren't working right anymore because she hasn't been taking care of herself, but that's nothing new. She's never taken much care of herself, as far as I can tell. At least she's with people now. She's living in a halfway house."

For a few seconds I couldn't say anything else. I just stood there staring. Finally I managed to ask, "Why didn't you tell me?"

"I was trying to keep you safe."

"Safe? From my own mother?"

Brenda closed her eyes. "Listen, I . . . I know she's my daughter, and I'll always love her, but believe me when I tell you that Jess isn't like you and never was. You have a selfless heart and a bright future. I know it sounds unkind, but things might have worked out for the best when she left. There, I've said it. Now you can go ahead and think of me as a bad person, but one thing I've learned is that life isn't always simple."

"But, Brenda, you could have told me all of this! You could have said something two months ago!"

"I could have," she said. "But the truth is, your mother asked me not to. She told me she wanted to write you but she wasn't ready just yet. She begged me to give her a little more time, so I did." At last Brenda looked at me. "Olivia, before you go and get yourself too involved with Jess, you should know that you'll be opening up a world of trouble and grief for yourself."

I didn't answer. What could I say?

She eyed me like she was trying to read my mind. "But you're not going to take my advice and stay away, are you? You're going to go and see her." She sighed. "I can't say I blame you. It's only natural for a girl to want to know her mother."

I took a step back. And then another. She was

talking as if I'd already decided what to do. To me it felt like the whole room was rocking. All I wanted was to get out of there. I backed away and ran to my room, slamming the door. That's where I still am. I'm furious, but I don't know who to be furious at. Brenda? My mother? You? I don't know. There are way too many moving parts here. It's too much to wrap my mind around.

My entire life is exploding and the only thing I understand is that I don't understand anything.

WEN
Toddlers with a Bowl of Spaghetti

After the *American Pop Sensation* thing, we had a small cult following all over the country. It wasn't *huge* or anything, but for the first time we had a fan base that went beyond the borders of Rhode Island. And yet, just like after the lemonade machine incident at the end of the recent school year, once again most of the media attention focused on the controversy instead of our music, with headlines like, "The Lemon That Roared" and "Rhode Island Kids Stand Up To 'Cruel' *APS* Judges." I kept remembering how Mrs. Reznik was always reminding us that it's the *music* that matters above all else. True, our performance got rave reviews in a few small music magazines and blogs. A handful of independent college radio stations even started playing our songs. But for the most part, people thought of us as a novelty story for the slower-news summer months.

I have to admit, as exciting as things were getting, that part was kind of a disappointment.

We were all at Bruno's Pizza Planet one afternoon, for example, listening to Mo read an article from the *Cleveland Chronicle*. It didn't even say that we were a band. It only referred to us as "five high school students with a penchant for civility."

"Typical!" Stella said when Mo finished. "What did they think we were doing up there in the first place, loitering? Didn't they notice our instruments? Didn't they hear our song? Why didn't they write *that*?"

When we mentioned this to Mr. Decker he didn't think it was a big deal. "Don't worry," he told us. "Any press is good press."

I tried to believe it, but it wasn't easy.

Now, there's been a lot of heated speculation about this next part, about how and why the events that followed could ever have happened in the first place. The thing to keep in mind is that we were all brand-new at this, and there was a lot of other distracting stuff happening in our lives. Even though my dad was working like a dog, his wiener business was struggling. Turns out my father was great with people, but he might have overestimated their willingness to eat wieners for lunch every day. So now he was asking for a lot more of my help. Mo was doing extra hours at her family's store, Stella was off in her own little world with Rajeev, and Charlie was on some weird mission he'd devised for himself, spending all his free hours trying things he didn't normally do, like baking cookies, rollerblading or building gigantic castles out of sand and shells. "There's something missing, Wen," he told me as he filmed a video of a cloud drifting across the sky, "something I have to figure out. How am I going to find what I need if I don't look for it?"

Typical Charlie. I would have laughed if I didn't think he was serious.

As for Olivia, I knew something was up with her even though she was still refusing to admit it. I felt this weird distance between us, and it was beginning to bug me. If she was mad at me, why didn't she just say so and tell my why? Why did she have to keep herself so bottled up? I know it sounds selfish, but I didn't understand, and I was starting to lose my patience.

So yeah, maybe we should all have seen the trouble coming, but I think we were each a little blinded by other things and ended up getting swept away in the moment. And anyhow, it wasn't like any of us had a crystal ball.

One day the five of us gathered in Stella's living room for yet another video link with Mr. Decker. He told us he had some big news. Chet Anders, the television talk-show host, had called him. His show, which aired late at night and was known for its edgy, anything-goes attitude, had been featuring the clip of our appearance on *APS,* playing it over and over again for comic value, and it was getting such a great reception from viewers that Chet had invited us to be guests for an interview on the show.

"And that's not the only big news," Mr. Decker told us as the monitor filled with his cigar smoke. "Zephyr Stick, the lip balm company, wants to sponsor you. They like the band's attitude and the image you can project for them, so they want to feature you in an upcoming ad campaign. I'm telling you, this is big. It'll go a long way toward solidifying Lemonade Mouth's national presence. It'll also set you up for even more sponsorships going forward."

I glanced around. Everybody looked stunned.

"The best part is that you kids won't have to do anything for this. The company already saw the band photos we took a few weeks ago, and they've picked one they want to use. It's all upside, guys. A no-brainer."

Stella's boot tapped as she brushed back a strand of her pink hair. "Wait, let me get this straight. They want to use us in an ad for *lip balm*? Is that really such a good idea?"

I was wondering the same thing.

"Um, this is only a question," Charlie asked, looking just as uncertain, "but, like, whenever anyone thinks of Lemonade Mouth, do we really want them associating us with chapped lips?"

Mr. Decker chuckled and took another puff on his cigar. "Guys, guys . . . you gotta be more forward-thinking than that. This is the music business—the real world. I didn't make the rules, but we have to play by them if we want to get ahead. A sponsorship means money for building the band's future. And don't worry. This ad is going to be young. It'll be hip. It'll be fresh." He leaned back in his chair. "You kids are going to love it. Trust me."

After the video link ended, the five of us had a long, tense discussion. On the one hand, this was starting to feel suspiciously like compromising on our ideals, and Stella wasn't the only one who felt uneasy about that.

"We're a *band*," Mo mused aloud. "We make music. Shouldn't *that* be what we're all about?"

I admit, I might have been the one who pushed hardest for us to go ahead with the deal despite the uncertainty in my gut. "Sure," I said, "but you heard what Mr. Decker told us about the industry and our future. What if this is our one and only chance to make it big?" I could see it on everyone's faces that they were worried about the same thing.

It wasn't an easy decision. In the end I think the argument that tipped the scales was that this was what Earl Decker advised us to do. This was a guy who knew the music business inside and out and had guided countless other bands to stardom. If we weren't going to follow the instincts of the legendary Earl Decker, whose instincts were we supposed to follow?

As Olivia likes to say, nothing ever happens without a reason. It's easy to look back now and second-guess what we did, but believe me, things can be clearer in hindsight than they were at the moment they occurred. Don't forget that this was a whole new world for us and we were still learning. We were like toddlers playing with a bowl of spaghetti: we didn't know what we were doing, so in a way, it shouldn't be surprising that we ended up making a mess of things—a mess that soon landed all over us.

STELLA
Staring at the Warped Face of an Unhealthy Ideal

Now and then everybody does things they later regret. We're only human, so it's unavoidable that each and every one of us is going to screw up once in a while. Sometimes we'll recognize our lapses in judgment right away. Sometimes not. Rarely in life, though, do the results of our bad decisions appear before us in the form of a forty-eight-foot-wide full-color image posted against the morning sky for all to see, making the mistake so obvious that it cannot be ignored or denied.

This was one of those rare times.

It was early on a Wednesday morning. My mom called me from the highway, waking me from a much-needed restful sleep. She was driving into Providence to meet a Brown University research student but had suddenly felt an urgent need to grab her cell and shake up my world.

"You're not going to believe this!" her voice buzzed through the phone. Still mush-headed, I rubbed my bleary eyes and took in the numbers on the clock: 8:53 a.m. I feel there is a sacred rule that people should not be disturbed when trying to sleep in on their day off, but my mother continued, undaunted. "I was taking the ramp onto Route 114 when I looked up, and who do you think was looking back at me?"

I kept silent. I had no idea.

"*You*, Stella! It was you and your friends! The Zephyr Stick ad, it's already up! It's giant!"

Two or three full heartbeats passed before the full meaning of this made its way into my sleepy brain.

Moments later, completely awake, I stood in my socks beside my beloved new SISTA SLASH: FAMINE RELIEF NOW! poster (from Earl—he also said he'd work with a connection to set us all up with free tickets to Sista's upcoming Take Charge megaconcert. Life was sweet!) and sent a group message to my friends. Forty minutes after that, we all met in town. I was thrilled to see Rajeev tagging along with Mo. He wanted to see the sign as much as the rest of us did. It was warm that morning, and I noticed everybody was holding a familiar green and yellow Mel's cup. I wasn't the only one who'd stopped at Bruno's to pick up a lemonade.

The billboard stood next to the entrance of the highway on Wampanoag Road, not far from the Bernbaum Associates

Dental building. There the six of us stood speechless, taking in the humongous image. The shot was impressive, to say the least. They'd used one of the photographs from Boston, and it must have been taken toward the end of our photo session, because we were all looking comfortable with the camera as we leaned against a brick wall. Wen had even taken off his black jacket and was holding it over his shoulder like some kind of high-powered supermodel. We weren't frowning, exactly, but our expressions were intense. Above our heads were giant blue words:

JOIN THE REVOLUTION!
PUCKER UP WITH ZEPHYR STICK!

"Holy crap," Rajeev said under his breath.

I couldn't have put it better.

We practically glowed up there. Mo looked mysterious and exotic, leaning her head on Charlie's broad shoulder, while Wen and I were like stylish super-spies. Olivia was the centerpiece, staring straight at the camera like she had a secret she wasn't going to tell. I don't think I'd ever imagined us looking so perfect, like flawless specimens of teenage health and coolness. But I think that's a big part of why, as I gaped at the sign, my fist was clenching my Mel's cup and my blood was starting to boil. We looked *too* perfect.

So perfect, in fact, that it wasn't really *us* up there.

The image had been altered.

Olivia's thighs were too skinny, like Barbie-doll legs. They must have been airbrushed. I'd been slimmed way down too, and there was something weird going on with my lips. They were puffy and pursed in a way that wasn't at all like the real me. Wen's slight acne, which I distinctly remembered he'd had during the photo shoot (the result of too many overheated hours in the wiener outfit), had been digitally cleared, and Mo's brown eyes were now a striking green. Even Charlie's uncontrollable mop had been altered. On the billboard his hair looked tidy—even (dare I say it?) *trendy*.

All of these changes were subtle, but then again, they weren't. Not if you were familiar with what we *really* looked like.

"I don't believe it," I said, unable to hold back. "This is outrageous! They've changed us to look like perfect little spokesmannequins! They've turned us into plastic dolls!"

"Uh . . . I don't know, Stella," Wen said. "I think I look kind of hot."

I rolled my eyes. "Wen, don't take this the wrong way, but that's not you up there. It's not any of us. We don't look like that. Sure, it might be a common practice in the advertising industry, but what kind of message does changing our appearance send?"

I looked around at the blank faces.

"Don't you see?" I asked, trying to keep my voice calm but failing miserably. "They're *using* us to promote a twisted image of life just like a zillion other ads do, a world of skeletal cover girls and synthetic faces! It makes people believe they need these products because it preys on everybody's insecurities, making real people feel like failures just because they don't look like this warped, unrealistic ideal. Come on, guys!" I said, jabbing my finger toward the freakish glowing kids that weren't really us. "Look at our faces! Look at Olivia's legs! No wonder there are so many kids with self-image issues and eating disorders! Normal, healthy people don't look like that!"

Mo's answer was quiet and reasonable, as if she was

worried I might bite someone. "Stella, the ad is already out there. I'm sure it's in magazines all over the country. It's done."

"But it's another form of oppression! A clear case of manipulation on a grand scale!"

There was a long quiet moment after that. Rajeev shifted his weight beside me, and I could hear Olivia breathing. In the distance, a dog barked.

I was sure I knew what my friends were thinking. I could imagine them saying to themselves, *Oh no, here we go again. Look out! Stella's about to unleash another of her wild ideas! Here comes more trouble!* And it's true that I was burning up over this. I wanted to tear that sign down. I wanted to make my feelings known to the world somehow. But I also felt that this time my friends were right to be frustrated with me. Sure, we'd all agreed to this together, but deep down I felt like I should have been the one to say no. I should never have allowed this deal to happen in the first place, but I guess I'd let my guard down and this was the result. And now it was too late to fix it. We were powerless to fight back. How do you take on a multibillion-dollar industry?

I couldn't ask my friends to fight a battle we couldn't win.

I gazed again at my altered face. My alien lips. My perfect, sculpted eyebrows. A distorted version of my own eyes stared back at me, taunting me. I was furious, but I also knew that if nobody else felt this way, then it didn't matter. From everyone's silence, I suspected I was alone.

But I was wrong.

For the record, it wasn't me who spoke up next, stirring up our collective emotions and setting off the hurricane of events that followed. It was Charlie.

"You know what?" he said. "I hate to admit it, but Stella's right. I didn't even notice it at first, but now that I do, I think it's totally uncool that they changed us." He gestured toward the billboard. "Sure, we agreed to let them do an ad—but we didn't say they could do *that*."

Everybody stared at the image again. Olivia took a step back. She studied it. After a moment she said, "I agree. What's up there is wrong. It's a lie."

Mo nodded too.

"Okay," Wen said. "But . . . um . . . what are we supposed to do about it?"

The wind picked up, a warm gust like the start of a summer storm. Everybody looked at me.

Devoted followers, I confess that I, your own normally outspoken Sista Stella, had no answer to give. What's more, I was too overwhelmed even to talk. I could hardly believe what I was hearing, the direction everybody seemed to be going in, even without me urging them on. Waves of emotion were welling up inside me. My band mates, my *friends*—they *got* it.

How could I ever have doubted them?

"All right, so we don't know what we can do about this yet," Charlie said, "but we'll think of something, right? The point is, they say they want a revolution, so let's bring it to them. Are we all in?"

Rajeev took my hand and squeezed it as, one by one, everybody raised their Mel's cups into the air. Not only was I still unable to speak, but by then I was too choked up to even make a sound.

MOHINI
A Short Conversation Across Four Thousand Miles

This is big. My house is closest, so we all head there to think things through. Maa and Baba have already gone to the store and Madhu's at an overnight with a friend, so the house is empty. As soon as we step through the front door, Rajeev announces he's got letters to write. It's obvious he's just making an excuse to give us space, and that's nice of him but not necessary. Everyone tells him he's welcome to join us, but he disappears anyway. The rest of us sit around the picnic table in the backyard, where I set out cheese sandwiches, little bowls of rice and reheated rogan josh left over from last night's dinner. The aroma of spice fills the air, even outside.

Our first idea is simple: we talk to Mr. Decker, tell him we don't want to be a part of this sponsorship deal anymore and ask him to help us figure out how to get out of it. It won't be an easy conversation, of course, but there's no other choice. We don't have a Plan B.

As it happens, Mr. Decker is in Germany with Tommy Bellclanger and the Ringtones—one of Decker and Smythe's biggest clients—for the kickoff of their giant new European tour. It takes a few calls to his office and some waiting around, but at last we manage a video link to his laptop in the lobby of his hotel.

Mr. Decker is not sympathetic.

"Guys, calm down," he says, frowning into the screen as we all stand around the computer on Maa's cramped little desk. "There's no backing out of this. Zephyr Stick is putting up big money for you. They're gonna front a lot of the cost for the August tour, where, need I remind you,

136

Lemonade Mouth is scheduled to do ten already-sold-out shows opening for Too Shy to Cry. We don't want to rock this boat. Your debut album is coming out, and that ad goes a long way toward building your presence. It's a gift straight from promotions heaven."

"Yes, Mr. Decker," Stella says, obviously trying her best to stay composed and tactful despite herself, "but it also sends out a bogus subliminal message that exploits kids and ignores the fact that there are lots of different ways to be beautiful. We never agreed to be part of that. It's a sham."

Mr. Decker strokes his scruffy beard. He checks his watch. "Look, you know I admire your spirit, guys. It's part of what makes your band what it is. But that doesn't mean any of us can change the way things work. The world spins the way it spins, and you should consider yourselves lucky to be on the side of the people who happen to have their hands on the wheel."

Over his shoulder we can see a youngish, slick-haired man in an expensive-looking suit. He's been talking on a cell phone, but now he steps closer and whispers into Mr. Decker's ear.

"One second," Mr. Decker says to him in a low voice, and then to us he says, "Listen, I gotta end this. The Lord Mayor of Heidelberg is throwing a meet-and-greet with Tommy and the boys. I'm already late for—"

"But the ad—" I start to interrupt. I can't believe he's about to cut us off. There's so much more we still want to say! Mr. Decker holds up his hand, though, and for an instant I'm almost sure I see irritation flash in his eyes.

"Sorry, out of time, kids," he says. "Just remember this: there are zillions of unknown bands out there, and out of all of them, yours is getting a measure of recognition across the country. With my help, Lemonade Mouth is about to take the world by storm. Believe me, it's gonna happen—I have it all planned out. I'll be back in the office in a couple days and then I'll fill you in." He's reaching toward the keyboard now.

"Mr. Decker, this is important. Wait!"

"Good luck with Chet Anders tomorrow night," he says as if he doesn't hear us. "Tell him I said hello."

And then he's gone.

The five of us are left gaping at the screen. My neck muscles are tense, and Olivia's face is turning the color of overboiled beets. Lemonade Mouth has been changed into something we never wanted to be, and it's clear we can't rely on Mr. Decker to help us set things right again.

WEN
Plan B—The War Room

One of the things about Lemonade Mouth that people don't always seem to realize is that if it hadn't been for the support of the people around us, our families and friends, the things that happened could never have played out the way they did. For example, we couldn't have signed with Decker and Smythe in the first place if our parents hadn't let us. It couldn't have been an easy decision for them, but in the end every single parent gave us the freedom to see how far this band thing could go, at least for the time being. And we all appreciated that.

But their help didn't end there.

Some people might be surprised to learn that after that Zephyr Stick ad came out, when we told our families about our feelings and explained our reasons, they took us seriously right away. In fact, they all agreed to meet that same evening for a big gathering in Stella's living room. All our families were there, plus Lyle, Naomi, Rajeev and Mrs. Reznik. The battle lines had been drawn, it seemed; it was time to gather our allies and plan a strategy.

The thing was, Mo, Charlie, Olivia, Stella and I had come up with a new idea. It was kind of a *risky* idea, though, and maybe even a little crazy, and it made each of us nervous just to think about it. Which was why we wanted to go over it with everyone. Before we ended up making a huge, stupid mistake, we wanted to know what our friends and families thought.

Everybody listened as we walked them through what had happened with the ad and our conversation with Mr. Decker. We told them the new idea and asked for their opinions.

It would be a lie to say that there weren't mixed feelings.

"This is serious stuff. You do realize that, don't you?" Stella's mother glanced meaningfully toward Charlie, as if she thought he'd be the most likely of us to see reason. I guess it made sense. Out of the five of us he generally *was* the calmest and tended to keep his head during tense moments. But right then he looked as unsure as the rest of us. "Even if you kids can pull this off," she continued, "you need to realize that there'll probably be repercussions."

Mo's mother was just as concerned. "Don't you think you've caused enough trouble for yourselves? Monu, you can't fight every battle that comes your way. When does it stop?"

"But, Maa," Mo answered, "didn't you and Baba always teach me to do the right thing even when it isn't easy? Well, this might not be easy, but we think it's important."

Even Mrs. Reznik had her doubts. "I don't know," she

said. "Your hearts are in the right place, but I wonder if you're taking on more than you realize here. And doing this would require an awful lot of work in a very short time."

But we knew that. We all understood.

There were more than twenty people in the room that night, and the whole group talked it over for more than an hour. Believe it or not, the one who spoke up for us first, the person who sort of turned the tide in our direction, was Mo's dad.

"Here's what I think," he said, and right away everyone else went quiet, because until then he hadn't said a word. "I think I have never been prouder of my daughter and her friends than I am right now. If Lemonade Mouth can do this, I say let them. And I will help in any way I can." A hush fell over the room. This was *Mo's dad*, probably the most conservative person there, a man who seemed to have a hard time saying okay to *anything*. A yes from him was a big deal.

Mo stared, her lip quivering.

After that it wasn't long before we had the go-ahead. Lyle, Naomi and Rajeev were with us from the start, of course, and the younger kids in the room—Mo's sister, Madhu; Stella's little stepbrothers, Tim and Andy; and my own little brother, George—were practically bouncing off the walls with excitement. What was more, everyone said they were all in this with us. Everybody would pitch in to help.

Which was good news.

We were going to need all the help we could get.

Before our plan had any chance of working, we still needed approval from one last person. It was Stella who called the production office of *After Midnight with Chet Anders*. We assumed we'd have to leave a message, but somebody answered. Stella explained to the receptionist who she was and that she had an emergency situation to discuss with the producers. To our surprise, after a few phone transfers we found ourselves on the line with none other than Chet himself.

Try to imagine it.

There we were, five kids from Rhode Island, standing around a speakerphone talking with Chet Anders, the subversive underground hero of late-late-night television. And yet as unbelievable as it felt, it happened, and Chet turned out to be a nice guy.

"So I hear you kids are having some issues and need to talk," he said. "What's up?"

Mr. Decker had already arranged all the particulars of our upcoming appearance. The plan was that we would do a short interview with Chet and then perform "Let Us Begin." But now, in a tone that sounded surprisingly levelheaded for Stella, she explained to him what was going on and told him our new plan. Chet listened. As the details came out, we heard him start to chuckle. I knew we had him then. He liked the idea.

By the time we hung up, we had his approval.

There was a part of me that felt almost disappointed when he said yes. If he'd said no, things would have been easier and a lot less risky. In a way, it would have been a relief. Instead, things had just gotten serious. We were going for it.

All I could do now was hope we didn't screw it up.

141

CHAPTER 6

Far better is it to dare mighty things,
to win glorious triumphs, even though
checkered by failure, than to take up ranks
with those poor spirits who neither enjoy much
nor suffer much, because they live in the gray
twilight that knows neither victory nor defeat.
—Theodore Roosevelt

RAJEEV KUMAR
Master Guru of Dance

Putting me in charge of the volunteer dancers was Stella's idea. The plan was for Lemonade Mouth to put together a special performance for a television show called *After Midnight with Chet Anders,* and my job was to choreograph a routine for the new song the band had written. Everything had to come together—the song, the costumes, the dancing—in only one day.

The pressure was rather intense.

I felt glad Stella had so much confidence in me, but I was secretly panicking. I'd never choreographed anything like this before—a dance for nondancers to perform on a show that would be seen across the whole country. How on earth was I going to pull this off?

But then I remembered being on the movie set with the great choreographer Shiamak Davar. I had spent two whole days watching him and studying his methods. Surrounded by chaos, movie executives and hundreds of dancers, Shiamak had been like a tranquil guru, the calm master of his art in the center of a mighty storm of activity. Three or four times I watched him retreat to a corner to meditate for a short while, and each time he disappeared he would then return with a new idea.

So that is how I decided to begin.

I set to work as soon as I arrived home with the Banerjees after the meeting in Stella's living room. First I removed my shoes. I sat myself cross-legged on the floor and closed my eyes. It was already late at night, and I do not know how long I stayed that way, taking slow breaths and stripping away my terrified thoughts one by one. But it worked. In time my panic faded, which meant I was able to concentrate only on the new song. Stella had given me a rough recording—they had written it that afternoon—and despite the poor recording quality, the music itself was wonderful, with a strong, almost Middle Eastern beat, like a cobra slinking through the sand. A year earlier I'd gone with an older cousin to a dance club in Khulna, where the music was raw and wild and nobody left the dance floor all evening. This song reminded me of that.

For me music is all about movement. As much as I hear it, I also *feel* it. Now, as Lemonade Mouth's new song played through my earphones, my head wanted to spin back and forth to the beat. With each rattle of Charlie's vibraslap, my body yearned to duck and slide.

Crassssh. Boom, boom. Spin. Tappa-tappa.
Crassssh. Boom, boom. Sliiiiiide. Tappa-tappa.

In my mind I was imagining turns and flips. I knew we would not have any professional dancers for the show, of course, so I needed to keep things simple, yet somehow still visually impressive. To accomplish this, all I had at my disposal was the music and my own instincts. And one day.

This was my challenge. This was my moment.

Everything that mattered came down to that.

Crassssh. Boom, boom. Drop-lock. Tappa-tappa.

Jump. Boom, boom. Sliiiiiide. Tappa-tappa.

With my eyes still closed I rose to a standing position. It was time to let my body do the thinking. At first I simply swayed back and forth, shifting my weight and taking in the coolness of the floor against my bare feet. I raised my arms slightly, like a bird lifting its wings. I was calm. It must sound strange, but as I stood there alone in my temporary bedroom far away from home, I could almost feel the energy flowing through me. I was focused and ready—at least as ready as I would ever be.

I opened my eyes.

For most of that night I stayed up, working. Long after everyone else had gone to sleep, I was still awake in my room, mapping out moves and ideas.

Early Thursday morning another crowd gathered, this time behind the high school. This second gathering had even more people than the first. Apparently Naomi and Lyle had made phone calls to put the word out, and by eight a.m.— a time when many American kids would still have been sleeping, I'm sure—the field by the school parking lot was swarming with activity. People arrived by the carload. Adults and kids, all friends of Lemonade Mouth who were there because they wanted to help the band. It was remarkable to watch. Naomi walked around with a clipboard and organized everyone into teams, each concentrating on a different aspect of the preparations for the show. Some were to create costumes with Sydney, others would help make props or work with the band's equipment, and still others would run errands or gather materials—or whatever else was required. When Naomi saw me she pointed to an area near the band's equipment. There were already eleven volunteers there, waiting for me.

My dancers.

"Go get 'em, Rajeev!" Stella whispered. "Show 'em how they do it in Bollywood!"

"Um, okay," I whispered back. "I will do my best."

My earlier panic had snuck up inside me again. I looked into the line of eager faces waiting for me to start giving instructions. Stella squeezed my arm and showed me the thumbs-up sign, and just looking at her made my heart do a double skip.

I took a deep breath.

It's incredible how everything can change in only a few weeks. Even as I began to talk, explaining my vision for the dance, I was remembering how just a month earlier I had been dreading my move to America. For a long time I had been sure this was going to be the worst summer of my entire life.

I was wrong. As it turned out, I was enjoying every minute of it.

LIZZIE DELUCIA
Organized Chaos

I got the message from Naomi Fishmeier the night before. Lemonade Mouth needed help, she said, and they were asking for volunteers to meet them the next morning. She told me it was important.

I didn't need any persuading.

Lemonade Mouth is a very big deal to me and a lot of kids I know. That past year they were at the center of the storm at our school. They'd changed things and made them better—and had even inspired me to take up an instrument. I'd bought myself a bass guitar and was taking lessons, all because of them. If those kids needed help, I was glad to give it. And besides, I knew that whatever Lemonade Mouth was planning, it was bound to be a good time.

First thing I did was call Scott to tell him he should come along. Just as I knew he would, he hesitated, saying that he wanted to but he felt weird about it because of all the stuff that had happened between Lemonade Mouth and Mudslide Crush during the school year.

"Mo's gonna be there," he said, as if somehow that closed the door for him.

"Don't be ridiculous. Mo's gonna be fine with it. She's with Charlie now, and you're with me, and everybody knows that. It's time to put the past behind you. Come with me tomorrow," I said. "You'll be glad you did."

There was a pause before he answered. I knew he thought I was a little headstrong sometimes, but think he secretly liked that about me. People always think of Scott Pickett as this confident, cocky guy, but believe me, he's supersensitive and a lot less self-assured than he comes off.

The next morning, when we arrived at the field behind the high school, there were at least fifty volunteers already there, most of them kids I knew from school, with more still arriving.

It was amazing to watch them pour in.

Naomi came over to thank us for coming and to explain what was going on. They had a bunch of different project teams for people to work on. As soon as Wen Gifford's dad saw us, he ran over to ask Scott if he would please help him at the wiener van. "A big crowd of people are coming to pitch in," he said, "and I need somebody to help me with Penelope so we can be sure no one goes hungry or thirsty." Since the wiener job was already sort of Scott's area of expertise, he was happy to oblige.

I glanced at Naomi's clipboard and saw an open slot on a list labeled "Costumes." Since I run a quilting club at school, I figured that was the place for me.

Turned out, the leader of the costume team was Wen's stepmom, Sydney, the same person who'd created that fantastic hot dog outfit I kept seeing Wen wearing on street corners around town. I'd never met her before, but she was very nice. A true artist too. She'd made drawings of the costumes we were about to create, and I was floored by the bold designs she'd come up with using only a few cheap materials and a bunch of odds and ends. There were five in our group—Mrs. Reznik, Richie Benedetti, Beverly DeVito (a nice lady who knew Stella from working at Stella's mother's lab), Sydney and me—and all of us got to work right away. We laid out two long fold-up tables at the edge of the high school parking lot with a couple of extension cords, two sewing machines, a staple gun, five big rolls of colored foam rubber, a crate of plastic tubing and some assorted stuff from the theater supply room.

All around us, other project groups were also getting down to work: prepping sound and light equipment, hammering strips of plywood together, packing boxes and generally doing whatever Lyle and Naomi said needed to be done.

It was organized chaos, and all to help Lemonade Mouth prepare for their big TV appearance that night. Nearby, the band itself was practicing a brand-new song they'd written, while the dancers—kids like Manny Valdez and Delila Czerwinski and a few others I recognized from the various basement clubs at school—were learning steps from this tall Indian kid, Rajeev. It was a great song too, with a good beat, a catchy chorus and words that left my jaw on the table the first time I heard them. Pretty soon people were nodding their heads and moving in time to the rhythm as we all ran around doing whatever we were doing.

The entire crowd of volunteers—over a hundred Lemonheads (I don't know who came up with that name for all the Lemonade Mouth fans, but I think that was the day it first stuck)—worked through the morning and into the early part of the afternoon. Even though it was hard work with a tight deadline, it didn't feel like a chore. With the music blasting and everyone grinning, the excitement grew. I think to a lot of us it kind of felt like we were taking part in something bigger than ourselves, you know? Like we were in the front lines of a movement.

Just as I was crouching to cut another sheet of yellow foam rubber, I noticed Scott about halfway across the field. He was walking around handing out hot dogs and lemonade. The band was taking a quick break at the time, and I saw that Charlie, Mo and Wen happened to be wandering in Scott's direction. When they noticed him they sort of stopped short. It was obvious they hadn't realized he was there—he'd spent most of the time by the van—and I guess they must have been surprised to see him. Then there was a brief weird moment. Wen kind of turned and drifted away, but not Charlie or Mo. After a pause they continued walking, going straight up to Scott and talking with him.

I crossed my fingers.

I was too far away to hear what they were saying, but nobody was shouting or pointing fingers or anything, which was a good sign. When Scott happened to glance in my direction, our eyes met. I waited, hoping he would give me a signal or something. Was everything all right? Had I been wrong to urge him to come? I knew how much this Lemonade Mouth situation had been weighing on him over the past few weeks, but Scott *realized* he'd done some stupid things, and everybody makes mistakes, right? I was proud of him for making the effort to show Lemonade Mouth that he got it and he wanted to move on. I knew it wasn't easy for him to come to the field that day.

I could only hope Mo and Charlie got it too.

I watched them talk for a little while, and then it happened: I saw Mo smile. Charlie put his hand on Scott's shoulder, and not in a threatening way or anything. They weren't mad. Scott looked embarrassed, but I knew he was happy, because he was doing that adorable half-grin thing he does sometimes. I know it might seem like no big deal, but to me it felt huge, as if a dark cloud was clearing in front of my eyes. Suddenly I could breathe again.

We worked all morning, and then a little after midday, I noticed something odd: we were being watched. At the top of the sloping road behind the high school field sat a rusty old red Ford Focus with hand-painted racing stripes—Ray Beech's car. Ray used to be in Scott's old band, Mudslide

Crush, but they'd broken up after he and Scott had a blow-out and now they weren't talking. And yet there he was. Even from so far away I could make out Ray's big head. He was just sitting there alone, staring out the window, looking at all the activity from a distance. After a while Scott must have seen him too, because he started up the hill toward him, probably to ask him what he was doing. As soon as Ray saw him coming, though, he drove off.

The whole thing was weird. Why was Ray watching us? Was he up to something?

I had no idea and I didn't have long to think about it. All of us were crazy busy, and then around one o'clock a limo pulled into the parking lot to take the band down to New York. That set off a panic. I guess we'd lost track of time somehow, and now everybody started rushing around packing stuff up. Sydney said we had to stop working even though some of the costumes still needed finishing touches.

"We're out of time!" she called over her shoulder as she crammed a sewing machine into the trunk of her Ford Fiesta. "If we don't leave now, we risk being late! Anything left to do, we'll just have to do at the studio!"

All around us people were snatching up equipment and stuffing things into boxes. The plan was to take all the key volunteers down to New York in five separate cars, each driven by a volunteer parent. But there was a problem. Even though not everybody was traveling with us, it soon became clear that we hadn't arranged for enough vehicles to hold all the extra people and equipment we needed. There wasn't any time to make a bunch of new phone calls either. This sudden realization set off yet another panic, and I could see in the anxious faces of the band and their parents, who stood staring at the final unpacked load of giant props, that they weren't sure what to do.

That was when Scott stepped in.

"Um . . . I have an idea," he offered. "What about Penelope? The passenger seats are removable, so we could take them out and pack the stuff in there."

"In the wiener van?" Sydney asked, her forehead wrinkling as she fiddled with a loose lock of her hair. "But it'd have to go all the way down to New York, and besides, we don't have a driver."

Scott shrugged. "Her exterior is old but her engine is solid. She can make it. And if you need a driver, how about me?"

Everybody stared at that yellow monstrosity with its patches of rust and that humongous plastic hot dog mounted across on top. If there was ever a rock-and-roll vehicle, this was definitely *not* it. But the truth was that it did have a big storage area and there really wasn't time to rustle up anything else.

Wen's dad grinned. "It's a good idea, Scott. As long as it's okay with your parents, I say let's do it."

I felt a rush of emotion—for Scott and for all of us. Scott called home and got the okay, and a few minutes later the Lemonade Mouth convoy was on its way to New York: three cars, two minivans, a limo, a refurbished ice cream van, twelve dancers, fourteen volunteer assistants and drivers and a band of revolutionaries. I was riding shotgun with Scott. We had three hours, just enough time to get to the studio on schedule. My adrenaline was pumping. I couldn't remember a time when I'd ever felt so excited to be part of something.

We blasted the music as we hit the highway.

People ask me why I did it. Why would I allow Lemonade Mouth to go ahead with such a crazy idea when I knew there might be a backlash? I tell them that our show has always prided itself on taking risks. We air in the wee hours of the night, so our viewership isn't the largest out there, but that's why we can sometimes get away with things other shows can't. Besides, our fans tend to be young and hip and college-aged—exactly the demographics the network wants to attract, so even though I realized I'd probably hear from the bigwigs in the morning, I also felt certain I'd get away with this, as long as I promised when it was over never to try anything like it again.

But I had another reason too. Even as an entertainer on a graveyard-shift talk show, it's always been my secret goal to do television that *matters*, that makes a difference in the world, and I guess I had an inkling about those Lemonade Mouth kids. I admired their nerve and I liked what they had to say.

That was the real reason I decided to take the risk.

Before we taped the show, my staff assigned Lemonade Mouth to wait in greenroom C, the biggest prep area we have, because they'd brought a lot of people and equipment with them. I checked in on them a few minutes before the final call time. At first they didn't notice me standing in the doorway. Even at that point, just a few minutes until we started taping, the group seemed to be in a frenzy of preparation. There were dancers practicing steps, rubber costumes being adjusted, people calling out instructions from clipboards. The five band members themselves were sitting in the center of it all, looking pale and terrified.

At last somebody noticed me and said hello. Everyone looked up and the whole room went quiet. It's silly, really, how people treat you like royalty just because you're on television every night, but there it is.

"Hi, guys," I said. "Just wanted to make sure you're all set."

All around the room, scared-looking teenagers nodded. I noticed that Olivia Whitehead, the lead singer, was in the middle of some kind of deep-breathing exercise, and for a moment I wondered if she was going to be sick. But she nodded too, so I assumed she was okay.

"I'm not much of one for pep talks," I said, "but I'm not worried, so you don't need to be either. Really. The rehearsal went well, and I'm sure you'll do great. Just have fun out there. That's all that really counts to the cameras."

More anxious stares. I figured I'd better quit while I was ahead, so I wished them luck, smiled and left. In just a few minutes the studio audience would be ushered in. After that we'd be ready to start. Even as I stood for my sound and makeup check, though, my thoughts were still on the kids back in greenroom C.

I'll let you in on a secret: I'd told a little white lie. After seeing the grim looks on their faces, I *was* just a little worried.

NAOMI FISHMEIER
Pandemonium

The tension backstage was almost unbearable. Everyone had the jitters, and Olivia, poor kid, looked ready to fall apart. There was nothing else I could do to help her, though, and my job back there was done. With showtime approaching, it seemed best to give the performers a little space before they went on.

All I could do now was take my seat in the audience and cross my fingers.

The crowd was in a party mood. Even though the program was broadcast late at night, they actually taped the show in the early evening. Before they began the main event, a couple of comedians came out to warm up the crowd. I must admit, Dear Reader, that I had a difficult time paying attention to them, talented comics though they may have been. My heart was pounding and my mind was decidedly elsewhere.

At last the house band started playing the theme music.

The real show was beginning.

Chet Anders strolled onto the stage, flashing his trademark gap-toothed grin at the cheering audience. He came across like a friendly neighbor, the kind of guy you could imagine pouring your heart out to just as easily as you could imagine inviting him to a barbecue. He pretended to pitch an invisible baseball into the still-applauding crowd and grinned again. The man was a pro at this. I, on the other hand, was new to this world, and so nail-bitingly nervous that I don't even remember most of his opening monologue. Only when he started listing his guests for the evening did I realize I was digging my fingernails into the seat.

"And we have a special treat this evening," he was saying. "Remember that band of high-school kids who stood up to the judges of *American Pop Sensation*?" On the overhead screens they showed a few seconds of the video clip. The audience laughed. Of *course* they remembered—Chet had been playing the clip as a running gag just about every night since it'd happened. "Well, they're here with us tonight, folks. Lemonade Mouth is waiting backstage!"

After a few more seconds of applause he nodded to one of his directors. The stage lights started to dim. I knew this was it—the beginning of the introduction they'd practiced. My guts twisted. It felt like everything was at risk now. The future of Lemonade Mouth was on the line.

Chet stood in the spotlight, his expression theatrically serious. The audience went quiet as he began to explain about his recent phone call from the quirky band from Rhode Island, how the kids had requested a change in tonight's format due to their recent indoctrination into the world of advertising. He held up a copy of the Zephyr Stick ad from one of the many magazines it had appeared in. The camera closed in on it.

"You've seen this, haven't you? It just came out and already I've been spotting it everywhere I look. Anyone else?" The audience clapped—yes, many of them were familiar with the ad. "Well, believe it or not, the band wanted to mark this grand event on my show, here, tonight, with a brand-new song they've written just for the occasion." He raised an eyebrow. "These kids take their newfound visibility very seriously, and I commend them for their thoughtful musical commentary. And now," he said, gesturing toward the curtains behind him, "*After Midnight* is proud to bring you . . . *Lemonade Mouth*!"

He stepped out of the light and the curtains opened. There was Lemonade Mouth. Except for the instruments in their hands, the band was posed exactly as they appeared in the ad—the same clothes, the same expressions—while the ad itself was projected behind them on a big screen. Seeing them this way, it was obvious that the kids in the photo and in real life were not the same.

I held my breath.

The song began with a pulsing bass line and a syncopated beat that Charlie played on a big funky-looking aluminum drum that was strapped to his side. Stella's distorted ukulele groove oozed with cool. The effect was like a storm about to break, a riotous party on the verge of busting open. Around me I saw heads starting to bob to the rhythm. With the ad image visible over her shoulder, Olivia began to sing:

> *I'm so slender . . .*
> *No lies, lies, lies*
> *I haven't eaten in days—*
> *Just look at my pencil thighs. . . .*

Stella came next, sweeping the audience with her gaze as she sang:

> *I'm so sultry . . .*
> *Look at my dainty hips.*
> *I scream and shout, d'you like my pout?*
> *'Cause I got inflatable lips. . . .*

Then Mo:

> *I'm so exotic!*
> *My brown eyes are freaky green!*
> *Take me to your leader—*
> *I'm a dreamy Martian queen!*

Charlie and Wen's part was a chant they did together, like a robotic chorus line, as the music increased in urgency:

> *Freaky, fakey, phony, baby!*
> *Let them give us what they got!*
> *Let the media decide for us*
> *What's hot and what is not!*

Glancing around, I noticed a few mouths drop open. I think a lot of people had probably had these same secret thoughts—I know *I* sure had—but I doubt anyone ever expected to hear them expressed aloud on television, and with music that was so crazy fun and danceable that it was impossible not to want to move your feet. With each new verse the camera alternated between the ad and the real person so that the difference between them was obvious, and judging by the astonished expressions, I had the feeling that people *got* it. They understood even if they were still too stunned to react.

Now it was time to hit them with the chorus. Stella's chords were coming faster and harder, a hurricane unleashed. Olivia stepped back up to the mike.

> *Freaky, fakey, phony, baby!*
> *So what if it's unhealthy?*
> *As long as we all keep lapping it up*
> *We're making someone wealthy!*
> *Freaky, fakey, phony, baby!*
> *Looking like a skeleton toy!*
> *Can't think for myself, can't be who I am*
> *I gotta beeee . . .*
> *Freakyyy! Fakeyyy! Phooonyyyyyyyyy!!*

Wen raised his trumpet and let out a flurry of notes like a rogue merry-go-round. In the row ahead of me, a large, middle-aged woman in pearls was listening wide-eyed. She wasn't the only one.

"Don't buy into the lies!" Charlie and Wen called out together.

"Don't fall for somebody else's idea of what's pretty or cool!" shouted Mo and Olivia.

Stella leaned into the mike, still strumming her uke to the jungle rhythm. "So maybe we're not rail-thin!" she shouted. "Maybe we don't have perfect hair or skin or bodies! But who decides what 'perfect' even *means,* anyway—to you, to me? Isn't that *your* decision and mine? And isn't it our little so-called imperfections that make all of us who we are? That make all of us *beautiful?*"

There was a growing clamor from the audience. Ahead and to my left a threesome of wiry, bespectacled guys in college T-shirts were craning forward in their chairs. The woman in pearls sat frozen, hanging on their every word. I'm almost sure I saw her lip quivering.

But Stella wasn't done.

"This is the real world, folks! Look around! *This* is what actual people look like! They're *you*! They're *us*! Not the fake images you see in certain advertisements! And if you ask *us*, being cool shouldn't mean having to change yourself into something you're not!"

Boom! A final slap from Charlie's drum echoed through the room, and all at once the music stopped.

"Because if you ask *us*," said Stella, "we'd say you guys are already looking plenty cool—*just the way you are!*"

The crowd went nuts. The woman in pearls raised her

fists in the air and gave out a war whoop. All around me, people started to cheer.

On beat, the music kicked in again, full-force, only now it unleashed an all-out, pulsing, whirling party. The woman in pearls leapt to her feet and began what looked like a victory dance, shaking her sizeable hips like there was no tomorrow. Near the front, a group of pimple-faced teenage girls joined in, whipping their long hair in wild circles. The college guys stood too, giving each other high fives. I gaped at the scene unfolding all around me. Pandemonium. Everywhere I turned, people were moving to the rhythm or pumping their fists and calling out their approval. I knew this would mean trouble for them later, but for now it was clear that Lemonade Mouth had tapped into something important, something unspoken that must have been simmering just under the surface, waiting to be expressed.

No longer did it feel like I was witnessing a television show. This was more like an explosion—the first spark of a giant new rebellion.

SCOTT PICKETT
Welcome to the Revolution

Just when it seemed like things couldn't get any crazier, the curtains on either side of the stage parted and I heard a bunch of people gasp. Lizzie and I were at the back of the audience, so we had a good view of the whole place.

The dancers came out in two rows, twirling and dipping and moving in formation as they filed onstage in giant foam costumes. There were about a dozen different ones—all of them oversized puppet-people. An eight-foot-tall girl with nerdy glasses. A giant bucktoothed boy with red-button zits. A matching bikini girl and surfer dude with oversized metal braces and poufy hairdos. There was even a wooden-framed two-person outfit that looked like a human-sized magazine. On the "cover" was a real face—one of the dancers, this kid Debbie Bloom from school—but she had a fake body with puppet arms and legs as thin as pipe cleaners. It was hilarious. And all the costumed dancers were stomping and gliding and spinning around the band. Once every two measures Charlie would move from the aluminum darbuka drum he was playing to a vibraslap, making a rattling sound, and the entire crowd of foam heads would dip and slide to the left in formation. It sounded and looked . . . well, *amazing*. Just *amazing*. Pretty soon Lizzie and I were doing it too, along with the rest of the audience.

If the excitement had already been high before the dancers came, it was in the stratosphere now.

I admit that when I'd first heard that Lemonade Mouth wanted to add costumed dancers to their act, I'd had my doubts. But now there was no denying that it turned out to have been a stroke of genius. That kid Rajeev—what can I say? He was brilliant. A phenomenon all on his own. I'd watched how he'd coached Debbie Bloom and Terry Cabeleira and the others, just regular kids, to do all of those crazy moves together. It'd seemed impossible that it would work out, and yet somehow he'd pulled it off. The whole effect was jaw-dropping.

When the instrumental part ended Olivia picked up the chorus again:

Freaky, fakey, phony, baby!
Gotta-gotta set myself free!
Thanks for the thought, but I like what I got
Don't need to beeee . . .
Freakyyy! Fakeyyy! Phooonyyyyyyyyy!!

Glancing at the pulsing scene around me, I couldn't help thinking how different things were now, compared with just a few weeks earlier. When I'd left my old band, Mudslide Crush, because I wasn't happy with the direction it was taking, things were pretty bad. Overnight my former band mate and best buddy, Ray, wouldn't even give me the time of day. Look, I know a lot of people thought Ray was a jerk, but deep down I knew better than anyone that he wasn't as bad as he came off—not all the time, anyway. I'm not making excuses for him, but with his troubled family and especially that domineering father of his, it was no wonder the kid was a little messed up. Plus, we'd been friends since nursery school, so it was hard for me to lose that.

But soon I'd started hanging out with Lizzie, this amazing girl, and I found myself with a whole new perspective on things. Lizzie made me *happy*, you know? When you're happy I guess it's easier to see stuff clearer. Someday I hoped Ray could be happy too, and that he'd get over his hurt pride so we could be friends again.

Despite everything, I still loved the guy.

Lizzie squeezed my arm. Chet Anders himself had joined Lemonade Mouth onstage now, laughing as he danced with a giant foam puppet of an old lady in gym shorts. Then the song ended and the audience went bonkers. I'd never experienced anything like this. I knew it was a big risk for

161

Lemonade Mouth to stand up to their sponsor like this on national television (even if it was just a funky late-night talk show watched only by insomniacs and college students), but for now it seemed to have paid off. The music was over but the room was still rocking, with everybody on their feet screaming and clapping and calling out to the band as the five of them just stood there blinking back at everyone. I think even they were surprised at the effect their song had. As for me, I could feel my blood rushing. I felt totally *alive*. I can't explain it better than him.

That's when Lizzie whispered in my ear.

"Welcome to the revolution, Scotty. You and me, we're part of it as much as anyone else." She squeezed my arm again. "I'm so glad you came along."

It was a powerful moment where everything felt right. I was on my feet and cheering along with everyone else, Lizzie was at my side, and Lemonade Mouth was on top of the world with a future that all of a sudden looked brighter than ever. And weird as it sounds, considering my history with them, I was *glad* about it.

Really and honestly glad.

If only things could have stayed that good. Looking back, I think it was a surprise to all of us that they didn't. How could anyone have been prepared for how quickly things were about to change?

CHAPTER 7

The sky clouded over and our
hearts grew heavy.
−Pliny the Tremulous

MOHINI
The Pilots of Destiny

We're on the road again. Hardly an hour into the long ride home, Stella's phone pings with a text message. It's Mr. Decker.

SAW THE SHOW. I'M
NOT HAPPY. I'M BACK
IN BOSTON 2MRRW.
CALL ME @ 10 AM.
WE NEED 2 TALK.

Our initial reaction is silence. Even though we all knew from the beginning that Mr. Decker wasn't going to be pleased, seeing it in glowing letters on Stella's phone makes it real, and all at once my mood is sinking into my shoes. I'm a little kid again. I'm in big trouble. I try to remind myself that we only did what we thought was right, but that doesn't help much.

In hushed voices we make a decision. The conversation we need to have with Mr. Decker is far too important to have over the phone. If we're going to figure out a better way to work with his agency, if we're going to talk this through with him and make sure we're all on the same page in the future, then that discussion should happen in person. So even though we arrive home late and exhausted, all five of us drag ourselves out of bed early the next morning. We're going to Boston.

"Are you all right, Monu?" my dad asks from the front passenger seat of the Penns' station wagon. Stella's mom is driving. "You're very quiet."

"Yes, Baba. Just a little nervous."

"Of course you are," he says. "Do your best, that's all. Be clear with him. Speak your mind." And then he adds, "I know you kids want to do this yourselves, but don't forget that Mrs. Penn and I are here if you need us."

I nod. I know they're there for us and I'm grateful, but my friends and I feel like this is *our* problem and we should try to fix it ourselves. I force a smile. I don't want him to see how terrified I am that everything is about to fall apart. Charlie, Olivia and Wen are staring out the windows like zombies. Stella's silent too, but her knee bounces up and down with nervous energy.

We arrive in Boston a few minutes early. To kill time we each grab a Mel's from the little convenience store across the street, which turns out to be a good thing, because the feel of the familiar green and yellow paper cup in my hands seems to calm me a little. The pretty girl at the desk buzzes Mr. Decker that we're here. After a pause she tells us we can take seats in the lobby, and once again we're waiting in that giant room with rock legends staring down at us like gods. Mr. Decker makes us wait for what feels like forever.

Not a good sign.

At last we're called in to see him. Mr. Decker is standing at his giant panoramic window with a view of Boston Harbor behind him. He's silent as we enter, and his arms are crossed. I've never seen him wearing glasses before. Black frames with a line of silver across the top, they give him the vibe of an aging hippie professor. He looks tired. He gestures for us to take a seat around the oak table, but he doesn't say a word. He doesn't join us at the table either.

"So . . . ," Stella begins, breaking the weird silence. "We . . . uh . . . got your message, Mr. Decker. We came here in person because we want to talk this through, face to face."

"We know you're not happy," Charlie adds. "We totally get that."

"You *get* that?" Mr. Decker repeats quietly. He wrinkles his brow as if weighing the idea in his mind. "No, I really *don't* think you get it, Charlie. That performance you guys put on last night? That little circus act? To me it didn't look at *all* like you understood what we're trying to do here." He scratches his beard. "Gotta be honest, this isn't good. Not good at all. The one silver lining is that you didn't disparage the product *itself.* I'm thankful for that, at least. It leaves an opening for us. You're lucky. I believe I might still be able to manage this situation."

I'm staring at my Mel's cup, which is almost empty now. I keep my expression blank, but inside, I'm relieved. I thought Mr. Decker wasn't going to want to represent us anymore, but if he's talking about managing the situation it means he isn't about to drop us. Despite everything, I can't squelch the part of me that wants Lemonade Mouth to be huge, that wants our music out in the world for everyone to hear. I know we all feel that way, even Olivia. She might not like the spotlight, but I know she wants our music to be heard, and we all know that Mr. Decker is still the best shot we've got.

To my left, at the far edge of my vision, I see Mrs. Penn shift in her seat. Instead of sitting at the table, she and my dad took chairs by the door. "*Manage* this situation?" she asks. "What does that mean, exactly?"

"As it happens, I have a good relationship with the Zephyr Stick people. Their CEO and I sometimes play golf together. This morning I left a message with her office and we're scheduled to talk later today. I'm not saying it'll be easy, but I think I can smooth things over. *This* time. Going forward, though, you kids need to *stick to the game plan*. We spoke about this already, as you recall, but it seems that wasn't enough, so from now on we need a new rule: no more changes without talking to me *first*."

I don't move or look up. Mr. Decker isn't yelling, exactly, but his words are strained and it's clear we've pushed him close to his limit.

"But we tried to talk to you, Mr. Decker," Wen says, his voice low. "Don't you remember? We called you but you wouldn't—"

"This isn't amateur night, guys," Mr. Decker continues as if he doesn't hear. He's pacing the length of the table now. "This is the big leagues, don't forget that. Everything we do follows a careful strategy. We're creating a *brand*—an image that positions Lemonade Mouth in the music marketplace. You're nerdy-cool. You're the outsider kids. You wear great clothes. Do you think it's *easy* to make a new product take hold in the minds of consumers? Do you think it happens by *luck*? No, it happens only because we've *thought things through*." He jabs his finger into the air. "It happens only when everybody sticks to the *same message*."

There's a battle going on inside me. I want to speak up and defend what we did, but I also know that Mr. Decker is right, in a way. He *is* the expert at this. And as long as he's still willing to work with us, maybe I'm better off keeping my mouth shut before I make things worse. We've already made our point. Why push him further?

In the end, though, I can't stop myself. I can't sit back without opening up my big mouth.

"Okay, we get it, but shouldn't Lemonade Mouth's message come from us? The band?" Everyone turns to me. I can almost feel the heat in Mr. Decker's gaze. I don't mean for my words to go quieter after that, they just do. "I mean, it's not like we're really a product, right? Like a pair of sneakers or something?"

Mr. Decker is gaping at me like I'm the Queen of the Clueless. "Of course a band is a product," he says. "From a marketing perspective, Lemonade Mouth is *exactly* like a pair of sneakers, or a bar of soap, or a roll of toilet paper, or"—his eyes fall on our Mel's cups—"or even that lemonade slush you kids like. I've said it before and I'll say it again—I didn't make up the rules, I just know what they are and that we all need to play by them. And this means not doing anything *stupid*." He slaps the table. "It means never again publicly questioning the actions of our *sponsor*. After all, they're the people with the *checkbooks*!"

I stay quiet. I want to shrink into my chair.

"Look," he says, breaking the tension with a sigh,

"there's a disconnect here and we need to resolve it." He removes his glasses, rubs his eyes and at last takes a seat at the table across from us. He folds his hands. "I know this is still a learning experience for you kids. I get that. If I didn't see real potential here I might've dropped you as clients for what you did, but instead I'm going to give this one more shot. If you want to keep working with me, you gotta promise you'll play by the rules. That's all I ask. No more surprises. No more childish stunts. Believe me, I know how to get Lemonade Mouth where we all want it to be. Bestselling albums. Stadiums filled with fans. You guys want these things, right? Well, I've mapped out a course that can make it all happen for you. All *you* have to do is stick to my map."

I'm still staring at the tabletop. What Mr. Decker is asking for doesn't sound like a lot, I guess, considering where he can take us, and yet, I don't know, it still feels unsatisfying somehow. Part of me thinks I should be happy. We made our big statement on television last night and it looks like we're getting away without having to pay too big a price for it. Promising Mr. Decker we'll follow his map should be no big deal, right?

So what's the problem?

Why do I still feel bad about it?

I'm surprised when it's Olivia who opens her mouth next, but as soon as she does I'm once again grateful that she's one of us. More than anybody else I know, she has a knack for finding the right words. Her soft, gravelly voice cuts through the quiet.

"But Mr. Decker," she says, "what if we don't *like* your map?"

His expression darkens. His hands are still folded on the table, but as I watch, the knuckles grow whiter.

168

"*Like* it?" he asks. "Olivia, I've been doing this for decades. Do you think you and your friends know better than *I* do how to position a band in this market? I've been turning nobodies into stars since long before you were born."

His face is red. I've never seen him so irritated. It's obvious that Mr. Decker isn't accustomed to having his judgment questioned by a bunch of kids. My father promised not to interfere unless he had to, but I guess this is too much for him. His words are polite enough, but I know my dad and I can tell when he's on the verge of losing his temper.

"There must be some misunderstanding, Mr. Decker. Surely you wouldn't ask Lemonade Mouth—a group of *children*— to do something they don't believe in?"

"Let me make this clear, then," he says, leveling his gaze at Baba. "Let me outline the obvious so there can't be any misunderstanding. If it weren't for Decker and Smythe, Lemonade Mouth would still be playing at local clam festivals. We've been honing their image. We've been positioning them for the media. We own everything from the new recordings right down to their new signature clothes." He sits back in his chair and eyes us. "Face it, we can ask Lemonade Mouth to do anything we want. We *own* Lemonade Mouth."

At first I think maybe I didn't hear him right, but I see in his face that he's serious.

Can it be true? Is it possible?

All at once the atmosphere in the room changes. My heart is going a mile a minute. This is the legendary Earl Decker? This is how things work in the big leagues? I look around at my friends and see the same confusion and panic I'm feeling. If Decker and Smythe own Lemonade Mouth, what does that mean for us? What do we do about it? My dad and Mrs. Penn both look ready to boil over. They're about to take over for us, I'm positive of this. They're getting ready to tell Mr. Decker what he can do with his map and his new signature clothes.

But they don't get a chance.

Just as my father opens his mouth, just as Mrs. Penn starts to raise an angry finger toward Mr. Decker, Stella holds up her hand to both of them as if to say, *I got this.*

For a heartbeat the whole world is frozen in place.

My dad and Mrs. Penn hesitate. Stella glares at Mr. Decker, who's surveying this whole scene from across the table. Something about Stella's manner must be impressive to my dad and Mrs. Penn, though, or maybe it's just that she startled them, but whatever it is, they both back down, sinking once again into their seats. Everyone's focused on Stella now. Her jaw is set. There's a steely look in her eyes and it's fixed like a death ray on Mr. Decker.

I hold my breath. I have no idea what's about to happen.

Like a statesman, Stella rises from her chair. "Let *me* make this clear, *Earl.* Let me outline it so there can be no misunderstanding." She leans across the table, her palms pressed to the oak. "*Nobody* owns Lemonade Mouth."

"I beg to differ, Stella. A contract is a contract. Unless you guys are okay with fading back into insignificance and obscurity with no hope that anyone else will ever pick you up in the future, your course is already set."

Stella looks around at us. It's then that I have this sudden sick feeling because I realize what's about to happen, but there's no other choice. It's what we *must* do.

Stella is the first of us to turn our backs to him. She doesn't shout or pound the table or anything, she just calmly picks up her empty cup and starts for the door. The rest of us do the same.

"Uh . . . where are you guys going?" Mr. Decker sounds different now. Not quite as sure.

We stop and turn back toward him. "Didn't somebody once tell us *we're* the pilots of our own destiny?" Charlie says. "We're charting a different course now."

I nod. "We're out of here."

"Oh, I get it," he says, his lips going pale. "So it's back to changing the world again? 'Don't Stop the Revolution' and all that crap? Well, before you saunter out that door, *children,* think carefully about what you're doing. The days when bands could thumb their noses at the system and ignore business realities are long over. Once you leave this office there's no coming back. You'll be scratched from the Too Shy to Cry tour. Your new recordings will never see the light of day. You'll disappear from the magazines, vanish from the spotlight, and no other promoter or record company will touch you. If you walk out on me, then by the end of the summer Lemonade Mouth will already be a fading memory."

Stella's voice is steady, but I think I hear a hint of sadness. "I used to admire you, Earl," she says. "You're fired. Goodbye."

From their expressions I think even my dad and Mrs. Penn are taken by surprise. We're not done yet, though—not quite. Before we walk out the door all five of us glance at each other, and then we raise our Mel's cups, almost as if we planned it. It's a last revolutionary salute, our one final act of defiance toward the great Earl Decker.

It doesn't change anything, but it feels good.

We hold them high. We raise them up.

Now, I need to say this: It isn't like we're natural-born rebels. We're not. We haven't been looking for trouble. Until moments ago we were hoping things could still work out with Decker and Smythe. Now each of us knows all too well that by walking out we're closing the door not only on Earl Decker, but on our own dreams. It's not a good feeling, but we can't change what we believe in and we won't pretend to. Not for anything.

I'm sure Mr. Decker is gaping at our backs as we walk through his door and out of his office.🎸

STELLA
Gloom Sets In

Friends and coconspirators, it would be difficult to convey the full depth of disappointment that soon enveloped the hearts of your pink-haired protagonist and her beleaguered band of rock-and-roll outcasts. It wasn't merely the loss of their once-idolized promoter. One theory holds that people who choose to perform on a stage are really just looking for a way to be loved, and maybe that was a little bit true for Lemonade Mouth. Maybe acceptance was part of what they were looking for. So can you imagine, then, the despair it brought them to hear from one of their former rock-and-roll heroes, a respected music insider, that he would do everything in his power to make sure nobody in the industry would ever want anything to do with them?

It was no joy-fest. Let me assure you.

The drive home after that last meeting with Mr. Decker was a miserable experience. Each of us was still shaken by the immensity of what we'd done. There we'd been, in possession of our very own ticket to fame and glory, and what had we done with it? Tossed it out the window. Now we had no choice but to face the dreary reality that our big chance was behind us and would never, ever return. Is it any wonder that we started to second-guess ourselves?

What had come over us?

Had we just made the biggest, dumbest mistake of our lives?

Had we lost our minds?

But there was no turning back. Without Decker and Smythe behind the scenes pushing the high-level buttons of the big media outlets, our phones soon stopped ringing and our lives plummeted back to their former ordinariness. Within days we felt like zombies, shuffling through our everyday jobs and obligations. I remember stopping by Mo's store and discovering her hunched in a chair, dismal and alone, staring at a wall. Olivia all but disappeared from view, retreating into her house like a turtle into its shell. Charlie's reaction was perhaps the most telling. For two days he wouldn't talk—I mean at *all*—and when I asked him why, he reached dejectedly into his pocket and pulled out a preprinted card that explained how Buddhist monks often use silence as a way to center the mind in times of turmoil. I knew Charlie had been on his self-imposed mission to find life's answers or whatever, but—wow.

This just seemed too sad for words.

As for me, my situation was no less depressing. At the height of our Decker excitement I'd cut back my hours at my mother's lab, but now, with no other commitment stopping me, I had no excuse not to return to the old schedule. So once again, bright and early every morning, I found myself stationed at the Reception Desk of Purgatory. I spent a lot of that time with my cheek planted on the desktop.

"Cheer up, Stella," my mother said one morning, setting

a cinnamon bun in front of my nose. "Better to be an almost-was than a never-could-have-been. At least you have your health."

I swiveled a bleary eye toward her. My *health*? Seriously?

Yes, I snarfed down the cinnamon bun (why waste it?), but clearing the fog of my despair was going to require a power beyond that of a mere pastry.

As if matters needed worsening, the Decker and Smythe situation wasn't the sole dark cloud hovering in my sky. First, with our Earl connection cut, my free tickets to Sista Slash's Take Charge Festival were gone. I'd also missed my opportunity to *buy* tickets, because the entire superhyped festival was sold out. In my frustration I resorted to calling in to WRIZ radio contests when they'd given away pairs of tickets, but I'd found no luck there either—the gods of speed-dialing hadn't smiled on me.

After all my efforts, it made me want to scream.

Second (and this, in all honesty, was the bigger drag on my soul), Rajeev's six-week stay in Rhode Island was nearing its end. The boy who had dropped from the sky to shake up my world and steal my heart would soon have to fly far away to his family's new home in Lubbock, Texas. The thing was, Rajeev and I had grown incredibly close during his stay. We'd shared secrets that neither of us had ever shared with anyone else. It hurt to even *think* of being apart. And I knew he felt the same. We had just a few days left, and then what? Sure, we could call and text and video chat, but it wouldn't be the same as having him here in person.

Would he and I ever be together again?

Would life ever be the same after he was gone?

My mother must have read my thoughts, because before

leaving me to head deeper into the lab, she gave my shoulder a sympathetic squeeze and said, "Don't worry, hon. I'm sure he'll be here any minute."

She was right, of course. Whenever I worked at the lab, Rajeev almost always stopped by to hang out with me. It was the one bright spot that made the job tolerable. But today I knew it would be hard to feel cheerful, even for him. When he arrived at my desk a few minutes later he was holding his hand behind his back. His expression was serious.

"I brought something for you," he said.

"You did?" I tried not to sound quite as downhearted as I felt. "What is it?"

"A surprise. A high-tech mood booster to make up for all you've lost."

I looked up. All right, I was intrigued.

At last he set it on the desktop. It was a bobblehead of Elvis. With a gentle flick of Rajeev's finger the king of rock and roll bounced and nodded at me, a tiny pompadoured stud muffin in a dance frenzy. I looked back at Rajeev. He was waiting for my reaction.

Despite everything, I smiled.

What can I say? The boy knew the way to my heart.

It was Lyle's idea not to wallow in our misery. "You gotta throw yourselves right back in it," he urged soon after the Decker debacle. "Let's finish the old recordings. There isn't much left, just a few cleanup tracks and maybe some over-dubs. But at least it's something to do instead of sitting around moping." We agreed, but it was kind of a downer to return to the makeshift studio after working on a big-time project at a real, high-tech operation. Our dreams had been so big, and now we were back to standing around in a sweaty garage?

It was hard not to feel discouraged.

But at least there was *some* good news. Starting the day after our appearance on *After Midnight with Chet Anders,* our official website (yep, it turned out we had one. Lyle and Naomi had put it up only a day before our careers crashed and burned. How ironic was *that?*) started receiving appreciative messages from people who'd seen the show.

> Dear Lemonade Mouth,
> As a 45-year-old professor in a lifelong battle with my weight, I want to let you know that I got so emotional during your appearance with Chet that I actually cried. Thank you for making it okay to be me.
> —Marjorie Chi, Mobile, AL

> LEMONADE MOUTH! DUUDES!! A bunch of us from my dorm r making a statue of u guys out of toilet paper rolls & those s2pid magazine ads where everybody looks fake. We'll send a pic when it's done! Glad 2 hav somebody on OUR side for a change! U GUYS ROCK!!!!!!
> —Dave McQuilkin, Ida College of Art, Ida, OR

I read maybe a couple dozen messages like that, most from ordinary people who'd struggled for one reason or another to accept themselves and wanted to let us know they liked our music and appreciated what we'd said. Which was nice to hear.

If that was the only good thing that came out of what happened, at least it was something we could be proud of.

The other positive news was that Lyle turned out to be right—going back to our old recordings was a welcome distraction. The Decker incident had left a certain amount of unspoken tension among us, but now that we were back in Lyle's garage and making our own musical production decisions, we started remembering how we used to feel when we were making music just for ourselves. The garage setting was far more casual than that stuffy studio with Mr. Decker's stressed-out producer. Here we felt like we were just hanging with friends and having fun, which of course was exactly what we were doing.

This arrangement was a lot more comfortable. It felt *right*.

Maybe it was having Lyle and Naomi helping us again, or maybe it was just where we happened to be emotionally and artistically, I don't know, but somehow being more relaxed made the whole process not only easier, but *faster* too. It was as if our version of the music had been bottled up inside us, waiting to get out. Without really thinking about it, we completed all the remaining overdubs from the earlier songs in just two intense afternoon sessions. Then, in a third session, we added two additional new songs—"Ninja Earthquake" and "Bounce in All Directions," both recorded in single takes, with all of us playing our instruments together, like in a live show.

For us, those few afternoons in Lyle's messy garage were like an oasis in the desert. They helped us forget, at least for a while, all the bad stuff that had happened, and they gave us something to look forward to. I think we were all relieved just to be having fun again, and I think that energy came through in the music we made. In my humble opinion, the results were better than any of Decker's studio recordings.

The big difference, of course, was that the Decker recordings would have gotten exposure to millions while these tracks, proud as we were of them, had little hope of being heard by anyone beyond a small number of local fans.

A few days later, I arranged for the five of us to meet at Bruno's so we could figure things out. You know, the future of the band and how we were going to move forward, stuff like that. I was trying to stay positive. It was clear on everybody's faces, though, that the flash of joy that had briefly returned to us in Lyle's garage had been beaten down again as the hopeless reality of our situation set in.

So much for moving forward.

Everyone arrived at Bruno's looking as enthusiastic as cold, wet blankets. And there seemed to be something uncool brewing between Olivia and Wen. First of all, Olivia showed up almost an hour late. A day earlier we'd texted her about meeting, but none of us had seen her since. Then, when we asked Wen if he knew where she was and where she'd gone (we figured he was the most likely of us to know, right?), he said he had no idea and his face practically morphed into a tomato.

Perfect, I thought. Relationship troubles. That's all we needed.

How many zillions of bands have imploded over the years because of some stupid love spat?

At last Olivia turned up, and she looked exhausted. She was apologetic but vague about what had happened, saying only that she'd been away, and nobody pushed her to say more because it was obvious she didn't want to. No surprise there. This was Olivia, after all; mystery seemed to follow the girl around like a shadow. We all knew that if there was something important she wanted to tell us, she'd get to it when she was ready.

But I could see there was something still going on with Wen. The whole time we were there, he hardly even looked at her.

CHARLIE
The Fickle Hand of Fate

EXTERIOR. ROOF OF CHARLIE'S HOUSE—EARLY MORNING

Charlie is seated in the lotus position on the near-flat roof of his house. His eyes are closed. Wind ruffles his hair. He holds his hands out with palms upward, ready to receive the elusive wisdom of the Universe.

> CHARLIE (V.O.)
> It was a time of intense spiritual upheaval. It felt like things were coming to an end, and music, which had always been the central calming force in my life, had now become a source of turmoil and sadness. And under it all, that vague imbalance that'd been simmering in me, that feeling that there was something important I was missing and needed to find, wasn't going away. Which was why I'd been stepping up my search a notch or two. I tried everything I could think of that might help me uncover the answers I was looking for.

INTERIOR. HINDU TEMPLE—MORNING

Charlie kneels alongside Mo and her family as a skinny old man in white chants in Sanskrit. A service is under way, and the place is decorated with fruits and flowers. As other worshipers chant responses, Charlie does his best to follow along.

CHARLIE (V.O.)

I went with Mo and her family to their temple. It was very cool, with lots of statues and burning incense and altars to different Hindu gods. I didn't understand most of what was going on, but everybody made me feel welcome. Mo's dad, especially, seemed happy that I wanted to come. It was an amazing experience but, sad to say, whatever I was searching for, I didn't find it there.

Dissolve to . . .

INTERIOR. STELLA'S BASEMENT—EVENING

Charlie is seated in the middle of a crowded sofa with Stella, Rajeev and Stella's older sister, Clea. Stella and Rajeev are sharing popcorn, while Clea is painting her nails. They're all watching television together. There's thunder and eerie music as the light flickers across their faces. Charlie stares at the screen, a look of terror in his eyes.

CHARLIE (V.O.)

Stella tried to help me. She knew I liked watching TV and she said that sometimes when she feels like her life is on shaky ground, it helps her to stay at home and watch vampire movies all day. So that's what we did. I think I saw more fangs that afternoon than a dentist sees teeth in a whole week. Some of the movies were okay, but I wouldn't say any of them actually *helped* me much.

Dissolve to . . .

EXTERIOR. CHARLIE'S FRONT PORCH—AFTERNOON

Charlie is on his front steps reading an old, ragged book.

CHARLIE (V.O.)

Olivia called what I was going through an "existential crisis," and she loaned me this book called *New Perspectives: A History of People and Ideas That Changed the World.* She said it might give me new ideas for my search.

180

REVERSE ON: A page of the book. Lots of words and a black-and-white image of an olden-days dude with an enormous bushy mustache.

> CHARLIE (V.O.)
> I read about this one philosopher guy in the eighteen hundreds named Friedrich Nietzsche. Nietzsche had this idea that there's a big difference between how people *want* the world to work, like being fair and stuff, and how it *really* works, and he figured that because of this difference, human existence must be meaningless. It was kind of a downer idea. I spent a long time trying to wrap my head around it.

REVERSE ON: Charlie. He lowers the book from his face, sets it on his lap, and gazes thoughtfully across the street. Little kids are playing with a dog. There's pop music coming from somewhere in the distance. A car drives past.

> CHARLIE (V.O.)
> I tried to imagine everyone in the world, all the zillions of people on this huge planet, living their lives and doing their own stuff every day, while all the time there's other stuff happening, some of it good and some not so good, and sometimes we're happy and sometimes we're not, and none of it, not one tiny bit of it, will ever matter in the grand scheme of the Universe. Wow. Did I really want to believe such a depressing thing? Could I believe it?

Dissolve to . . .

EXTERIOR. OPEQUONSETT TOWN CENTER—LATE MORNING

A wide shot of the storefronts at the north end of Wampanoag Road. At one end of the screen we see Charlie ambling along the sidewalk toward Wen, who is half a block away, near the center of the frame. Wen is in his wiener outfit but he isn't jumping around or anything. In fact, he isn't moving at all. He's staring into space looking depressed.

> CHARLIE (V.O.)
> We'd finished our recordings in Lyle's garage, but now the days felt bleaker than ever because our brief moment

of relief was over. The project had at least been something to work on, and now Lemonade Mouth's future seemed nothing but empty. The weight on all of us was starting to show. Especially on Wen. A few hours after the five of us met at Bruno's, I decided to take a walk into town to catch him before he finished his wiener shift.

Charlie is near Wen now, and the camera has been slowly closing in on them. They exchange nods of greeting, but otherwise Wen hardly moves and his cheerless expression remains. Charlie remains silent. The two friends gaze across the traffic together, a picture of quiet sadness.

                    CHARLIE (V.O.) (CONT'D)
It was pretty obvious to me that something was up with him and Olivia, and being the only other guy in the band, I wanted to let him know I was there for him if he wanted to talk about . . . you know . . . anything.

                            WEN
          (softly, almost to himself, still not looking at
          Charlie)
What does it mean when a girl keeps so many secrets? Sometimes I don't even know what to think. I have no idea where I stand with her.

                          CHARLIE
Dude, you're nuts. She's crazy about you. Anybody can see that.

                            WEN
Oh yeah? Then why did she stand me up last night? We were supposed to go to the movies together, but she didn't show. She never answered my calls either. Or my texts.

                          CHARLIE
          (takes this in)
Um, I don't know. I really don't. But I'm sure there was a reason. Something must have happened.

WEN

Right . . . well . . . maybe I'd feel better about it if she just told me what it was. Or maybe I could laugh it off if weird stuff didn't keep happening all the time with her. But it does, Charlie. When something's wrong she won't admit it. She bottles herself up and won't let me in. I don't know if she's mad at me or . . . or what.

CHARLIE

Listen to you. You're driving yourself crazy. Wen, whatever this is, I'm sure she'll tell you eventually. She's just one of those people who has a hard time opening up about certain things. You know that. It's how she is. It's how she's always been.

WEN
             (unconvinced)
Yeah, I know. I know . . .
             (sighs)
. . . and I get it, I do. She doesn't have to tell me what's going on. Why should she? It's not like I'm even her boyfriend or anything. To her I'm just another friend, I guess. A regular friend, and that's better than nothing, right? Why should we have to be more than that? It's no big deal. . . .

CHARLIE (V.O.)

This was even worse than I thought. Wen was a complete mess, and it was hard to watch. It was obvious he was hurting.

A passing car honks and somebody calls a greeting to them as they continue driving past. Wen dutifully holds up the WIENERS ON WHEELS sign and waves his huge rubber hand, but the effect is nothing less than pathetic. Through the wiener costume's face hole we can see his expression. There's no joy in him right now. As he continues to stare blankly ahead, Charlie looks on in dismay.

CHARLIE (V.O.) (CONT'D)

I wanted to help him. I wanted to fix this somehow, but I knew there was nothing I could say or do to make him feel any better at that moment. He wasn't going to listen.

183

Wen's cell phone alarm goes off, a short, complicated trumpet solo.

CHARLIE

What was that?

WEN

(yanking one of his gloves off)
"Salt Peanuts." Dizzy Gillespie. It means my shift is finally over and I can go home.

As Wen starts taking off his other glove, we see Charlie's mind working, still searching for a way to help.

CHARLIE

Hey, I know—why don't we head over to Goldy Records and look through their old LPs? We both love that, and it'll get our minds off . . . well, everything else.

Wen looks over at him. His expression changes. For the first time in the whole conversation he looks almost excited about something.

WEN

That's actually a good idea, Charlie. Let's do it.

CHARLIE (V.O.)

But it was not to be, because just at that moment, like an untimely grenade tossed at us by the fickle hand of fate, who was to appear over his shoulder but Olivia. She was rushing toward us with her accordion case gripped in her hand.

Wen notices the direction of Charlie's gaze. Now he sees her too. His distant expression returns.

OLIVIA

(still approaching, a little out of breath)
Looks like I just made it in time! Guys, I have a new riff idea I want to play for you. Can you stick around a little longer and work on it with me?

CHARLIE

Hey, Olivia.

Olivia sets down her case and, crouching, starts to open it. Wen's face is stony.

                              WEN
              So are you going to tell me what happened last night?
                         (off her blank look)
              The movies? Remember?

By her expression it's clear that she's only now remembering and feels terrible about it. She stands up again.

                            OLIVIA
              Oh no. Wen. I'm so sorry. I completely forgot.

                              WEN
              And the messages I left for you? You didn't get those?

Olivia appears confused at first, and then suddenly realizes . . .

                            OLIVIA
              Oh no. I'd turned my phone off . . .
                         (checks it)
              . . . and look, it's still off. Oh . . . hey, you must be mad.
              I get that. I deserve it. Listen, I really am sorry. I never
              meant—

                              WEN
                    (holds up his hand to cut her off)
              It's no big deal, Olivia. It's okay. You don't have to explain
              what happened or where you were. Now or ever. It's not
              like I have any special claim to your trust or your time. You
              were busy, that's all. The details are none of my business.
              I don't want to pry.

                            OLIVIA
              What? No, Wen . . . I—

                              WEN
              Look, I gotta go. There's a bunch of stuff I gotta do. See
              you guys later.

He spins his still-costumed body around and stalks away.

OLIVIA

Wen . . .

CHARLIE

Come on, Wen. Don't.

But he's still going. Olivia's frozen, staring at his back.

CHARLIE (CONT'D)

Are you okay, Olivia?

OLIVIA

(quiet, looking away from him)

Yeah, I'll be fine. I . . . I have to go now, though. Bye, Charlie.

She snatches up her accordion, and before Charlie can stop her she's already disappearing down the sidewalk, head low, rushing back the way she came.

CHARLIE (V.O.)

There I was, stuck in the middle as two of the closest friends I'd ever had stormed off in opposite directions, furious with each other. I wanted to shout, "Wen! Olivia! Stop! Please don't fight!" But it was no use.

The camera backs slowly away as the distance between Wen and Olivia widens.

CHARLIE (V.O.) (CONT'D)

Sometimes you can be right there watching while your friends, who you know care deeply about each other, make a big mistake, but there's nothing you can do to fix the situation. Stuff happens. That's just the way life is. I was sad not only for them, but for all of us. This was bigger than any lost contract. Before my eyes, Lemonade Mouth was falling apart.

186

WEN
One Burning Question

"What's going on, Wen? It's a beautiful day and you've been flopping on that sofa doing nothing for ages. It's kind of dark in there too. Everything okay?"

"Peachy," I answered, not even bothering to look up. "Everything's just grand."

In my peripheral vision I could see Sydney considering my answer for a moment, but that was when the person on the other end of the phone (Sydney was on hold during a long business call with an antiques buyer) must have come back, because Sydney ducked into the kitchen again and started talking about Victorian chamber pots. Which was good. I didn't want to speak with her or anyone else. My trumpet was nearby, but I didn't want to play it. I didn't want to do anything. Which was why I'd retreated into my dad's little office off our kitchen, pulled down the shades and thrown myself onto the ancient excuse for a couch my dad kept in there.

Nothing in my life was working out.

Lemonade Mouth? A complete wash with no future. My dad's business? Failing. Nobody was admitting it out loud yet, but despite how hard my dad was working, it was pretty obvious from his phone calls that selling hot dogs wasn't bringing in enough money to pay all the bills. My own personal prospects? Ha. Put it this way: despite everything, I was still a big goofy frankfurter waving at traffic on a street corner. 'Nuff said.

And then, of course, there was Olivia.

My concern for her had been growing through most of July. There was something happening with her, but I couldn't do anything to help if I didn't know what it was. And then she disappeared for a whole day and conveniently forgot to mention it to me, even though we had plans? What was up with that? Did I do something wrong? Was she mad at me? I just think that if a person who cares about you is upset with you they ought to tell you so. Was that asking too much?

But at the center of it all was one issue, the burning question I kept coming back to even though it was eating me up inside: how can anybody ever get close to a person who keeps you at a distance? Okay, so maybe I wasn't her official boyfriend or anything, but I cared about her. A lot.

And that's why, when there was a knock at the door, I was sitting in a dark room staring into space and wondering if anything in my life would ever make sense. I noticed George padding past, and a minute later his head reappeared in the office doorway.

"Somebody's here for you," he said.

"Yeah?" I asked, only vaguely curious. "Who?"

"Olivia."

The information worked its way through the fog of my brain, and then I leapt up from the sofa so fast that it made me dizzy. When that passed, I straightened my T-shirt and went out to meet her. There she was on the front steps. As soon as she saw me her forehead wrinkled. She was looking at me like I had an extra nose.

"Olivia. What's wrong?"

"Your hair," she said. "I don't think I've ever seen it do that before."

I touched it with my hand, immediately realizing that one side of it was flat to my head and part of it was sticking up. "I was on the sofa," I admitted. "Resting, sort of."

She nodded.

"Um . . . want to come in?"

There was a blast of electronic sound behind me—George, firing up a noisy video game. Olivia leaned around my shoulder to glance inside.

"No, I don't think so," she said after a moment. "Not here. Come walk with me? We need to talk."

My stomach sank. Whenever my dad said "we need to talk" it was never, *ever* good news. But I nodded.

A minute later, after I took a few seconds to comb my hair, we were walking quietly down my street in the direction of the beach. And when I say quietly, I mean we weren't talking—not at all. I was waiting for Olivia to begin but she wasn't doing it, and the tension just got worse and worse. It was horrible. I could pretty much guess what was going on. I wasn't even sure if it was technically possible to break up with someone you weren't officially going out with in the first place, and yet I felt positive that that was exactly what was about to happen. My world was teetering and my mouth was dry and I wanted to curl up and hide. I told myself to put on a game face, as if I didn't care about anything and nobody could hurt me.

If she wasn't going to talk, then I wasn't either.

Finally we reached the beach. We walked to the far end beyond the big boulders to an area where few people ever go, and that's where we sat down in the sand. I tried to stay calm even as my throat was tightening and the world was about to fall apart. We were alone, just Olivia and me, gazing out at the water with the smell of sea salt in the air and a gentle breeze in our faces. Behind us, the sun was on its way down.

"I know I haven't been very open with you," she said at last, running her fingers through the sand, "but this has been a weird time for me. I'm sorry. I really am. But I want you to know that it's never been about trust. I trust you. It's just that having a hard time trusting others is something that's been going on throughout my entire life and . . . well . . . old habits die hard."

"Okay . . . ," I said, trying to understand.

"The reason I was away yesterday, the reason I forgot about going to the movies with you and ended up being so exhausted this morning that I slept through my alarm, was that I was in Massachusetts. I was visiting my mother."

It was like an explosion that hit me in waves. At first I wasn't sure I'd heard her right. Olivia's mother had disappeared when she was really young. This was big. Huge.

"Your *mother*? Oh my god, Olivia."

She nodded. "I told you. The past few weeks have been . . . weird."

With her arms wrapped around her knees, she explained to me how she'd heard from her mom, whose name was Jess, and how her grandmother had known that she'd been back for a while but hadn't said anything. I listened, but I had a hard time taking it all in. No wonder it wasn't easy for her to talk about this stuff. A thing like this would have been an emotional roller coaster for anyone, but it must have tied Olivia in knots. I wanted to reach out to her, to somehow show her that she wasn't alone.

"It's okay," I said, resting my hand on her shoulder. "I get it. You don't have to say any more, Olivia. I understand."

She spun on me, and without warning there was an edge to her voice. "No, you don't, Wen. You really don't. You have no idea what it was like to meet Jess after all this time. You have no idea how it felt—how it still feels. But I *want* you to understand. That's the thing. I really do. Except I'm no good at this. For me, things don't come across right when I just blurt them out. And that's why I went back home after I saw you this afternoon. I had to go get something and bring it back to show you."

She reached into her pocket and pulled out a little gray book. Its binding was frayed and some of the pages were folded at the corners.

"This is my diary. These are my thoughts. It's all here," she said, holding it toward me. "I want you to read it."

I glanced at the scribbled handwriting. She'd opened it to an entry marked *Tuesday, August 3,* which was two days earlier. "Your *diary?* Are you . . . *sure?*"

"Positive."

I felt kind of weird about it. I'd never kept a diary, but I knew they were supposed to be kind of sacred places where people wrote things that weren't supposed to be read by anybody else. Looking into Olivia's diary would sort of be like sneaking into her private thoughts. But the way she was looking at me, I could tell she wasn't doing this on a whim. This really was what she wanted. So what could I do? I took the diary.

And then for the next few minutes, with Olivia next to me staring at the ocean, I read.

OLIVIA
The Stranger

TUESDAY, AUGUST 3

It's almost midnight and I can't sleep. For days

I've been thinking and thinking about Jess, and now I'm picturing her in my mind. She's standing in front of a mirror brushing back her long dark hair, and when she notices me watching, she smiles. Every time I close my eyes I see her. Which is ridiculous, since I really don't have any idea what she looks like now, or who she is, or anything at all about her. All I have is a faded old photograph, a few foggy memories I probably made up and the stupid letter she sent me a month ago. That's it.

So why can't I just forget about her and go to sleep?

I'm going to put down my pen and try.

WEDNESDAY, AUGUST 4

It's past 2 a.m. Still awake.

Daisy's curled up in the corner of my room. I see her eyes on me and I can't help wondering what she's thinking. There's something very peculiar about that cat. Today she decided to claim all of the food bowls as her own, standing guard over them and hissing whenever the other cats tried to come near. But as much as Daisy drives Brenda and me up the wall, as selfish and wild as she can be, there's also something special about her. I see it in her eyes right now, a look of understanding, as if she knows what I'm going through. She might be a baby, but she's got a strong spirit, and I get the feeling she has an old, old soul.

I've given up on trying not to think about Jess. I've taken out the photograph of my parents again. I'm staring at it.

8:05 A.M.

I made up my mind. There are so many questions I don't want to stay unanswered for the rest of my life. I want to know what happened. I have to find out why she left and where she went and what exactly was going through her head when she left me to grow up without a mother. Because no matter what else she is, she is that—my mother. And Pittsfield, Massachusetts, is only two and half hours away.

Despite everything she did, or maybe because of it, I have to go see her. We need to talk.

9:45 A.M.

I can't believe it. It's really going to happen. I told Brenda what I decided and she wasn't happy but she didn't argue. "If that's what you want," she said, "then there's no point in putting off the inevitable." There's a bus leaving from Providence at two o'clock this afternoon. I don't think it's fully sunk into my head yet. We're going. Today is the day.

10:10 A.M.

I'm amazed to be writing this, but I'm actually worrying about what I should wear. What's the rule for something like this? Do I dress up? Do I put on a skirt and blouse, maybe even a pretty dress for her, trying to look my best? Or do I just go as I am and not worry what the heck she thinks when she first sees me? After all, she had her chance to see me at my best, my worst and everything in between, and she decided to turn it all down. Maybe showing up in ripped jeans and a nasty old T-shirt would make a statement.

1:00 P.M.

I'm a total mess. I didn't even want to eat lunch but Brenda insisted, which I guess was good because now we're heading to catch the shuttle to Providence. Brenda called ahead to let Jess know we're coming, so now she's expecting us. She even told Brenda that she's excited to meet me. Just looking at those words on the page totally weirds me out.

My mother is out there somewhere.
She's expecting us.
She's excited to meet me.
Me. My mother. Mine.

3:50 P.M.

We're somewhere in central Massachusetts. It's drizzling outside and Brenda's asleep beside me, and somebody nearby has a radio playing softly. I brought a book to read but it's no use. I can't concentrate. I keep thinking about all the things I don't know about her and all the things she doesn't know about me. The music I like. The books I read. My friends. My favorite foods. I'm not even sure she knows where I went to elementary school. What will she ask me first? What will I ask her? Where to even begin filling in the gaps?

I also keep thinking about Lemonade Mouth and how everybody's so unhappy right now. This has been the strangest summer I could have ever imagined, and it's not about to let up. I wish my friends were here with me now. Especially Wen. He has a way of making me feel calm and safe. But even if I could have found the courage to talk with him and the others about this, I also know that whatever happens today, this is something that has to be between Jess and me. I know I should be excited—and I am, in a way—but I'm also dreading this. After all these years without her I'm less than an hour away from meeting the woman I barely remember, the woman I almost remember waving to from the window just before she got into that taxi and disappeared from my life.

My palms are sweating. My whole world is hanging by a thread.

9:25 P.M.

On the bus again. It's dark outside and we're on our way home. I want to set down my thoughts while they're fresh, but I'm not sure I have the words. Everything is all jumbled. It's like I had an old storage attic where I kept things locked carefully away but now somebody's gone in and messed it all up, leaving me with a huge pile of stuff to sort through. I don't even know where to begin.

So, yeah, I met her. It's done. Only, it was completely different from anything I ever imagined it would be. Or maybe it was exactly what I'd imagined. I don't know. I'm so tired and empty.

Now I really wish Wen was here. Talking to him would calm me and maybe even help me get my thoughts in order. So I'm going to pretend he's sitting next to me. I'm writing this to you, Wen, even though I might not ever show it to you. You're here and I'm talking and you're listening. I can already tell this is a good idea. Just writing it down is making me feel a little better.

My mother lives in a halfway house called
Sunshine Haven, a three-story brick building on a
busy street opposite a public park with a little pond.
You know that building we bike past when we go to
Muffit's Music in Riverside? The one with the lion
sculptures and the hedge like a staircase? Well,
it reminded me of that. Sunshine Haven is a sort
of stepping-stone home for women in transition.
My mom's there because of the type of life she's
been living and because she's sick. She's getting
treatment at a local hospital because her kidneys
aren't working as well as they used to.

Brenda and I had to sign in when we got there,
and then a lady showed us to a room on the second
floor. The whole place smelled of disinfectant. We
opened the door and there sat my mother on a
chair by a window, waiting for us.

The first thing I thought when I saw her was
that we were in the wrong room. I guess I'd been
expecting to see the girl from the picture I've kept
by my bed since forever, but instead here was this
short-haired lady in a frumpy flowered skirt. She
was skin and bones, with dark circles under her
eyes. She looked fragile. She didn't even get up from
her chair the whole time. But when she put her
hand to her mouth and said, "Oh, Olivia, honey!
You're even prettier in person than you are on TV!"
I knew this really must be her. For a few seconds

I just stood in the doorway. Brenda stepped in and asked how she was and she said fine as they gave each other a hug. I think I said something polite like "It's nice to meet you," but on the inside I was just overwhelmed and still taking in this stranger, this alien from outer space who has everything to do with my life and yet nothing to do with it.

"Well, don't just stand there like a statue, sweetheart," she said. "Come on in. Let me get a look at you."

I did what she asked. I stood in front of her and let her study me even as my face got warm. Inside, I was furious at myself. This woman left me when I was still practically a baby and here I was like a kid from a Dickens novel, presenting myself to her for inspection. What was wrong with me? But as much as I hated to admit it, I guess I really did care what she thought, because I'd picked out a nice dress, my knee-length pale blue one, simple but pretty, just for her.

"Wow," she said with a glance toward Brenda, "it's like I'm looking at you again, Ma. I'm staring at another version of my own friggin' mother."

I had no idea what to say to that. Brenda just smiled and then asked, "How are you doing with your appointments, Jess? Are you showing up for dialysis?"

"Yeah, yeah, I've been going," she said with a flash of irritation. "Don't nag."

There was only one other seat in the room, so I let Brenda have it while I took the edge of the bed. Then we talked, sort of. It was pretty awkward. Brenda started telling her about me and my life and Jess just nodded without saying much. I said even less.

"Is she always this quiet?" Jess interrupted after a while, looking at Brenda but nodding in my direction. "That's her dad all over again, I suppose."

There was another silence and then Brenda clasped her hands together. "You know, I think I'm going to step out for a while. Give you two some time."

I start to panic. I wasn't sure I wanted to be left alone with Jess. Jess seemed to feel the same way, because she gave Brenda a worried look and said, "No, Ma, stay here. I don't think you should go."

But Brenda had already grabbed her walking stick and was heading toward the door. "I need a little fresh air," she told us. "I won't be long." It was a lie, of course, and everyone knew it. She was just trying to get us to talk to each other.

So then I found myself alone with my mother. I had no idea what to say. My eyes fell to the bedside table next to her, where there were maybe a dozen photographs. They were mostly of Jess herself, which I thought was interesting, and most looked like they'd been taken a few years ago, because she appeared younger and her hair was longer. There was my mother sunning herself in a beach chair. In another she was smiling on a porch swing. In yet another she was twirling around in a red dress at what looked like a dance club. There were only a couple where she was posing with anyone else, and I didn't know them.

"You like pictures?" Jess asked, following the direction of my gaze. "Me too. I only have these, but I always keep them with me. They bring back memories."

"Who's that?" I asked, pointing to a shot of Jess standing at the edge of a cliff with a beefy bearded guy wearing a headscarf.

She looked at the picture and frowned. "Oh, that's just me with Dylan, my off-again on-again. Mostly off-again now. We were at the Grand Canyon. But this one," she said, picking up a photograph where her hair was poufy and she was grinning at the camera while straddling a huge black motorcycle, "is me in my glory, back when I lived in Memphis for a while—the happiest days of my life. This one's my favorite. Every time I look at it I smile."

I felt a flash of something I couldn't name—Sadness? Frustration? Something else?—and I almost asked her where the heck were the pictures of my dad and me. But I didn't.

"I'm glad you came, Olivia," she said. "This must all be pretty weird for you."

Ya think? Was she trying for the understatement of the year?

It occurred to me that maybe it was good that Brenda had left. I realized that while a part of me was feeling like a lost little kid, another part of me was quietly fuming, and being alone with my mother had made me remember why I'd come all this way. I decided to concentrate only on that.

"I have some questions for you," I said more forcefully than I meant to. "That's really the only reason I'm here. I just want to understand some things about what happened. I want to know why everything . . . you know . . . played out the way it did."

She studied me. "You want to know why I left."

I nodded.

"Olivia, hon. I was never meant to be a mom. I would have been terrible at it."

"How do you know?"

She waved her hand as if it was a dumb question. "My mother always said I was born selfish. I guess it's kind of true."

"And that's it? That's why you disappeared out of my life?"

She shrugged. "Yeah, that was part of it."

"So what was the other part?"

201

She looked at me like I was asking a lot, as if I was pushing some kind of limit, but I didn't care. I stared right back at her. I wanted to know.

"All right, then," she said. "If that's what you came here to find out, then I'll give you your answer. I'll tell you how it was."

And so she told me the story. She started by talking about things I already knew, like how she was barely seventeen when she had me and how my dad was only a year older, and how it wasn't easy for them. But then she told me some things I didn't know, like how all her life, ever since she could remember, she'd had panic attacks. As you know, Wen, I sometimes get them too, so I guess now I know where I get them from, except my mother's sound like they were much more severe than mine. At times, she said, she'd get really angry at people, especially Brenda, who was raising Jess alone. Jess told me she would throw things at her and call her every bad name she could think of. She'd been taken to doctors who'd called her unstable and had given her medications to help with her mood swings, but she didn't like how the pills made her feel so she didn't always take them.

I knew my mother had issues, but I was surprised to learn they were that bad.

She told me that starting even before she was a teen, she was sneaking out to parties, drinking and going out with older boys. "I was a hellion back then, there's no denying it," she said with the faintest of smiles. "I've never been one to let anybody control me." Things got worse and worse as she got into her teens. Drugs. More alcohol. Fighting. According to my mother, she sometimes had blackout periods when she wouldn't remember what happened. At fifteen she ran away and was picked up six days later in Albany, New York, by the police, who found her sleeping under a bridge. She told me she didn't even remember leaving home.

In retrospect, it should have been obvious she needed more help than she was getting, but it's easy to look back and criticize. Brenda did her best with her, I'm sure.

And then my mom met my dad and got pregnant, and suddenly Jess was terrified. My dad didn't run, though. To her surprise, he moved in with her. Jess said there was a time when she thought maybe things were going to get better because of the baby, but it turned out she was wrong. Having a newborn in the house was hard. My mother hadn't really changed, and my dad was in and out of trouble with the police, so he wasn't always around. And when they were together they were fighting all the time. For almost two years the arrangement worked, sort of, but mostly because they had Brenda helping.

"But one night," my mother said, "when Brenda was away and your dad had stormed out yet again, all up in arms about something I can't even remember anymore, I decided to invite some friends over, and pretty soon we had quite a party going. You were less than two years old and you were sleeping in the next room." She'd been looking toward the window but now she turned to me. "Olivia, I don't remember much from that night, only that I woke up the next morning all alone beside a Dumpster off Atwells Avenue in Providence with the sun shining on my face."

I waited for her to continue but she took her time, gathering her thoughts. Meanwhile, I was gripping the edge of the mattress.

"Now, I'm not the best person in the world and I know it," she went on, "but I'm telling you, my first thought was of you and whether or not you were okay. I realized I must have left you all on your own at home. What if something had happened to you? I panicked. I had no money. Nothing. Somehow I managed to hitch a ride back to Opequonsett. I ran back to the house. I threw open the door. My friends were all gone, the place was a friggin' disaster, but you were okay, thank god. I found you still in your crib, holding on to the wooden bars and looking out at me. You were crying your little head off but otherwise fine. You were scared, that's all. And I was too. If anything had happened to you, I swear I don't know what I would have done. So I picked you up and I held you close. My heart was racing. And that's when it hit me: my whole life was a roller coaster and it wasn't about to change. So for the sake of my daughter, I knew I couldn't stay." She looked up at me again. "I just knew it, Olivia. I had to go."

"But why? Why couldn't you have just made the decision not to do those things anymore?"

Again she didn't answer for a while. "Honey," she said finally, "even back then I knew who I was and who I wasn't. You've got to understand, there's always been something inside me, a little voice in my head telling me I gotta go live my life. I wasn't going to suddenly transform into a responsible mother, and I knew it as well as anyone could know anything. But that didn't mean you stopped being my little girl."

She leaned toward me then and put her hand on my arm. She was looking at me, and I didn't know what to say. I wanted to believe she cared about me. I wanted it so much, Wen, and yet how could I forget everything I've been through all these years?

"I don't buy it!" I snapped, pulling my arm away. I surprised even myself with the sudden bitterness in my voice. "I think you could have at least tried to be a good mother."

"Olivia . . . ," she said, leaning back in her chair again. Her smile faded.

But my blood was racing and I was just getting started. "Do you have any idea how hard it was to grow up without you?" I asked her. "I needed a mom, Jess. I needed you there, but you didn't care enough to even pick up the phone to talk to me. Would that have been so difficult? Was it such a big deal to write a letter every now and then, or maybe send a postcard just to let me know where you were? That you were even alive?"

"I understand you're mad," she said quietly, her face darkening. "I don't blame you. But don't think my own life has been a slice of cherry pie. People don't end up in places like this because they want to. I'm not going to spell it all out for you, Olivia, but let's just say that bridge in Albany wasn't the only one I ever slept under. I know I'm no angel, but not everything in life is in our control."

"That's crap! That's just an excuse!"

I couldn't believe I was saying these things. I'd come to get answers, not to argue with her, and yet I couldn't stop myself. My eyes were stinging and my throat was tightening up, but I choked it all back because one thing I refused to do was show her any tears. After all these years without her, I wasn't going to start crying in front of her now.

Jess's lips went tight, and for a moment I saw the girl from the picture again, the determined kid who knew what she wanted and wasn't going to take no for an answer. I thought she was getting ready to shout back at me. In a way, I wanted her to so we could have it all out and then maybe I'd feel better. But instead she just went quiet, her face all red and her eyes still on me as her fingers adjusted and readjusted the folds in her flowered skirt. At last she reached out her hand again, this time to brush back a lock of hair that had fallen in front of my eyes. She tucked it behind my ear.

"I'm real tired, Olivia. I think you better go."

"What? But we're not done!"

"I think we are. It was sure nice of you to come visit me."

I almost wanted to laugh. It was ridiculous. I'd been there less than an hour. But she was serious—she really was sending me away. So what could I do except stand up and head out?

"Tell your grandmother I'm sorry," she said to my back. "Tell her I'll see her next time, and shut the door behind, will you?"

And that was it. For a while I stood in the hallway feeling like my insides had just been ripped from me. I was so angry and sad and confused. I couldn't have talked if I'd tried. I stumbled down the corridor and found my way downstairs, and there was Brenda sitting in the little lobby area, waiting for me.

So now we're on the bus again, and all this time I've been going over and over the things we said. Why did I have to go and tell her I needed her? It's not true! Brenda is great and I have my dad and I have my friends and that's good enough. One thing I understand now is that my mother is not a well person, and it isn't just her kidneys either. She's not well in the head, which makes me feel sad for her. But that's still not an excuse for the things she did and didn't do. If she's not responsible for her actions, who is? She may be my mother, but in some ways she's more like a kid than I am.

In any case, I'm glad I wrote all this down, because now I'm too exhausted to feel much of anything. I'm done crying. I'm too spent to think. I'm going to stare out the window and watch the lights go past until we get home. ✿

WEN
All That Really Mattered

I set the diary down. A few feet away, Olivia was still hugging her knees to her chest, staring out across the water.

"I had no idea you were going through all this," I said. "Are you okay?"

She shrugged. "I'm fine."

I tried to imagine how it must feel to be her. I wish she'd told me sooner, but at least now I understood a little better. "So, are you glad you went to see her?"

"Not sure," she said after a pause. "I thought I'd feel relieved in some way, you know? Like talking with her would resolve something. But it didn't. My visit only ended up raising more questions than it answered, and when I think about all this stuff, I still feel . . . I don't know . . . kind of empty." She looked out at the water again. "Maybe Brenda was right after all. Maybe it would have been better if I hadn't gone."

She picked up a piece of broken shell and tossed it into the water. The air smelled of the ocean, and from somewhere far to my left came the distant sounds of little kids playing in the waves.

"I'm sorry I waited so long to tell you," she said at last.

"Why? This was never about me. You had to do whatever was right for you."

"I'm not saying I should have done it for you, exactly. Looking back over these past few weeks, I think talking to you sooner would have made the whole thing easier. For *me,* I mean. I guess I was just . . ." She seemed to search for the right word.

"Scared?"

She nodded. "Like I said, old habits die hard."

We sat there quietly a while longer, but then she stood up. After brushing the sand from her legs, she tucked the diary back in her pocket and then reached for my hand. Without a word we started walking along the water together. The tide was going out, and after a few steps we took off our shoes so we could go barefoot, letting the waves roll over our feet in the soft wet sand. There was a sailboat in the distance. Behind it, a line of pink puffy clouds looked like the castle wall of a faraway country. We stopped to look.

"Do you ever feel lonely?" she asked. "Like we're just small parts in a giant, complicated universe?"

"I'm not lonely," I said. "I'm here with you."

She blinked at me, and then something unexpected happened. She reached out and touched my cheek, staring right into my eyes, and then she kissed me. And I kissed back. It was a real kiss, gentle and quiet, the kind that gets your blood racing and your head spinning, and when it was done I just stood there, surprised, looking at her.

And she was looking back at me.

A warm breeze blew a few strands of her hair into her face and she swept them aside with her fingers and took a step back. She turned and walked away, continuing along the edge of the water, almost daring me not to follow. But I didn't wait. I caught up with her and took her hand and we kept walking. No need to talk. No need to pick through the exact meaning of what had just happened. We both knew. I was her boyfriend. She was my girlfriend. Maybe we'd already been that, but now it was official. And the sun was shining and the sand was soggy and cool under our feet and the world was full of mysteries yet to be explored. We were together and it felt good. It felt right. And that was all that really mattered.

STELLA
A Break in the Proverbial Clouds

Picture the scene: There sat your troubled troubadour in depressed silence on the steps in front of the local Honey Fields Mini-Mart, having just received a call from Charlie with the disturbing news of Olivia and Wen's recent blowup. Thank goodness Rajeev was there to console her with a bag of salted veggie chips. It felt like storms were swirling and the end of Lemonade Mouth was in sight. The band had nothing scheduled, no prospects, and now this newest debacle threatened to become the final nail in their sad, citrusy coffin.

Yet, unbeknownst to your somber Sista, change was in the air. Little did she suspect just how close she and her friends were to a break in the proverbial clouds—a small one, perhaps, but at this point any tiny glimmer of hope was better than no glimmer at all.

Just as Rajeev and I were finishing the last of the crispy veggie treats I got a message from Lyle.

> Guys, can evry1 pls come 2 my house?
> U have 2 see something.

It was vague but intriguing. I texted back to ask what it was but he didn't answer, so Rajeev and I set out at once for Lyle's place, which, unfortunately, was about a twenty-minute walk away.

We were the last to arrive, right behind Olivia and Wen, who were walking up the driveway just as we approached the house. I noticed they were hand in hand. I had no idea what exactly had gone on between them, but I was relieved to see that the recent trouble seemed to be over.

"All right, Lyle," I called. He was in his garage, sitting in front of a crate with his laptop. Charlie, Mo and Naomi were already there, standing behind him. "So what's the big mystery?"

"I was waiting to tell you guys," he said, running his fingers through his thick mess of hair. "I didn't want to get anyone's hopes up if it was only going to end up being a short-term thing."

"What are you talking about?"

"Our website. I told you I posted a couple of tracks from the new recordings, right? Well, since your Chet Anders appearance I guess curiosity about Lemonade Mouth has been growing. I expected a surge in site visits for a couple of days, maybe, but I assumed it'd drop away after that. It hasn't." He pointed to the screen, where there was a picture of us and an area where people could get free downloads of two of our new songs—"Let Us Begin" and "Freaky Fakey Phony." "Our daily visitor count has been rising, not dropping. Over the past twenty-four hours alone we got more hits than our server could handle. Earlier this afternoon the whole site crashed. I just had to upgrade it to a more powerful platform."

We all stared at each other. "So . . . uh . . . what does this mean, exactly?" Mo asked.

Naomi grinned. "It *means* that even without Decker and Smythe, the word is still getting out about Lemonade Mouth."

CHAPTER 8

*What does not destroy me,
makes me stronger.*
—Friedrich Nietzsche

CHARLIE
The New Cool

Lemonade Mouth's "Ninja Earthquake"—an up-tempo dance
rocker—plays over a montage of short, grainy black-and-white film
clips of some of the stuff from Olivia's book *New Perspectives:
People and Ideas That Changed the World:*

A. 1955: ROSA PARKS, the future icon of civil rights, stands alone
   at a bus stop on a drizzly day in Montgomery, Alabama. A white
   couple walks past, ignoring her, as a bus approaches.

B. 1936: The astronaut NEIL ARMSTRONG, still a little kid, gazes
   at the sky as his arguing parents change a flat tire behind him.

> CHARLIE (V.O. while the clips
> continue)
> Things happen for a reason. Sometimes a new idea, like a
> rocket, takes a little time fizzing quietly in the background
> just before it blasts off and demands our attention.

C. 1902: THE WRIGHT BROTHERS, soon-to-be inventors of the
airplane, try unsuccessfully to fly a crazy-looking jalopy, kind
of like a giant lobster trap on wheels. It rolls for a distance
but doesn't leave the dusty ground. A solitary newspaperman
shakes his head and walks away.

D. 1860: ABRAHAM LINCOLN, future president and world
changer, wipes the sweat from his brow as he hammers up a
sign announcing that he's running for president. Behind him we
see the sidewalk of a bustling town. People rush past without
even looking.

E. ONE MILLION YEARS AGO: A bunch of CAVEMEN in a
frozen landscape look bored and cold as another caveman
rubs two sticks together to make fire. There's a sudden spark,
but only one or two of the cavemen see it. Most don't even
notice.

The music fades to . . .

EXTERIOR. A QUIET BEACH—EARLY MORNING, THREE
YEARS FROM NOW

Barefoot Charlie strolls along the empty beach talking to the
camera.

> CHARLIE
> The online notes thanking us for our Chet Anders
> appearance were still coming in, more and more of
> them each day. It was as if no one was used to hearing a
> message like ours and people needed time to process it
> before they were ready to react.

Hands in pockets, he continues walking in thoughtful silence. A
seagull calls. Waves crash. Close to the camera, Charlie stops.

CHARLIE (CONT'D)

But then, to our surprise, *Howit Iz,* the third-largest
independent news and culture magazine in the country,
ran an opinion piece about us, calling us "champions
for the unappreciated, a long-missing voice for the
unpretentious."
        (a pause . . .)
I had to look up what that even meant.

INTERIOR. BRUNO'S PIZZA PLANET—AFTERNOON

Naomi Fishmeier holds open a copy of *Howit Iz* and reads aloud
as the members of Lemonade Mouth, sitting with her in a
semicircular booth, listen in stunned silence.

NAOMI

"Whether you're tall or short, skinny or full-figured,
bespectacled, bedraggled or bald, Lemonade Mouth
wants you to know that *this is your moment.* The
until recently unknown high school band from Rhode
Island . . ."

INTERIOR. SMALL, MESSY LIVING ROOM, OPEQUONSETT,
RI—AFTERNOON

Lemonade Mouth's old nemesis, RAY BEECH, oversized and
sad-looking in a faded Mudslide Crush T-shirt, sits at one end
of a worn-out sofa. In his hand he holds the same article, and he
reads it with an expression of both shock and defeat. Perched
beside him on the sofa, oddly enough, is a large pink pig. The
pig gazes over Ray's shoulder at the article and seems just as
forlorn as Ray.

RAY (V.O.)

". . . has just opened the door for all of us, challenging
people everywhere to redefine who and what we
accept as cool, to take on the narrow notions of style
and beauty that have been handed down to us from the
bigwigs at . . ."

INTERIOR. THE OFFICES OF DECKER AND SMYTHE, BOSTON, MA—AFTERNOON

JENNIFER SWEET, assistant to Earl Decker, swivels her computer monitor slightly so Earl won't see what she's looking at—an online version of the same article. Earl is nearby, visible in his office, talking angrily on the phone. Jennifer continues to read silently, leaning into the screen.

> JENNIFER (V.O.)
> ". . . self-interested corporations. These kids seem to be saying that women don't have to . . ."

INTERIOR. MUSIC ROOM, BLOCKSTON BAPTIST CHURCH, BLOCKSTON, DE—EVENING

In the out-of-focus background, church musicians are setting up for practice. In the foreground, GLENDA MAY and GLENDA LEE PUTRIDGE, the solidly built banjo-playing twins from *American Pop Sensation,* are seated cross-legged on the floor with their banjos at their sides. They're staring at the *Howit Iz* article.

> GLENDA MAY AND GLENDA LEE
> (V.O.)
> ". . . have hourglass figures to be attractive, and men don't have to be body builders."

INTERIOR. BIOCHEMICAL LABORATORY, OPEQUONSETT, RI— MORNING

While BEVERLY DeVITO, lab tech at Stella's mom's lab (twentysomething, glasses, heavyset, friendly face), waits for a plant cell test to run, her rapt attention is on the article.

> BEVERLY (V.O.)
> "So you don't own all the latest fashions? So your cheekbones aren't prominent? Stand proud!"

EXTERIOR. A SMALL BOAT ON WHITEFISH LAKE, WHITEFISH, MT—MORNING

Fishing alone in the middle of a peaceful lake surrounded by mountains, Opequonsett High School's vice principal,

MR. BRENIGAN, appears stunned at the article he's stumbled onto. Even vacationing in an isolated part of the country, he hasn't escaped Lemonade Mouth. He gapes at the page.

> MR. BRENIGAN (V.O.)
> "So your hair isn't perfect? So you're not as young as you used to be? Hold your head high!"

INTERIOR. HIGH-RISE OFFICE, NEW YORK, NY—MIDDAY

With his feet up on his messy desk and a view of New York City skyscrapers, Chet Anders chuckles to himself. He's reading the article too.

> CHET (V.O.)
> "The New Cool has arrived. Lemonade Mouth has ushered in a new era, and we are all invited to join them in being fabulous—just the way we are."

INTERIOR. BRUNO'S PIZZA PLANET—AFTERNOON

Still in the booth listening to Naomi read, the members of Lemonade Mouth appear to be at a loss for words—except maybe Stella, who fidgets as if getting ready to say something. Naomi holds up her hand to stop her.

> NAOMI
> Hold on, Stella, there's more.
>   (pause)
> "And if that kind of revolution still isn't enough for you, just wait until you check out the sound track. Lemonade Mouth's mix of oddball instruments, together with their honest, emotional approach, creates a musical vibe that transcends description. It's a sonic boom, a wild riot and a bright summer day all rolled into one. It's quirky, raw and utterly unlike anything you've ever heard before—not to mention danceable as all get-out. So hold it high! Raise it up, America! Prepare yourselves for the revolution!"

Naomi lowers the article and sweeps her eyes across the five faces of Lemonade Mouth, who are all too dumbstruck to speak.

NAOMI (CONT'D)
(dead serious)
Guys, strap yourselves in. I believe you're about to take off.

DISSOLVE INTO: A television set. Three beautiful women stand at a podium in the front of a crowded room. The women are surrounded by microphones, reporters and flashing cameras.

CHARLIE (V.O.)
(over the television sound, which is inaudible)
It was just the beginning. A few days later, three of the most famous supermodels in the world—Jara Shé, Rubia and Karen Sasky—got together for the first time ever to make a big announcement. The media was all over it.

SUPERMODEL #1: JARA SHÉ
After years of abusing our bodies through chronic starve-dieting, unnecessary surgeries and other unhealthy behavior, all just so we could achieve an unnatural look we were told was required by the industry, we are now announcing the launch of a new movement . . . a movement that demands change!

The crowd cheers. Fist-pumping.

SUPERMODEL #2: RUBIA
(thick Brazilian accent)
We here to protest the kind of corporate manipulation that idealizes a warped reality! We not gonna go along with it no more! We here to promote consumer demand for *healthier* body images in the media!

More shouts of approval. More camera flashes. The audience is eating this up.

SUPERMODEL #3: KAREN SASKY
Join us! Celebrate your individuality—the real, natural, beautiful *you*! Because nobody needs to be what they're not! And none of us need to be . . .

(dramatic pause)
... *Freaky Fakey Phony*!

The crowd goes nuts. Behind the models a curtain rises, revealing a lineup of ordinary-looking people—women and men, boys and girls—all smiling and looking confident in their ordinariness. Above them a giant sign reads: SNaP! REAL IS THE NEW BEAUTIFUL! Cameras flash like crazy.

> CHARLIE (V.O.)
> They didn't mention us by name, but it was obvious where the idea came from. They called themselves "Supermodels for the New Pretty," or "SNaP," and they urged everyone, no matter their age, size or shape, to tap into their "inner supermodel."

As the cheering and applause continues, we see a montage of shots of people watching the scene on TV:

A. Somewhere in middle America, four or five scruffy-looking truckers in a donut shop diner, all of them staring in disbelief at a screen above the counter.

B. Somewhere else, a group of preteen girls at a sleepover party, all arranged on a carpet lined with pillows. Their eyes are wide as they watch.

C. Seated on a leopard-spotted sofa, SISTA SLASH, Stella's activist/anarchist, guitar-slinging hero (late thirties, spiky black hair with orange stripes, biker-tough), takes a bite from an apple and studies the television with interest. At her knee is an open copy of *Howit Iz*. Behind her we can see her huge, fancy-glitzy living room, which is decorated with dozens of wild-looking guitars and mementos from her impressive career. Far away, near the opposite wall, a young worker-guy vacuums a rug.

Back to ...

The TV screen with the grinning supermodels. They've joined the line of ordinary people, and all of them are now waving at the ecstatic crowd.

219

CHARLIE (V.O.)

Watching all this play out . . . well, it was incredible. And surprising, even for us. It wasn't like any of us ever *expected* our song would set off that kind of a reaction.

EXTERIOR. QUIET BEACH—EARLY MORNING, THREE YEARS FROM NOW

Barefoot Charlie, deep in thought, is strolling along the waterline again, except this time the camera is at his side and moving along with him, with the ocean as the backdrop.

CHARLIE (CONT'D)

> (to the camera, like a conversation with a
> . friend)

It was like we'd tapped into a well of pent-up emotion across the country. And with all this publicity, our songs were getting an increasing number of downloads—not *chart-busting* numbers, but still. For a bunch of kids with no corporate backing it was more than we'd dared to hope for.

He looks out across the water. The wind ruffles his hair.

CHARLIE (CONT'D)

But as amazing as all of this was, our excitement was tinged with sadness. The time had come to say farewell to a friend.🎥

MOHINI
Might As Well Be the Moon

🐦 Rajeev's stay in Rhode Island is over. All of us are accompanying him to the airport, where he's flying off to his new life in faraway Lubbock, Texas. Nine of us are here: Lemonade Mouth plus my family plus Rajeev. There are too many of us to fit in our Volvo, so the Hirshes have lent my parents their Caravan, which was nice of them.

220

But this is no small goodbye. We all feel it's important to be here.

The closer we move to the gate, the slower all of us walk and the quieter our conversation becomes. We're like a band of heavy-hearted mourners, shuffling along the industrial carpeting while an overhead electronic voice announces arrivals and departures. Too soon, we reach the security gate. This is as far as the friends and family of passengers are allowed to come. But we've run out of ways to delay the inevitable. Rajeev already has his seat assignment. His bags are already checked. We linger a little while longer, but there's no denying the truth.

There's nothing left to do but say goodbye.

Rajeev starts by thanking my parents for maybe the hundredth time. He hugs Maa and then Baba and then Madhu (she's biting her bottom lip and looking like a cloudy day) and then me.

"Stay in touch, Monu," he whispers in my ear, giving me a squeeze.

"Of course" is all I can manage because of the heat in my eyes and the rock that seems to be weighing down my stomach. Saying goodbye to Rajeev feels worse than I ever would have imagined less than two months ago, back when I actually hid in my room just to avoid meeting him. In the weeks since then, I've grown accustomed to having him around. I already know I'll miss his weird sense of humor and his water fights and the way he can make Madhu smile just by making a face at her. I'll miss our easy conversations, the way I never have to explain certain things to him because we both grew up with the same kind of parents.

I feel like I'm saying goodbye to the brother I never had.

It's Charlie's turn next. He and Rajeev do one of those

guy-handshake things that involve a long series of complicated steps and end in bear hugs. It's sweet to watch, especially after the uncomfortable start I know Charlie had when Rajeev first arrived. That's one of the things I love most about Charlie, how even when he feels strongly about something he's still open enough to realize that his opinions might need adjusting. He takes himself seriously, but in a way, he kind of doesn't. Charlie knows how to laugh things off and move on.

Rajeev is finished spending his final moments with Wen and then Olivia. Next comes the part I'm sure will be the hardest.

All week I think everybody has been feeling bad for Stella. Not that she's been walking around in a depressed fog or anything. Olivia and Stella and I got together at Olivia's two nights ago to listen to music and talk, and Stella seemed cheerful enough. But it doesn't take a relationship expert to see that this is going to be hard for the girl. She and Rajeev have not only fallen headlong for each other, but even though I never would have guessed it, they turned out to be an incredible couple. Like curried chickpeas and hot sauce, they just go together.

Watching the two of them at this moment brings another lump to my throat. They both look haunted, like they can't believe they're saying goodbye. They're gazing into each other's eyes and holding hands. Not a word passes between them, and yet I can tell there's real communication happening. It's amazing to watch.

At last he kisses her forehead.

She puts her hand on his cheek.

He takes a step back.

After a heartbeat he turns and walks away, his expression resolute as he moves through the gate.

There. It's over now. All of us step closer to Stella. Her eyes are red rimmed. Wen rests his hand on her shoulder. I hear Olivia whisper in her ear, "He'll be back. Don't worry, Stella. We'll see him again soon."

I want to believe it, but I don't. I've never met Rajeev's family—well, not recently, anyway—but I know how things are. Rajeev's parents are superconservative, and they just arrived in this country. Stella is wonderful, but they don't know that. Plus, Stella and Rajeev are going to be two thousand miles apart.

If you ask me, Lubbock might as well be the moon.

Everybody's quiet as we watch Rajeev work his way through the short line, wheeling his carry-on luggage behind him. He steps through the metal detector. He's on the other side now but he still hasn't looked back at us. He's walking farther away down the long hallway. It hurts. It feels like we're watching a part of Lemonade Mouth disappear, like he belonged with us and is now being ripped away. Stella's face is ashen. Charlie squeezes my hand and I can't help feeling grateful that at least *he* isn't going anywhere.

I can't believe Rajeev still hasn't looked back at us, but then, just as he's about to turn the corner and out of sight, he spins around in a cool robot dance move that's somehow both choppy and graceful at the same time, and he's facing us again. He lifts an invisible lemonade cup into the air.

"Hold it high!" he calls out with a grin. "Raise it up!"

Even though my throat is tight and I feel my eyes welling, I smile. I think each of us feels the same way. We do what he asks. We all return the salute of our new, dear friend, holding up our invisible cups. Even Madhu, Baba and Maa.

I have no idea what's going to happen to any of us next. Whatever it is, though, I can't help thinking things won't be the same without him.

CHARLIE
The Message That Changed Everything

EXTERIOR. QUIET BEACH—EARLY MORNING, THREE YEARS FROM NOW

Barefoot Charlie is walking along the shore again, hands in pockets.

>   CHARLIE
> It was a roller-coaster ride. Even as we said our sad farewell to Rajeev, the media firestorm we'd set off was still raging. After the *Howit Iz* article and the SNaP announcement, the online messages started pouring in. I mean, *loads* of them—it was nuts. Lyle wouldn't admit it, but I think he was getting overwhelmed.

Charlie stops. He looks out across the water, which sparkles with sunlight.

>   CHARLIE (CONT'D)
> And that's when we got the message that changed everything. It was only a day or two after Rajeev left, and in the slew of other emails, we almost didn't see it for what it was. We didn't believe it was real.

INTERIOR. SOUND ROOM—EVENING, THREE YEARS FROM NOW

At a huge control board surrounded by stacks of amazing-looking sound equipment, Lyle Dwarkin, disheveled as ever, is being interviewed.

Uncomfortable in the spotlight, his voice is quiet as he talks with an off-screen interviewer.

> LYLE
>
> I thought it was a joke at first. Through the website we received a private fan message from somebody who claimed to be Sista Slash. You know, *the* Sista Slash, the protest rocker. I figured for sure it must be bogus, somebody trying to fake us out by using the name of a celebrity. But . . . well, a couple more messages came through and I looked into it, and . . . yeah. Turned out it really was her.
>
> (shakes his head, still wowed by the memory)
>
> She said she was impressed by what Lemonade Mouth was doing. She said she wanted to arrange a meeting.

There's a pause as Lyle lets the enormity of that statement hover in the air.

> INTERVIEWER (OFF-SCREEN)
>
> So what happened when you told everyone?

> LYLE
>
> (shrugs)
>
> Well . . . they could hardly believe it, of course. Especially Stella, who was like the biggest Sista Slash fan ever. After I showed her the message she didn't speak for, I don't know, maybe three whole minutes. I thought she was going to pass out.

OLIVIA
Barbecued Zucchini with a Rock-and-Roll Anarchist

Dear Ted,

I don't know whether to feel good or to scream. My life just jumped into scary overdrive, and yet as

I'm writing this I'm wondering how much you even know. Have you even received my last letter, the one where I told you that we were going to meet with Sista Slash?

Well, now we have. And boy, what a day it's been.

We met her in a restaurant in Providence. She's in New England anyway because the Take Charge Festival is this weekend (even you must have heard about that—the huge multiband benefit concert in Vermont? It's all over the news), and since she's putting up the money for the whole thing, she's spending the week up in Vermont organizing the final preparations. She said she wanted to come down to Rhode Island to meet us, though, and in her message she said she'd be at a place called the Lone Star Veggie, a little vegetarian Texas barbecue restaurant on Federal Hill.

It was a good thing the trip from Opequonsett wasn't long. For the whole ride into Providence, Stella was working up a major freak-out. "Are we going to be late?" she kept asking. "Oh god oh god oh god, can you believe this is happening?"

When we stepped into the restaurant, there she was, Sista Slash, the Lawless Queen of Anarchy. She was alone at a booth waiting for us. We recognized her right away, not only because a solidly built middle-aged rocker with spiky black hair striped with orange is kind of hard to miss, but also because there weren't any other customers in the place at the time. When she realized how many of us had come (eight—us five plus Lyle, Naomi and Mrs. Penn, who drove) she started moving tables so we could all sit together.

Now, I'll be honest. From what little I knew about Sista Slash—her shock-and-blast music; her reputation as a reckless, in-your-face crusader for a zillion different causes; even her whole retro-tough studded-jeans-and-leather look—I was secretly worried she would turn out to be a loudmouthed, full-of-herself, rock-diva type. But she wasn't. She seemed genuinely thrilled to meet us. In fact, instead of talking about herself, she went on and on about how much she loves our music.

"Guys, I just have to get this out right from the get-go," she said (she has a Southern accent—I didn't know that, did you?), "I'm a huge fan of Lemonade Mouth. Your sound is outside of the everyday. It takes risks. It's got an edge, know what I mean? An attitude. And, girl," she said, turning to Stella, "I can't get over that uke of yours! Holy crap! That little thing rocks!"

Stella was speechless. She turned purple.

Believe it or not, Sista Slash was super charming the whole time we were with her. And funny! You should've heard her talk about all the trouble she has getting her hair to stay spiky after wearing a motorcycle helmet. ("This darn do takes up more of my time than I care to admit, but I'm not giving up my ride, and appearances must be maintained!") Or about how worried her accountant is because of the financial risk she's taking on the Take Charge concert. ("The man is so frightened of taking chances that I think even if he was about to burst he'd be too scared to pee in the dark.") Within minutes she had us all laughing and relaxed. The woman might have a pile of gold records, a Humanitarian of the Year award and the email address of the Dalai Lama, but Sista Slash is about as unassuming as they come. I began to see why Stella admires her so much. Even Mrs. Penn was impressed at how down-to-earth she was.

Sista introduced us to the restaurant owner, a tall, muscular guy named Pete (apparently Sista and Pete grew up together, another reason why she offered to make the trip down to Rhode Island), and he treated us like family. "Any friend of Sista's is a friend of mine," he said with the same Southern accent. After that he brought us plate after plate of the best vegetarian food I ever imagined. Who knew spicy barbecued zucchini with chipotle black beans would be delicious?

Then, about halfway through the meal, she dropped a bomb on us.

"Listen, guys," she said, wiping her mouth on a napkin, "I have an idea I want to run by you. What would you say if I told you I'd like to squeeze Lemonade Mouth into the lineup of bands performing at Take Charge?"

I'd just bitten into a deep-fried artichoke and I almost coughed it up. By the sudden silence around the table, I think everybody else was just as shocked.

"Think about it," she continued. "I'm talking maybe a fifteen-minute set, short but sweet. I know five days ain't a lot of notice, but it's an important cause and I think Lemonade Mouth would be a terrific addition to the festival. I'll help you, you help me. What do you guys say?"

I looked around. Stella's mom set down her fork. She looked too stunned to continue eating, and I guess she was waiting to see what everyone thought. But I knew exactly what my friends were thinking—that this was a colossal opportunity for us, that taking part in this huge event would bring us much further than <u>APS</u> or <u>After Midnight with Chet Anders</u> had. The Take Charge Festival is sure to be the biggest concert event of the whole year. Sharing the stage with famous, respected acts like the Swag Hags and Fade Out 321, not to mention Sista Slash herself, would establish us as real musicians, not just a novelty act of high school protesters. There would be worldwide satellite links and international coverage, and afterward, who knew what else? A retrospective concert album? Maybe even a documentary movie?

If ever there was a big time, this was it.

But needless to say, the idea scared the living crap out of me. My stomach had already tightened to the size of a marble and I had to fold my hands together in case they started to shake. Everyone stayed quiet. Stella, who probably wanted this more than anybody, looked at me and then quickly back down at the table, not pushing one way or the other. Wen squeezed my shoulder. I could tell none of them were even going to try to persuade me. They were just waiting to hear what I would say.

I think Sista Slash is a smart lady. I think she was aware of how we felt about the situation just from watching us.

"I understand about being scared," she said after a pause, her voice gentle, even motherly. She was looking around at everyone, but I felt sure she was actually talking to me. "I'll let you in on a secret. When I first started out I used to panic before every show I did. I'd break out in a cold sweat like you wouldn't believe, and it got worse as the venues I played started to get bigger. But then I decided I had something worthwhile to say and that nothing was going to stop me from saying it, especially not myself. You kids have something to say too, something people need to hear. The truth is, up until now I've been wondering whether your whole all-for-one-and-one-for-all thing was just a marketing trick, but now that I've met you guys I can see that it isn't. It's real. And it's exactly what Take Charge is meant to be all about."

At last she turned to me and she touched my hand.

"Olivia, hon," she said even more gently, "you can do this. I may have trouble balancing a checkbook, but trust me, I'm an excellent judge of character, and I firmly believe that you and your friends can do whatever you set your minds to."

I'd been staring down at the tablecloth but I looked up at her now, and in her eyes I saw that this wasn't about her trying to convince me to do her show. I could tell that she meant what she was saying. She really did understand the kinds of feelings I go through, and she wanted to help me. Realizing this, I felt my face heat up and I had to look away again. But when she squeezed my hand, I squeezed hers back.

The Universe really is a mystery, Daddy. Earl Decker is gone, but they say sometimes when a door closes a window opens. Maybe that's what's happening here. I'm told there are Take Charge posters not only all over the country but all over the world, each showing Sista Slash with her fist in the air and the slogan ACTIVISM MEANS DOING SOMETHING! IT'S YOUR WORLD! TAKE CHARGE! There'll be over fifty thousand people in the live audience this Saturday. Tens of millions more are going to watch across the country and around the globe, from Burbank to Boston to Brussels to Bombay.

And Lemonade Mouth is going to be a small but real part of it.

We're scheduled to play four songs.

We start at about 12:20 in the afternoon.

I can hear your voice now. You're telling me to stay calm. You're saying I need to take deep breaths and find some small part of this situation to focus on instead of letting the entirety of it overwhelm me. And, Daddy, that's what I'm doing. I'm thinking about my friends and how much this means to them. I plastered my bedroom walls with life-size printouts of faces, hundreds of strangers who are watching me even as I write this. That was Sista's suggestion. She told me that instead of trying to pretend the audience wasn't there, what worked for her was when she went the other way, trying to imagine that she was being watched all the time. I know it sounds crazy, but she said it made her get used to the idea and after a while it didn't affect her as much. Every now and then I look up at the images and I imagine they're real. I try to see them without seeing them, without catching my breath, without my hands starting to shake.

I don't know if it'll work, but nothing else has, so I'm giving it a shot.

We go on in five days.

P.S.

It's a couple hours later. You're not going to believe this, but we just heard from Jess. She called to ask Brenda for two hundred dollars, and when Brenda asked her why, she only said it was for bills. Can you believe the nerve of that woman? And Brenda says she's actually going to give it to her! I asked her why (it's not like we're rolling in spare money) and she told me it's because Jess is her daughter. I understand that, of course, but it still infuriates me. It's obvious that Jess uses people. When I said that to Brenda she just got mad.

"Don't be so judgmental," she said. "Neither of us can understand all the things she's gone through, and anyway, her health is more of an issue than you realize."

I was going to say something else but that last part made me stop. "What do you mean?"

Brenda sighed. She was opening cans to feed the cats at the time and she didn't look up. "Your mother isn't doing very well right now. Worse than normal, I mean. Her kidneys are failing and it looks like she's got a tough fight ahead. This is serious." She stopped what she was doing. She turned to me. *"What I'm saying, Olivia, is I don't know how long your mother's going to be around. Understand me? Maybe you ought to keep that in mind before you get too high and mighty about her."*

I shut my mouth. I had nothing to say to that. I had no idea.

Okay, so I'm keeping it in mind now. I'm imagining my mother's life as kind of like an iceberg, and I'm trying to picture the entire thing, not just the part I've seen, the part sticking out of the water. I'm working on it, but it isn't easy. Do you have any idea what it's like to finally get comfortable feeling mad at somebody, only to have something else happen that makes you feel bad for them? That makes you realize your own problems are nothing in comparison with theirs?

Not only is it ironic and scary, it's infuriating.

WEN
The Mystery of Ray Beech

Man, were we ever nervous. There was no denying this was huge for us. It wasn't a record deal, but it was still a big opportunity.

In the few days of practice leading up to the Take Charge Festival, Stella was in panic mode. "We have to get this right!" she kept saying. "We have to be better than tight! The breaks need to be super clean and we need to absolutely nail the starts and endings!"

We worked hard on our set. We'd decided to begin with "Blastoff Castaways" and then move on to "Let Us Begin," "Street Corner of Condiment Dreams," and "Zombietown." I knew this whole thing was tough for Olivia, but she seemed to be holding up. I was proud of her. We were sounding good too, and I was feeling pretty okay about how we were going to do.

And then an odd thing happened with Ray Beech.

It was the middle of the afternoon during a break from practicing in Lyle's garage, and I'd volunteered to shoot into town on my bike to grab everyone some snacks—we'd already raided Lyle's cabinets clean of chips and other munchies, so it was time to replenish the supply. Just as I turned the corner onto the pedestrian bridge over Warren Street, I noticed Ray Beech about a block away. From over the rails of the bridge I could see him standing on the sidewalk gazing through the display window of Goldy Records, probably checking out the new Dustbin Dukes poster.

Just then I heard a voice call out, "Ray! Long time no see, buddy! How's it going?" I recognized that voice.

Scott Pickett.

I slowed my bike, peering down from the bridge. Sure enough, there was Scott with his girlfriend, Lizzie DeLucia, about half a block closer to me but on the opposite side of the street from Ray.

I'm not going to lie. I was still having a hard time with the Scott Pickett thing. He hadn't stopped working for my dad, so I had to keep running into him, and it was always uncomfortable. Sure, he'd helped us with the *After Midnight* show and I knew that was good and everything, but come on, after all he'd done to us in the past, all of a sudden he was supposed to be our *friend* now? We were supposed to just forget everything? And yet everyone else seemed perfectly fine with it. They told me I was carrying the old grievance too long and that I should let it go. Even Mo.

I was trying not to make a big deal of it, but deep down it wasn't easy for me to make the shift.

Now, in the street below me, Ray turned to see who had called to him. When he saw Scott I could tell this was some kind of an uncomfortable moment for them, because they both sort of froze for a second. Ray looked a little surprised and Scott just stood there waiting for a response. Nobody noticed me on the bridge overhead. I was close enough to Ray, though, that I could see happiness flash across his face at first, like a part of him was glad to run into his old friend. But that didn't last. Just when I thought Ray was going to call out hello and maybe go over to talk, instead his expression went all dark and he stormed away in the opposite direction without saying a word. Only then did I notice that Scott and Lizzie were both wearing Lemonade Mouth T-shirts.

The entire incident couldn't have lasted more than a few seconds, and like I said, nobody even noticed I'd seen it. It might not have seemed like a big deal either, except Scott definitely looked deflated afterward. I couldn't hear him and Lizzie, but when they walked away they moved slowly, with Lizzie talking and Scott shaking his head and staring at the pavement. And that was it, it was over.

Still, it got me wondering. This wasn't the first time I'd seen Ray looking like a sad little kid who'd lost a friend and didn't know how to get him back. I remembered the morning in the high school field when everyone was helping us get ready for the *After Midnight* show, how I'd noticed him at the top of the hill watching us from his car. Eventually Scott had seen him too and started walking up to him, but just like today, Ray had left as soon as he realized people knew he was there.

So what was that about? What could it mean?

Could it be that Ray Beech, the biggest loudmouth I knew, wanted to mend fences but couldn't see a way to make it happen?

Was it even possible that Ray secretly wanted to join Scott with all the other Lemonheads but was too proud?

STELLA
Boulevard of Squashed Dreams

At last the enormous day arrived. Astonishing as it seemed to our five bewildered rabble-rousers (especially to your own Sista Stella, who had tried so long and hard to get the elusive Take Charge Festival tickets without any success), Lemonade Mouth was not only going to *attend* the massive concert event, they were going to be *part* of it. And all at the personal invitation of the great Sista Slash herself.

My friends, emotions rise and bubble at the mere memory.

And yet it would be false to suggest that my happiness was complete. Sure, I was excited—of *course* I was, who wouldn't be thrilled to have all their musical dreams come true? But I was also a nervous wreck, and my mind kept going back to how much I missed Rajeev. How much *more* glorious the day would have been, I kept thinking, if only he could've come with us.

Now, in case any of you out there are thinking that Rajeev

and I shared some unrealistic romantic delusion, that our relationship was just some blinding teenage summer crush gone sadly overboard, let me set the record straight once and for all about Rajeev and me, and how *we* saw ourselves: From the very beginning, Rajeev and I both recognized that we still had our whole lives ahead of us, and that teenage romances have a long history of fizzling out over time. We recognized this and accepted that the future—our future—was very much unwritten and still in question.

But that didn't mean our feelings weren't *real*.

Even though we couldn't have foreseen what, if anything, lay ahead, we knew that we'd found something in each other that was rare and special. We both realized that we wanted the same kind of magic in our lives—not the fairy-tale-fake kind of magic where people go nuts for each other like sharks at a feeding frenzy and then move on. No. We wanted the real thing, the kind based on true friendship and respect, and in our own way, that's what we were already building. Yes, there was a huge spark between us from the moment we first met, but somehow we knew to take things slowly, enjoying that fleeting moment for the true magic it was. I think that's what made our time together so powerful.

So on the morning of the Take Charge Festival, there I sat, sweaty-palmed and secretly pining for my lost Rajeev, as my family and friends and I were transported from the hotel in two stretch limos on our way to what was sure to be the biggest event of Lemonade Mouth's existence.

The festival was happening on a three-hundred-acre dairy farm in a tiny rural town called Stamford, Vermont. We were set to be the second act, squeezed in between Li'l Jedediah and the Blast Babies, and we were told to arrive two hours early. Unfortunately, everybody else seemed to have the same idea. The ride from the hotel should have taken thirty minutes (because we were a last-minute addition to the schedule, there were no hotel rooms available for us closer to Stamford), but it took us longer because even three hours before start time, the highway was already jammed with people on their way to the show.

At least we'd lucked out with the weather. It was a beautiful, cloudless day.

Finally we arrived at the festival grounds. The traffic cop waved us through the main gates, and we all went quiet as we took in the scene: a parking lot full of bicycles, buses and cars, and then, behind it, a giant bowl-shaped field swarming with people. The stage was set up in the center, surrounded by a patchwork of blankets and tents. Many of the concertgoers seemed to have camped overnight. It would be another hour and a half before the first act began and already the crowd was bigger than anything I'd pictured.

"Whoa," Mo said.

I glanced toward Olivia. Squeezed between Charlie and Mrs. Reznik, she had a determined look as her gaze stayed focused on her knees.

Our limo driver followed the directions of the traffic guys, weaving us slowly along a dirt path toward the back of the stage as people drifted all around us. In the line of food vendors to our far left I could see Penelope, the Wieners on Wheels van. The bright yellow wasn't hard to pick out. Wen's dad and Scott Pickett were already setting up to sell hot dogs. Wen had arranged this with Sista Slash, sort of a last-ditch attempt to help his father get the struggling business to catch on. There were advantages to having connections with the concert organizer. ("If this doesn't work, I don't think anything will," Wen had confided to me.) Closer to our limo, some of the people were holding up signs with slogans like:

ROCK THE BALLOT BOX!

SUPPORT HURRICANE DISASTER RELIEF!

WANT A BETTER WORLD?
THEN GET OFF YOUR BUTT AND DO SOMETHING!

Faces strained to see us through the limo's tinted glass. We were being treated like VIPs, and I admit, I loved every second of it. It was an amazing rush.

At last we reached an enclosed area near the stage. Roadies leapt from the chaos to help unload our stuff. Sista Slash was nowhere in sight (I later found out she was with one of the concert sound teams in another part of the giant field), so we were met instead by a guy named Al Pinkerton, who was in charge of all the incoming performers. He came over right away to introduce himself. A tall redhead with a wireless headset strapped to his ear, he was super nice and even had a copy of our first CD, *Live at the Bash*. He asked us to sign it for him.

"So great to meet you guys!" he said, reaching out to shake everybody's hands, starting with mine. "I'm a big fan—you have no idea how excited I was when Sista first told us you were going to play today." He really did know our music too, and to prove it he sang his own quick rendition of "Back Among the Walls," which was totally flattering.

I guess what I'm saying is that everything was going well. The morning wasn't even over yet and already the day looked like it was going to be the crowning achievement of our lives. We'd landed the gig of the year, our music was about to be legitimized in front of a gigantic, eager audience and the air practically vibrated with hopeful excitement, a general feeling of Great Things About to Happen. Even Olivia, who we'd all been worried about, seemed to be taking the chaos with surprising calmness.

And that's why it was such a crushing blow when it all started to crumble so quickly.

Disaster was already heading our way, preparing to slam us like an unstoppable freight train.

It started less than five minutes after the roadies unloaded all our instruments and equipment near the stage. We were just waiting for the tech crew to let us know they were ready for us. Other than the band members, nobody else needed to stick around, so our families and the rest of our entourage had started wandering away to check out everything happening out on the field.

That's when Olivia's cell phone rang. She looked surprised to hear it.

"I meant to switch my phone off," she said, and she seemed to hesitate as if considering whether or not to even answer it. But when she checked the screen she saw it was her grandmother, who'd stayed at home to watch us on TV because she'd been worried about doing a lot of walking on her bad legs. I figured she was calling to wish Olivia good luck.

Wen and I had been killing time leaning together against a giant crate, so we were right there with Olivia as she answered the phone. As soon as the conversation started I could tell from her expression that this wasn't a good-luck call. Something was wrong. Olivia drifted into a corner, away from the sounds of people talking and the equipment guys working. I couldn't hear what they said, but I noticed Olivia's hand rise to her mouth. There was a lot of listening and nodding. At last she put the phone away, and when she came back she looked as pale as a phantom.

"What's the matter?" Wen asked.

"Brenda just got a call from Sunshine Haven," she said, "the place where my mother lives." Olivia had told us earlier that week about her mom and how she'd come back after so long and all the stuff that was going on with her. It was mind-blowing. "It was one of the social workers there. They . . . um . . . they had to call an ambulance. My mother's on her way to the hospital."

That took a moment to sink in.

"Holy crap, Olivia! That's terrible!"

She nodded. I knew she was mad at her mom about a lot of things—and who could blame her? But now her arms were crossed and she was biting her lip as she stared at the ground. It looked like there was a battle going on inside her.

At the edge of the stage a few yards away, Al Pinkerton was calling out orders to his crew while somebody from Li'l Jedediah's backup band was tuning a twelve-string through a gigantic Marshall amp. Charlie and Mo weren't far. They'd been with a couple of the roadies—and Charlie had been taking a video of all the activity—but the two of them must have realized something was going on, because they came closer now. We filled them in.

"So, what does this mean?" Charlie asked. "Your mom's going to be *okay,* right?"

"I don't honestly know. All they could tell Brenda was that earlier this morning my mother seemed short of breath.

She insisted she was fine, but then a few minutes ago they found her collapsed on the floor. The social worker thinks she's been lying about going to her dialysis treatments." Olivia glanced around at us. I could see she was scared. "My grandmother's been hinting that something like this might happen. Now I guess the situation is really serious—maybe even life-threatening."

Mo's eyes went wide. "The social worker actually said that?"

Olivia nodded again. "She told Brenda that if the hospital can't clear her system fast enough, there's a chance that . . . well . . . that this could be really bad." She was hugging her shoulders tight and her gaze dropped to the ground again. She almost looked like she was getting smaller.

Mo stepped closer and wrapped her arms around Olivia's shoulders. Wen touched her arm. "Olivia," he said, "whatever you need, we're here for you. Just tell us what you want to do."

But in Olivia's expression I could pretty much see the answer. Her grandmother was at least three hours away from her daughter, almost certainly too far to arrive at the hospital in time to be with her during the crisis. From here in southern Vermont, though, the drive to Pittsfield would only be about an hour.

I glanced at Charlie, Wen and Mo. They seemed to be realizing the same thing I was—the same obvious truth Olivia was struggling to admit to us and maybe even to herself. In the distance the concert crowd was growing quickly. People were pouring in through the main gate and side entrances along the fence while recorded music started to play through the field speakers. Near the front of the stage a line of cameras and journalists was already beginning to buzz with

243

activity. I took a moment to grieve. We'd come so, so close. Painfully close. But Olivia was more important, and there was no question about what we needed to do. In the span of about three seconds, Mo, Charlie, Wen and I looked around at each other, each of us nodding one at a time.

We made our decision. Nobody even hesitated.

Wen was the one who broke the brief silence. "You need to be with her, don't you." It wasn't a question.

Olivia bit her lip. "I'm so sorry. I know it's crazy after . . . well, everything, but she's still my mother, and what if something bad happens? What if I don't ever see her again?"

"Olivia, you don't have to explain," I said. "Of *course* you need to be there with her. We're going to do everything we can to get you there."

Her eyes welled up. "Are you sure? We'll never make it back in time for our performance slot. We'll lose our one big chance."

"Doesn't matter," Charlie said. "If there's a way to get you to Pittsfield, you're going."

Olivia looked like she was going to cry. There was no time to stick around, though, and Charlie, Mo and I were already sprinting toward Al Pinkerton. We needed to let the concert organizers know what was going on, and to figure out how on earth we were going to do what we'd just promised. Al was finishing up with a couple of lighting equipment guys, and we quickly explained the situation to him. He listened quietly. We hated to disappoint him—and Sista Slash and everyone else—but this was bigger than a concert.

Al was surprised but he was really nice about it. "I'm sorry this is going on for you guys, but no worries at this end. We squeezed the schedule to fit you in, so now we'll just have to unsqueeze a little and adjust. Hey, this isn't the first change of the day and it won't be the last. When I explain it to Sista, I'm sure she'll understand."

Unfortunately, things were a little harder when we asked him if we could get Olivia a ride to the hospital.

"Look, guys," he said, suddenly uncomfortable. "I'm sorry, but we're moving a lot of bands today. I can spare one of the limos long enough to get you back to your own cars at your hotel, but I can't send it all the way to Pittsfield and back. I feel bad about that, but Sista Slash has a lot on the line here and we need all the transportation we have."

I realized this meant we had a big problem. Going all the way back to the hotel meant heading in the opposite direction from where Olivia needed to be. Plus, it meant we'd have to face the crawling traffic coming back toward the concert again. We didn't have that kind of time. Olivia needed to get to the hospital as soon as possible. But without another option, what could we do?

I looked across the field and saw Penelope. All at once I realized we did have another option, one that could get Olivia out of there fast. Long lines of customers were already forming at most of the other food vendors, but at Wieners on Wheels there was barely anyone. It felt like fate. That eyesore of a van might not have been much of a money maker, but this wouldn't be the first time she would come in handy.

So that's how it happened.

Minutes later we were strapping ourselves into the seats at the back of the wiener van—Olivia, Mo, Wen, Charlie and me (it wasn't like we were going to stick around at the festival and perform *without* her, right?), plus Mrs. Reznik, who happened to be nearby when we rushed over. Wen's dad was great. As soon as we told him the situation he closed up shop in a flash. Scott insisted on coming with us too. He was in the copilot seat. Out in the field, Al had a bullhorn and was calling for the crowd to clear a path for us. It was like the parting of the Red Sea. People stood on either side of the little grass boulevard they'd created, each of them staring in wonder at the curious VIP van with the giant wiener on top as we each said our silent, sad goodbyes to the Take Charge Festival. It was the last we'd see of the crowd that day.

WEN
Waiting for News

That was a long afternoon I'll never forget.

So, we left the festival behind us and headed to the hospital where Olivia's mom was being rushed for emergency treatment. We arrived just in time. Olivia's mother was already there and hooked up to a bunch of tubes and the doctors were about to transfer her into the intensive care ward. I saw her, but not for long. She was behind a curtain, so I got only a quick glimpse of a dark-haired lady on a hospital bed with machines all around her. But that was okay—it wasn't why we'd come. The point was that Olivia got a couple of minutes with her.

Olivia described to us afterward that her mother was short of breath and maybe a little confused, but she recognized Olivia and told her she was surprised to see her and grateful that she'd come. Olivia said she could tell that her mother meant it too—she truly was glad to see her. Which obviously was a big deal. Seeing the look on Olivia's face when she came back to the waiting area and told us all this, well, I think that one thing alone would have been enough to make it all worthwhile.

After that, we waited.

Olivia sat hunched beside me. Other than when she texted her grandmother with updates, she mostly stared at her feet. The rest of us did what we could to keep a conversation going, if only to distract Olivia from worrying too much. But really there wasn't anything anybody could do to help except be there with her. Overhead, the televisions were showing reruns of stupid old sitcoms. Their laugh tracks felt out of place against the harsh reality of sick people and anxious families all around us. The hospital was busy that day. Maybe it's like that every day. I don't know.

It seemed to take forever for the doctors to come out with more news and I kept glancing at Olivia. All this waiting seemed agonizing for her. Like I'd done so many times before, I tried to imagine what it must feel like to be her, to have lived her life and to have had the kinds of sad experiences and disappointments that I could barely conceive of.

"Thanks for . . . you know, doing this," she said to me quietly, reaching for my hand. "I'm grateful to all of you guys for being okay with this."

"Of course," I said. "You're our friend. I think it's great that you wanted to come, that you're here for her."

She shrugged. "She's my mom."

She went quiet again, but for a while I couldn't help mulling over what she'd just said and what it meant. It was finally hitting me, something I hadn't fully appreciated until that moment. This whole situation with her mom's reappearance had been so difficult for Olivia, a real struggle, and yet even though her mother had serious problems, even though

247

Olivia had plenty of reasons to be furious at her, she'd still wanted to come here to the hospital to be with her. Was that acceptance? Forgiveness?

I didn't know, but whatever it was, it struck me as amazing.

I looked around the room at all the other people who'd come to help support Olivia and my eyes lingered on Scott. He'd been quiet, sitting in a chair along with the rest of us, waiting for news. A few months ago I would never have imagined that Scott Pickett of Mudslide Crush would give a crap about anybody but himself. And yet there he was. It wasn't the first time either, although I'd been refusing to see it. I'd been simmering in my resentment about the past for so long, but now I had a new idea, an idea about forgiveness. It occurred to me that even though it isn't always easy, maybe it was better than letting bitterness and anger slowly eat me up from the inside.

It's funny how everything happens at once. Just as Olivia was finishing her zillionth update to her grandmother, I noticed through the big window that Sydney was walking across the parking lot to the main entrance. There was no mistaking her long stride and that cascade of black hair. Following behind her was a whole crowd of people, our families. They'd all left the Take Charge Festival to pick up the cars from the hotel and had finally made it through the traffic to join us here. I was happy to see them. I knew Olivia would be too. I was just about to point them out to everyone when, from the opposite end of the waiting area, the double doors opened and the doctor in charge of Olivia's mother appeared. She was looking right at Olivia.

All of us stood up.

It was clear she had news.

CHAPTER 9

What this power is I cannot say; all I know is
that it exists and it becomes available only
when a man is in that state of mind in which
he knows exactly what he wants and is fully
determined not to quit until he finds it.

–Alexander Graham Bell

MOHINI
The Laws of the Universe

It's a beautiful, lazy morning and I'm sitting at the kitchen table finishing a late breakfast with my family. Maa is sipping the last of her chai. Baba is lost in his newspaper. Madhu is chatting endlessly about a new pink blouse she saw in a store, a not-so-subtle attempt to convince my parents to rush out and buy it for her. The Take Charge Festival, only a few days in the past, is starting to feel like a fading dream.

At least, that's what I'm trying to tell myself.

Absently taking a bite of a crispy luchi (my mother makes the best), I look for the hundredth time toward the front window.

"Are you okay, Monu?" Maa asks. "You seem distracted."

"Just waiting for my friends to arrive. I'm fine."

And it's true, I *am* fine. More or less. Sure, my thoughts still drift every now and then to how things might have turned out if we hadn't missed our big chance at Take Charge, but as Charlie keeps pointing out, playing at that concert wasn't what destiny had in mind for us. I have no regrets. If the five of us were to somehow travel back in time to face that same morning by the Take Charge stage again, I'm positive we would all make the same decision.

The good news is that Olivia's mother is doing okay. The hospital kept her overnight, but she was much better the next day and they were able to release her. Now she has a nurse who watches her closely, double-checking on her dialysis routine and working with her to take better care of herself. "There's only so much anybody can do, though," Olivia told us. "Everyone wants the best for her, but in the end it's her own life and she's the only one who can really be in charge of it."

There was one good thing, at least, that came out of that experience: Olivia and her mom are now planning to stay in touch. Olivia says she'll go back out there next month for another visit.

So considering everything, things could have ended up a whole lot worse. I have many things to be thankful for. My friends and family are okay. I just got my schedule for the new school year and I made it into all the advanced classes I'd wanted, and I still have three whole weeks until the semester starts. Things are good. It's a warm summer morning and my life is pretty much back to the same old way it's always been. Normal. Comfortable. Low-key.

And yet . . .

And yet . . .

I'm glancing around at our kitchen and everything in my

world feels just a little . . . *off.* Unsettled, somehow. It takes me a moment to figure out why, but then I do. I realize that right now, a warm, do-nothing morning is exactly the kind of time when Rajeev would have instigated one of his massive water fights. Now that he's gone it's like there's a hole where he used to be. I miss him.

And then a very Charlie-like thought occurs to me: every upside has its downside. For instance, it's great that Rajeev came to visit us, but now I have to pay for that by feeling bad that he's no longer here. It's just the world's way of keeping an equilibrium. I make a mental note to tell Charlie about my revelation. "See? I'm getting it," I'll say. "Yin and yang. Balance in the Universe."

He'll be so pleased.

As if the Universe itself is trying to prove this point to me, my eyes happen to fall on an article on the back of the paper my father is reading. The headline says *Slash Out of Cash: The Queen of Rock Anarchy's Festival Proves a Musical Success but a Personal Financial Disaster.* This isn't the first time I've seen this story reported, how the concert was organized on a shoestring budget and how there ended up being insurance issues and lawsuits and other unexpected costs. Even though her festival brought a lot of money to a lot of causes, it looks like Sista Slash herself might end up broke. I don't know much about that kind of thing, only that it's sad.

She did something big, so now of course she has to get knocked back down to size in some way.

Upside. Downside.

Yin. Yang.

See, Charlie? I really get it.

A stack of yellow flyers with black printing appears in front of my face. "Since you'll be going through town

251

anyway, Mohini," Maa says, setting the flyers on the table in front me, "could you please hang a few of these up by the community center, and bring the rest to Mr. Taxiarchis at Paperback Joe's? He promised to pass them out."

"Sure," I say, taking in the jagged lettering across the top.

LEMONADE MOUTH PICNIC
Join us Saturday for an afternoon
of neighbors, fun and music!

It was the Lemonade Mouth parents who came up with the idea. It's basically a big party for our families and friends and anyone else who wants to join us in celebrating all the good things that happened, kind of a consolation prize for not being famous. It's going to be in the field behind the high school. People are being encouraged to set up barbecues, and there'll even be one of those bouncy castles for the little kids.

The five of us figure, why not? Any excuse for a party, right?

Plus, it'll give us a chance to perform our newest songs.

At last there's a knock at the door. I look up. There's Charlie, with his big goofy grin, waving at me through the window. As if by magic, the unsettled feeling I was just having fades away. Behind Charlie are Stella, Olivia and Wen. Scott's there too. I'm grateful for my friends, and all at once it occurs to me that my earlier revelation was only half complete, that the laws of the Universe work *both* ways.

For every downside, there's also an upside.

I grab the stack of flyers, thank Maa for breakfast and head for the door.

"Monu, where are you going?" my father asks, peering over his newspaper. It's as if he's been so lost in his reading that he's only just joined us.

"We're on a mission, Baba. We talked about this earlier, remember?"

His brow wrinkles, but then he does seem to recall. "Yes, yes. I forgot," he says. "Well . . . good luck." And he's back to his newspaper again.

Soon I'm outside with the others and we're heading down the street. We have a job to do.

STELLA
Springing a Big Idea

Now comes perhaps the least known and certainly one of the strangest episodes in the entire history of Lemonade Mouth. There trudged your dissident band of agitators, making their way across town on a sticky August morning to the one place you would never in a million years expect any of them to go.

It was Wen's idea.

Since the summer began, each of us had realized, of course, that Scott had been in kind of an uncomfortable position whenever the topic of Ray Beech came up. It was clear that Ray was a dark cloud issue for Scott, a longtime friend who'd fallen by the wayside, and one who didn't exactly bring warm and fuzzy memories for any of us, his new friends. So we all avoided the subject. Wen was the one who finally came to the rest of us and said it was time to talk with Scott about it. He had an idea how we might be able to help him out—as long as Scott *wanted* us to, that is.

I was surprised to hear Wen talk about helping Scott, of all people, considering how unhappy he'd been at having to work with him that summer. I also wasn't sure there was anything we really could do to fix the situation. But I figured as long as Wen and the others were willing to give it a shot, what the heck?

So we went to Scott. It wasn't the most comfortable conversation, especially at first, since I don't think Scott would ever in a zillion years have brought up the subject himself. But I guess he must have seen that we meant well, and eventually he opened up about all the bad feelings going on between him and Ray, how it had been hard for them both since Mudslide Crush broke up and how crappy he felt about losing his former best friend. Ray pushed him away whenever he tried to communicate.

Then Wen told him his idea.

After a long pause Scott looked around at us and said, "Really? You guys would do that?"

Let me stop here to point out that, like Ray, Scott had a history with Lemonade Mouth that was far from unblemished. There had been a time in the not-so-distant past, in fact, when I'd considered them both to be about as evolved as a Neanderthals. But since then time had marched on, and people, it seems, can be mysterious creatures. Over and over fate seemed to be making a special effort to throw Scott together with us, and I ended up seeing there was more to him than I'd recognized. Sure, he could come off as a little cocky sometimes, but he could also be thoughtful and loyal and, in his own way, kind of a sweet kid. I'd never seen a hint of disrespect toward Mo (which would have been a deal breaker), and for her part, Mo didn't seem to have any problem having him around.

Plus, there was no denying that Scott had come through for us a couple of times.

To my own astonishment, I found myself warming up to the guy.

So that's how we found ourselves following Scott Pickett, the former Mudslide Crush golden boy, as he led us to the lair of Lemonade Mouth's once-biggest tormentor, Ray Beech. The walk seemed to go on forever. Mo's mom had asked us to stop by to distribute picnic flyers at the community center and Paperback Joe's, and after that we continued down a turn off Wampanoag Road and Scott led us from there. Ray lived in the Claypit Farm area, a secluded and relatively rural part of Opequonsett at the opposite end of town, far from the main highway. In the entire year since I'd moved to Rhode Island I'd only passed through there two or three times.

While we hoofed it in near silence, I couldn't help noticing when Mo reached for Charlie's hand, or when Olivia rested her head on Wen's shoulder. I was happy for my friends, but for me these displays of affection were also painful reminders of how much I still missed Rajeev. We'd been calling and texting each other, but those things almost made it worse, kind of like describing water to a thirsty person. Tragically, I hadn't even thought to keep something of his, maybe a hoodie or a T-shirt or some other article of clothing I could have at least worn to remind myself of what being close to him felt like.

But I didn't dwell on this. I was making a conscious effort to live in the here and now; I refused to let self-pity get the better of me.

"There it is," Scott said at last. "Up ahead, where the road turns."

At first I was confused. All I saw was an abandoned gas station with boarded-up windows. It looked like it had been out of business for quite a while. Surely Ray didn't live there.

But then a hundred feet or so behind it I noticed a depressing little one-story brown house with a chain-link fence and a couple of rusty old cars on cinder blocks. It looked like a junkyard.

"That's it? *That's* where Ray Beech lives?"

Scott nodded. "Yup. When we were little we used to tie ropes to branches and swing from his roof. The place had more trees back then."

I took in the mounds of mud and unidentifiable crap scattered across the enormous backyard. Near the side fence there was a wooden hutch with a railed-off area in front of it, like an animal pen. Finally we reached the front gate, where we were welcomed by a sign with big red letters that said, PRIVATE PROPERTY, KEEP OUT! THAT MEANS YOU!

Scott must have noticed us staring at the unfriendly message. He shrugged.

"That's from Ray's dad. He can be kind of a . . ." He seemed to search for the word. ". . . character."

All any of us could do was nod. Ignoring the sign, Scott led us through the front gate. I glanced around in case we were about to be charged by attack dogs or something, but seconds later all of us stood huddled behind Scott on the front step of the house. I could hear the faint sound of a television. Somebody was home. My palms were sweating like crazy by then, and I don't think I was the only one. After all, this was the home turf of Ray Beech, a gorilla-sized kid with a mean streak and a grudge against Lemonade Mouth. There was no way to know for sure how he might react.

I hoped we weren't making a mistake. For all we knew, this was about to get ugly.

"Go ahead, Scott," Wen whispered. "Ring the bell."

We waited, but Scott was just standing there staring at the doorknob like it might bite him or something. He glanced back at us, and all at once I felt awful for him. For the first time I could see in his face just how hard losing his best friend must have been on him for the past few months. I realized how much he had at stake right now.

Mo gave his shoulder an encouraging squeeze. "It's okay. No matter what happens, we're right here."

He nodded. "I'm warning you guys. As soon as Ray sees me he'll probably slam the door in my face." He took a deep breath and rang the bell.

Moments later we heard footsteps, and then a series of clicking sounds—locks unlatching. By the number of them it must have been like Fort Knox in there. Finally the door swung open and we were looking at an all-too-familiar hulking figure, one that I associated with high school tyranny and oppression of the voiceless and powerless.

Ray Beech.

It would be an understatement to say that Ray appeared surprised to see Scott at his doorstep with Lemonade Mouth standing behind him. He blinked at us, looking disheveled and confused, as if he'd spent the morning with his head planted on a sofa only to find himself suddenly face to face with invaders from the planet What The Heck Is Going On Here? I thought he was going to get angry, but instead he glanced around at the junk piled on the patchy ground behind us and I'm pretty sure I saw his face turn pink. Maybe he was embarrassed at the state of his yard.

After that, Scott and Ray leveled their gazes on each other.

"So . . . I came by to see you," Scott began, "because I've been trying to talk with you even though you haven't been making it easy. It's been too long, man."

Ray curled his lip a little but didn't close the door. His voice was expressionless. "I see you brought some . . . friends."

"That's right."

Another uncomfortable silence passed, and then Wen spoke up. "Ray, we . . . uh, we came along because we wanted to let you know that even though things haven't always been great between you and us, we don't see any point in carrying the hard feelings forever. If you're up for it, we want to put all the bad stuff behind us and start over again. What do you say?"

Ray's jaw went even tighter. He seemed to eye us with suspicion, studying our faces one at a time. I could see he wasn't sold on the idea of letting bygones be bygones. After all, in his mind, Scott had betrayed him and we were the cause. It occurred to me that Ray might be about to go off like a bomb blast. At the very least, I expected to be sent packing.

But then something both bizarre and amazing happened.

"What's *that*?" Olivia asked out of nowhere.

Everyone turned to see her pointing toward the hutch near the fence. At that very moment I saw something move on the ground just outside of the open door of the pen. Whatever it was, it was very large and very pink and it made a sudden, loud snorting sound as an entire mound of dirt seemed to roll over. My friends, I'd been feeling jittery anyway, so that unexpected blast of noise sent my stomach into my throat. I was on the verge of making a run for it. The thing lifted its giant, hairy head, and then I recognized what it was—not an attack dog, but something weirder.

An enormous pig.

I stared. It didn't seem angry or anything. It was just lying there on a patch of grass. It looked like it was sunning itself. If a pig can smile lazily at a group of stunned high school musicians, this one did.

"Holy crap!" I heard myself whisper.

But far from seeming surprised, Scott looked thrilled. He hopped off the step and started ambling in the direction of the beast. "Bacon Sandwich!" he said. "How are you, girl?" And then back to Ray he called, "Dude, she's trimming down! She's looking good!"

Olivia followed him. It's no newsflash that the girl had a thing for animals, so I honestly think she couldn't help herself. Still in the doorway, Ray was watching all this without a word.

But not me. "You have a *pig*?" I asked, still gaping. "What is she, like . . . a pet?"

He narrowed his eyes. "Well, I'm never going to *eat* her, if that's what you mean, Stella. Yeah, she's a pet. So what?"

Before long, Charlie, Mo and Wen were heading over there too. I guess their curiosity got the best of them. But I stayed put. Let's just say that I'm not exactly a farm girl. I prefer to stay at a safe distance from anything that looks like it might want to swallow me.

Ray must have recognized my skittishness. "She's not going to hurt anyone," he said, chuckling. "She's a sweetheart. She's as gentle as they come."

The next thing I knew, he stepped through the doorway and sauntered past me, following everyone. By then the others were next to the giant animal. Scott looked like he was reconnecting with an old friend. For its part, the pig seemed just as happy as he was, and pleased to be getting so much attention. It sat up and snorted cheerfully, rubbing its snout against Scott's sleeve.

Yuck.

I wasn't comfortable being the only one still waiting by the house, though, so after a moment I decided to drift closer.

Closer, but not *too* close.

For the next few minutes we gathered around what turned out to be a two-hundred-pound porker with the temperament of a lazy dog. It was like the whole confrontation thing was temporarily put on hold. Ray just stood there while Scott told the story of where the pig came from. Apparently Ray's dad had brought her home years ago because he'd decided on a whim that it'd be fun to raise a pig for meat. But when the time came to do the deed, Ray, who was still a little kid, caused such a fuss of screaming and crying that his mom made his dad give her to him.

"Ray's done an amazing job with her," Scott told us, scratching behind her ears as the pig grunted. "He's always been great with animals. He raised rabbits and turtles and pigeons too. Bacon Sandwich here is my favorite, though. She's the smartest hog you'll ever meet. I've known her since she was a piglet. How long ago was that, Ray?"

"Seven years," he said quietly.

Olivia was thrilled. She squatted right down in the dirt beside it and started petting its neck. Mo and Charlie were right there with her. I, on the other hand, was still coming to terms with the revelation that Ray Beech, the loudmouth behemoth of Opequonsett High School, had a soft spot for animals. Who knew? I secretly studied him as he stood there watching all this affection get lavished on his hoofed companion, and I swear I saw the same kind of glow you see in a proud parent when his kid does something good.

And after a closer examination I couldn't deny that Bacon Sandwich *was* kind of cute. For a pig.

After a while Charlie, who can be a heck of a lot smarter than people give him credit for, casually turned to Ray and said, "Hey, listen, Ray, we never told you this, but all of us liked Mudslide Crush's music and we were sorry to hear that you guys stopped playing as a band."

Ray didn't answer. His face flushed again and his gaze dropped to the ground. Then I saw Mo look over at Wen, who seemed to understand. If ever there was a time to spring the big idea, this was it.

"Yeah, so . . . ," Wen said, picking it up from there, "we don't know if you've heard already, but we're throwing a big picnic event this Saturday and Lemonade Mouth is going to perform. The thing is, an entire afternoon is a whole lot of time for a single band to fill with music, so we were thinking that it sure would be nice to have another band there with us. You know, to break it up a little."

Ray looked up. Scott did too.

Other than the pig, everybody went quiet, waiting to hear what Ray would say. He was looking around at all of us as what we were saying finally sank in.

His stony expression started to fade.

WEN
Veering from the Expected Path

Saturday morning it drizzled on and off. There were a couple of panicked phone calls from the Hirshes and the Banerjees because rain hadn't been in the forecast.

'One thing I'll say about Sydney, she's cool in a crisis.

"It's going to clear," she assured them. "And if it doesn't, then we'll make the best of it. Everyone can just pack lunches and we'll move it into the gym. No big deal. We already have the okay to do that."

But I wasn't so sure moving the entire picnic into the high school would really end up being no big deal. For one thing, I doubted as many people would come. Who wants to picnic inside? Plus, my friends and I had been looking forward to playing an outdoor show.

The other thing weighing on me was something my dad had told us the previous night. He'd called us all to the kitchen table for a family meeting.

"Sydney and I have been spending a lot of time looking over our finances," he'd said. "Wieners on Wheels has been a fun experiment, but it's pretty clear that it's not going to take off the way we need it to."

"So . . . what are you saying?" I'd asked. "It's over? You're not going to do it anymore?"

He nodded. "The business just isn't sustainable. We're cutting our losses now before we end up getting deeper into debt than we already are. I already spoke with my old boss and he offered me my job back."

Sydney rubbed his shoulder sympathetically. "It wasn't an easy decision."

George kept quiet, but from his expression I could tell he understood this was a big deal. But something was bothering me. Not long ago the end of my dad's wiener business would have been exactly what I wanted, but now it didn't feel so good.

"So . . . you're going to be an insurance adjuster again, just like that?" I asked. "You're going back to your old life?"

"Not until September, when you kids are back in school.

Hey, don't look so glum, Wen. It's fine. I'm okay with it. Actually, I'm lucky. At least I have something to fall back on. Lots of people are out of work right now."

Later, I couldn't stop thinking about that conversation. My dad had said he was fine, but I was surprised at how hard the news was hitting me. Sure, I was glad my days of standing on the sidewalk dressed as finger food were ending, but I still couldn't help feeling bad about the whole thing. Terrible, actually. My father's new business was officially a failure. He'd worked hard trying to make a major change in his life only to have to go back to his old, unsatisfying job like a dog with his tail between his legs.

I didn't say so, but I had a hard time imagining how he could really be okay with that.

It turned out Sydney was right about the weather. By eleven o'clock, when a bunch of us showed up at the high school to start setting up barbecues and sound equipment, the sky had cleared. The rain had even washed away some of the humidity, making it more comfortable in the heat.

It was a beautiful day for a town picnic.

By the time we'd set up the instruments, the parking lot was already starting to fill, so I could tell we were going to have a decent turnout. I was just helping Mr. Banerjee set up a bathroom direction sign when I heard Naomi Fishmeier call out to me from across the field.

"Get 'em while you still can, Wen!" she said.

She and Lyle were holding up hot dogs that they must have just scored from the wiener van, which was behind them. My dad had brought Penelope out for this one last event before putting her up for sale. "She should be worth something," he'd explained to me. "Not only did I make a bunch of improvements to her as a food-service vehicle, but she could still be a good passenger van too. Who knows? We might even get some decent money for her."

I could only blink at him. Surely he was kidding. I tried to imagine who the heck would want to buy a rusty bright yellow van with a giant plastic hot dog welded to the roof. Is there really a market for a thing like that?

Plus, I wasn't going to admit it, but as surprising as it might sound, I had misgivings about getting rid of that crazy van. Penelope was so ancient and over-the-top ridiculous that in a weird way she actually had a certain kind of cool. I'd only recently come to realize that. She'd also been there for us when we'd needed her, and for that I kind of felt like she'd earned a special place with Lemonade Mouth, almost like a mascot. The five of us had joked about it, but I knew we all felt the same way.

I waved at Naomi and gave her a thumbs-up sign. I'd downed zillions of hot dogs that summer; what was one more? I had to pay my last respects.

Half an hour later the field was crammed with blankets and people. I guess the flyers worked, because more cars showed up than any of us had expected. Some families set up barbecues, others brought pizzas or coolers with sandwiches or whatever, and everybody settled in for what turned out to be quite a celebration. Someone had even made yellow T-shirts with a screenshot from our *American Pop Sensation* audition, so wherever I turned I was seeing images of my friends and me staring down those three surprised-looking judges. Since that time, after the media backlash from our audition, there'd been a noticeable shift in the tone of the show. The judges didn't always like the acts, but it was hard to miss that their criticism was now being delivered with a tad less venom.

I guess we felt just a little bit proud of that, and when we saw those T-shirts they kind of brought the point home. Below the screenshot of us, whoever made the shirts had added words in stark black letters:

"STAND UP FOR RESPECT!
LET THE WORLD SEE IT MEANS SOMETHING TO YOU!"
—LEMONADE MOUTH

Wow.

And that wasn't the only jaw dropper. Somebody else had gone to a printer and made a giant banner that now hung from one of the basketball nets. It was a blown-up image of the *Howit Iz* article—including a photo from our performance on *After Midnight with Chet Anders*. Above it in yellow and black marker somebody had written, *Thank you, Lemonade Mouth! Don't Stop the Revolution!*

When they first raised it up there, we all stared.

None of us had expected this.

I remember Charlie, Stella and me walking around in a daze as people kept coming up to us and saying things like "You guys rock!" or "Lemonade Mouth tells it like it is!" Word had gotten out about what happened at Take Charge, and there was a lot of sympathy about that, but to this crowd it didn't seem to matter that we never made it big. They treated us like celebrities anyway, raising their lemonade cups and telling us we'd made the town proud.

It was all pretty overwhelming. Sure, our parents had told

us this would be a Lemonade Mouth picnic, but we never imagined that people would show us that much support and respect. I didn't know what to say.

One of the things that struck me most, though, was when this little shaggy-haired kid I didn't even know came up to me with his mother and asked if I would please sign his T-shirt. He was maybe six years old or so, and super shy, but as I signed the shirt his mom explained to me that the kid was asking her for a trumpet now. He'd told her he wanted to learn to play it because he wanted to be like me.

I didn't even know how to answer. It was the first time anybody had ever said anything like that to me. It was a huge honor.

The little boy waved me closer. He wanted to whisper in my ear. "Somebody told me the revolution is over. It's not true, right?"

"No, buddy," I said. "Don't worry."

I didn't have the heart to tell him what I really thought, which was that Lemonade Mouth's brief moment in the spotlight was probably behind us.

Eventually my friends and I went to our instruments and the crowd settled down to hear us. I can honestly say that that afternoon was one of the most fun concerts we ever played. *Ever.* From the first notes of "Humanator," our opening song, the crowd started to cheer like crazy, and as soon as the chorus kicked in, pretty much everyone was dancing. Charlie did an extended funky solo in "Ninja Earthquake," and for "Monster Maker" Mrs. Reznik joined us onstage with a cello and harmonized with Mo's bass. The crowd went nuts. For an old lady, Mrs. Reznik can totally rock. Olivia had never sounded better either, and for the first time ever, she hardly seemed anxious at all. I'd never seen her so relaxed in front of a crowd. Now, I'm not saying everything was perfect from then on, or that she never got nervous in front of people again, but something had obviously happened to make her better able to deal with her feelings. And that was good.

I can't tell you how glad I was to see her this way, just singing and having a great time without worrying so much about everything.

After we finished our first set Lyle made an announcement to unveil the boxes of our new, completed recordings—our second official release. We'd all chipped in to have the CDs made, and we'd decided to call the album "Pucker Up!" Sydney had designed an eye-catching cover: a simple extreme close-up on pursed yellow lips against a checkered background. When you looked closely, though, each of the dark checkers was a black-and-white image of one of our five faces.

We were thrilled.

Okay, so this album wasn't going to get the Decker and Smythe national marketing treatment we'd once hoped for, but at least it was finally done. And the people at the picnic were gobbling it up.

As Olivia and I stuffed our faces with barbecue and corn on the cob, a few kids wandered through the crowd in some of the costumes from our appearance on *After Midnight with Chet Anders*. They looked hilarious. It was then that I caught sight of my dad, who was busy with the hot dogs, and I couldn't help remembering how he would soon be back to his old job again. But my thoughts didn't linger there for too long because all of a sudden a drumbeat was pulsing through the air. Ray and Scott were at their instruments.

Mudslide Crush was about to perform for the first time in ages.

The crowd started moving toward the stage again. Olivia and I were as excited as anybody else. Ray was at the microphone. It felt odd to admit it to myself, but it was good to see him up there again, and I was happy for his sake and ours that he'd agreed to do it. (He'd even toyed with the idea of bringing Bacon Sandwich to the festivities, but in the end he didn't, maybe because a barbecue wasn't the best place to bring a pet pig.) We cheered along with the rest of the crowd as Ray strutted back and forth like an oversized rooster with an attitude and a mud-brown Stratocaster. Acting cocky had always been part of his onstage persona, and it worked. He was fun to watch. Since Mudslide Crush's original bass player, Dean Eagler, had already moved away to Ohio for college, taking his place was Lizzie DeLucia, who gripped her new pink bass like she was holding on for dear life. Nervous as she looked, she was doing just fine. And then Ray kicked in a rocking guitar lick that made the crowd roar. There was no denying that this new Mudslide Crush lineup sounded terrific. At his drums, Scott looked like he might keel over from sheer happiness.

All this made me think of what Mo had said about time marching on. Back before the school year ended, who would have thought I'd ever be cheering for Scott Pickett, let alone Ray Beech? But I guess my dad was right about people changing. And I'm not just talking about Scott and Ray.

I looked again in my dad's direction. He was watching all this from the window of the wiener van. Seeing his grinning face, I realized he looked more relaxed than I'd seen in a long, long time, and all at once it struck me that maybe, just maybe, I understood why. After all, my father had done something few people ever dare to do. He'd taken a chance. He'd made a decision to step off the path everyone expected

268

him to follow and had taken a shot at going after his dreams. How many people can say that? And sure, his new business hadn't worked out the way he'd hoped, but that didn't mean the experience had been worthless to him. There I'd been feeling bad, thinking his life was going back to the way it once was, but now I understood that it just wasn't true. His life would *never* be the same again because *he* wasn't the same. While I'd been busy complaining, my father had been working his butt off to do something meaningful in his life. Something that was important to him.

And he had. Despite everything, I could see it on his face. He absolutely had.

More than ever it struck me that my dad is an amazing guy, and that I'm proud to be his son.

CHARLIE
Listening to the Cosmos

It was a couple of days after the picnic, and I was on the front steps of my house with Olivia's book and a tuna sandwich. For a long, long time, I just sat there. I do a lot of my best thinking on my front steps, and that morning my thoughts kept coming back to two things: Nietzsche and the meaninglessness of the Universe.

Look, I'm not saying we didn't have a great experience at the picnic. We did. It was amazing. But come on, that was just a town picnic, a small-time gig if ever there was one. After all that had happened that summer, I kind of felt like Lemonade Mouth had come close to something really, really big, only to have it snatched from us at the last second. Where was the meaning in that? It would be depressing to think Nietzsche was right, but what else was there to conclude? If the great forces of the cosmos were trying to say something, I sure as heck didn't know what it was.

Plus, the feeling that there was something I needed to find, something important that would help me sift through all the chaos of what had happened and somehow find order in it, was still needling me. The answer seemed so close, and yet weeks of trying to figure it out had brought me nothing.

Zippo.

Nada.

So if I was starting to feel a little like the center of futility in a pointless world, could you really blame me?

I guess sometimes I get so lost in my thoughts that I tune out everything around me, and I must have done that then, because after a while of sitting out there on the porch, I suddenly realized somebody was standing right in front of me. Somehow they'd come up close and I hadn't even noticed.

EXTERIOR. CHARLIE'S FRONT YARD—LATE MORNING

The camera sees what Charlie sees: a shadowy, indistinct image of a person only a few feet away on his front lawn. Slowly the slight angle of the frame straightens and the picture comes into focus. We see that it's a girl, and then we recognize her. It's Olivia. Her forehead is wrinkled with concern.

OLIVIA
Charlie? Were you sleeping?

REVERSE ON: Charlie. His hair is disheveled. He straightens up, rubbing his eyes.

CHARLIE
No, I don't think so. I was just . . . thinking. About stuff.

We see them both now. For a few seconds Olivia just stands there looking at him. From his expression it's clear that Charlie is glad to see her but is wondering why she's there. Then he appears to remember something. He reaches around, grabs Olivia's book and holds it out to her.

> CHARLIE
>
> Hey, I want to return this to you. I'm done with it. Thanks for the loan.

> OLIVIA
>
> No problem. Did you ever find what you were searching for?

> CHARLIE
>
> (shakes his head)
> I think maybe whatever I was searching for doesn't really exist.

> OLIVIA
>
> Oh. Sorry.

> CHARLIE
>
> (shrugs)
> It's okay.

> OLIVIA
>
> (fumbling with her Scooby-Doo backpack
> and slipping the book inside)
> Listen, I was just passing by on my way to the library and I saw you. If you're not too busy, want to come along?

Charlie thinks about it a moment and then gets up off the steps. In a single long shot we see him accompany Olivia across his yard and down the sidewalk. As they get smaller in the frame we hear Charlie's Voice-over:

> CHARLIE (V.O.)
>
> Now, normally I'm more of a TV guy than a library person, so I'm not sure why I agreed to go. I guess maybe I was feeling a little down and I was glad to have somebody to talk to. I told her about a new idea I'd thought of, an idea of writing everything down. At the end of the school year

271

I was forced to write an English Comp paper about how the five of us met and what happened to us that first year, and it had been complete torture writing it, but it also ended up helping me make sense of it all. So now I was amazed to find myself wondering if maybe I should try writing *another* school paper. Only this time not for school. Yeah, I know. It sounds ridiculous, but there it was.

The camera is following them again, this time with a medium shot as they amble up the sidewalk.

CHARLIE

It's just an idea, though, and probably a stupid one too, because first of all, I have no clue how I would even tell the story of our summer. So much happened at once. And anyway, the idea of filling up all those pages with paragraph after paragraph gives me a headache. I'm not really a writer. Maybe I shouldn't do it at all.

He waits for a response, but Olivia stares straight ahead, silent and unreadable, as she so often is. So he continues. . . .

CHARLIE (CONT'D)

Plus, I have no idea if I'll even *find* any meaning in what happened. It's not like we got famous or anything. What kind of a story is that? What was the point?

OLIVIA

(finally looking at him, she slows her pace)
The point? Of Lemonade Mouth?

CHARLIE

Yeah. So, we're all good friends and we play at a town picnic and have a good time. What the heck kind of lame ending is that? Where are our groupies and cool clothes? Where are our private jets? Where's the big concert at Madison Square Garden?

Olivia gives him a hard stare, and then . . .

OLIVIA

Charlie, this isn't a Disney movie.

CHARLIE

(a shrug)

Yeah, I know. But still, it would've been pretty cool, don't you think?

She rolls her eyes. With a shake of her head she turns and keeps walking. Charlie follows, and for a while the camera hangs back as they continue down the sidewalk in silence, each lost in their own thoughts.

Okay, so they say descriptions of screen action shouldn't include too much about a character's thoughts or backstory or stuff like that, but that's exactly what I want to put here, so that's why I'm breaking the rules and mixing different formats and stuff, which I've kind of been doing all along. (I guess I'm a rebel that way. Ha ha.) Plus, it just feels right switching to regular sentences for this next part.

So we finally got to the library, and that's when something weird happened to me. I don't normally get panic attacks or anything, but for some reason, being surrounded by so many shelves stuffed high with books and magazines, a sea of words in all directions, left me feeling like the walls were pressing in on me. The air smelled of homework, and all at once my mouth felt like sandpaper and my pulse was going like a burglar alarm.

I forced myself to keep cool.

Whatever was happening was weird, but I knew it was all in my head.

"I don't get what you see in this place," I whispered as we passed through the maze of bound paper volumes. "Hasn't anybody here heard of the digital revolution?"

"If you don't get it, then I'm not going to try to convince you," Olivia said.

I trailed along until she found an empty table. She set her stuff down and took one of the seats.

"You come here a lot?" I asked. "Even during the summer?"

She nodded.

"What for? What do you do?"

"I read, mostly. I also like to write here sometimes. It's big and quiet and it's good for working on my journal. You know, figuring stuff out." By then she'd reached into her backpack and pulled out two pencils and a spiral notebook. "Here," she said, ripping a few blank sheets from the notebook and holding them out to me, "you should give it a try. Just jot down your thoughts, whatever they are."

"I told you. I'm no good at that. I'm not really a writer."

"You just gotta keep at it. It gets easier, you know, the more you do it."

She was still holding the paper out to me, so after a while I took it. And then, for what felt like days, I sat at that table staring at those blank pages and wondering how on earth I was supposed to start. Beginnings are so hard. In the end I decided to scribble some words—any words—just to get me going. I wrote the first thing that came to my head:

Once upon a time . . .

And that's as far as I got. Only four words into my story and already I was disappointed. In my mind I could see Lemonade Mouth doing all the things we did that summer, and I could hear our voices saying all the things we said. If I was going to write the story, then I wanted it to somehow be like that—like how I was viewing it at that moment. Weird as it sounds, I realized that this was really important to me, that if I could do it, it could bring me the clarity I wanted. But how? No matter how hard I tried, I couldn't figure out what exactly I was looking for.

So eventually I gave up. I left the table and wandered around.

INTERIOR. PUBLIC LIBRARY—LATE MORNING

The library is almost silent except for Charlie's echoing footsteps. He drifts between endless stacks of bookshelves, warily scanning the bindings. We see him meander through the home repair section. Now he's exploring the art history section. He gazes at shelf after shelf but nothing grabs him, so he moves on.

Finally he comes to a little corridor of bookcases with an overhead sign that says MOVIES, TELEVISION AND THE CREATIVE ARTS. He stops. We see him read the sign.

CLOSE-UP ON: Charlie's finger. One by one it slides across titles like *Hollywood Ghouls and Monsters* and *The Golden Age of the Television Sitcom* and *A Dictionary of Literary Terms*. Finally his finger comes to a book called *Screenwriting: A Beginner's Guide*. It stops. After a pause, Charlie's hand pulls that one from the shelf.

REVERSE ON: Charlie. He's studying the cover. He opens it to a random page. He's taking it in, concentrating. Suddenly the silence is broken by an energetic tombak drum beat. Soft at first, it builds in volume. It's the opening riff of Lemonade Mouth's "Blastoff Castaways." After a while Charlie looks up, lost in thought.

We see him drift to an armchair and for a few measures we watch him sitting there, reading, with the book open on his lap.

A screaming electric ukulele joins the music—hot chords of triumphant energy. The bass and trumpet kick in too, and now the camera begins to slowly pull back. As the view widens away from Charlie, we see more and more of the library around him: An elderly couple peruses the shelves of a nearby bookcase. A teenage boy types at a laptop. A middle-aged woman reads a newspaper while, at her side, a little kid sits cross-legged on the floor with a picture book.

Smaller and smaller on the screen, Charlie remains motionless in the armchair. He's on the verge of a transformation. The world may be continuing around him unaware, but Charlie's universe has just spoken, sending him on an unexpected new journey of exploration and discovery.

The music takes over.

FADE OUT.

STELLA
The Great and Mysterious Conductor

The summer wasn't over yet, but already it had been a time of meteoric highs and desperate lows. Our music was still getting downloaded (Lyle told us "Zombietown" was starting to do especially well), but giving away music isn't exactly a long-term business strategy, and it wasn't like we were household names or anything.

Let's just say we didn't feel so overexposed that we needed disguises to leave the house.

Olivia once told me that everything that ever happens was always meant to be, that life's events, no matter how large or small, are like train stops on a journey where nobody but some great and mysterious conductor knows the route, let alone the final destination. Things might *seem* random and maybe even a little unfair at times, she said, but if we wait long enough, the grand purpose will eventually reveal itself. I never used to believe that, but when I look back at that chaotic time and its aftermath in the months that followed, I can't help but be amazed at how things played out in ways none of us could have predicted but that seem to have been inevitable.

Take Franco, for example.

After our appearance on *American Pop Sensation*, the backlash against him grew until finally, sometime in October, somebody somewhere uncovered an old video clip of Franco singing a Broadway tune called "Send in the Clowns" at a karaoke competition. It turned out that Franco had a singing voice like a drowning duck with a nasal problem. Both jaw-dropping and hilarious to watch, the video shot to the top of the most-watched rankings. Whoever uploaded it even took the trouble to add choice *APS* clips of Franco giving some of his most cutting insults, so he seemed to be tearing his own performance apart. After the revelation that Franco was no better than the acts he'd cruelly ridiculed, he became a national punch line and eventually resigned from the show in humiliation.

I actually felt sorry for the guy.

On the other hand, I hear he's doing all right now. He started a one-man lima bean farm in eastern Wyoming far from other people, where he practices meditation as a way of overcoming the inner anger he's carried since childhood. I'm told he's never been happier or more relaxed.

And then there was SNaP. That autumn I began to notice less-traditional models showing up in advertisements. Beautiful full-figured women in glamorous poses. Skinny academic-looking guys relaxing on the beach or posing as construction workers while attractive women eyed them appreciatively from afar. Kids with actual acne that hadn't been airbrushed away, and it wasn't being treated as something horrifying or even remarkable. At first it was hard to get used to but, boy, did it feel good.

It felt like Lemonade Mouth had been heard.

Perhaps the most gratifying moment for me, though, was seeing the smiling faces of Ruby, Glenda and Glenda on the magazine cover of *New Music Weekly*. The article inside told the story of how, after their *APS* appearances, Earl Decker had taken the three of them on as clients, combining them into a single act. The writer implied that signing the scrawny, birdlike girl and those stocky teen twins was just Earl's way of riding the new "Get Real" wave, but I didn't think so. Earl Decker may have been many things, but there's no denying he was a genius at recognizing musical potential, so when I read that article it hit me that he'd done it again. By blending little Ruby's incredible voice with the creative musicianship and backup vocals of those banjo-playing twins, Earl might just have created yet another pop sensation for the ages. And time proved him right. As everyone knows, that first album by Ruby and the Glendas went platinum and is already considered a classic. My friends and I couldn't be happier for them.

But all that came later, of course.

Compatriots, when I recall myself in the waning weeks of that momentous summer, I see a different girl from the one whose fingers trembled the first time she dialed the offices of Decker and Smythe. While it's true that I secretly still yearned for the elusive glory that comes from general acceptance, it's also true that playing gigantic stadiums or otherwise rising to the top of the music charts was no longer my central concern. No, my attention had moved on to more important matters, and even small-seeming moments now sometimes glittered with real, lasting significance.

Case in point:

A couple of days after the Lemonade Mouth picnic, I returned home from band practice to find my older sister and my two little brothers huddled around a large package that sat on the kitchen table. As soon as I stepped through the doorway, all three eager gazes moved from the package to me. Right away I knew something was up. It was as if they were expecting me to turn into a platypus or something.

"Um . . . what's going on?" I asked.

"This just got delivered," Clea informed me, barely hiding a smirk. "It's addressed to you."

I still didn't understand. I wasn't expecting a package and, in any case, so what? What was the big deal? But Tim cleared up that mystery by contorting his face into a fourth-grade version of a suggestive leer and saying, "We think it's from your *boyfriend*! Open it up, Stella! We want to see what it is!"

His equally sophisticated twin, Andy, started making loud kissy noises, which triggered peals of laughter from his brother. Even Clea seemed to fight back a snicker.

Now, by that time I was pretty much immune to their childish taunts, and anyway, I was too curious to care what they said. I ran to the box. There was no return address, but even before I recognized the familiar handwriting I noticed that the postmark said *Lubbock, TX,* which for me was evidence enough of who had sent it. My heart leapt.

Rajeev!

The package was big enough to hold a cocker spaniel but not heavy. I shook it a little. Nothing inside seemed to move.

"Go on," Clea urged. "What are you doing, savoring the moment? Open it."

So I did. I grabbed a pair of scissors from the kitchen

drawer, and a few seconds later all four of us were staring eagerly into the darkness of the box as I peeled back the top flaps and saw what it was.

A cowboy hat.

Dusty black with a weathered look, a pinch-front crown and a wide brim, it was like something you might see on a lone-wolf drifter in an old western.

There was also a handwritten note:

Howdy, pardner,

Please accept this token of esteem from me and the great state of Texas, where the sky goes on forever and the tumbleweeds drift free.

Yours even across a great distance,
—Rajeev

I lifted the hat from the box and held it in front of me. It was by far the coolest thing I'd ever seen in my whole life. I sent out a silent thank-you to the boy I missed with a fiery passion, the one who seemed to know me so well it was scary. And then, for the first time ever, I placed that amazing hat on my head and felt its untamed power settle over me.

Even my sister and stepbrothers were wowed into respectful silence.

The world is a mysterious place.

The very next night, with only two weeks before we had to return to school, when there was little reason to expect the summer would have anything else in store for us, my friends and I were hanging out listening to music in my basement when my phone rang. I almost hit the ceiling when I saw who it was.

Sista Slash.

Blunt and friendly as ever, Sista told us she was glad she'd reached us, and that she was sorry things hadn't worked out for us at the festival. She added that things hadn't worked out too well for her either. (Which we knew, of course, since it had been all over the news how she'd sunk a lot of her own money into that festival and had ended up losing it.)

"Believe it or not, my blasted accountant is telling me I'm practically broke, at least on paper," she said with a calmness I found hard to understand. "But that's rock and roll for you. One day you're soaring like a jet and the next day your engines burst into flames. No worries, though. I've been down once or twice before and I've always come back. No doubt I'll do it again. In the meantime," she said, "I have another idea, if you guys are interested."

While we crowded around the speakerphone, she explained that she'd decided to waste no time picking up the pieces and was getting right back into the game. If Sista Slash was anything, she was a survivor. She'd already scheduled a special end-of-summer engagement—three whirlwind evening gigs at a small club in her hometown of Sweetwater, Texas, where she'd gotten her start. Her plan was to record her next album there. She'd written more than a dozen new songs that she was going to record live in front of her most devoted fans, and a film crew was going to capture every onstage and offstage moment for a later video release.

Sista was calling us, she said, because she wanted to know if Lemonade Mouth would be interested in doing it with her. She wanted us to be her opening act.

"You kids are a perfect fit, and we've already seen how well you come off on camera," she said. "It's short notice again, I know, and the truth is I can't fly you guys down, but if you can convince your parents to get you and your instruments to the Lone Star State somehow, I have a friend with a gigantic house that we can all stay in together for a few days—you guys plus your families, whoever you want to bring along."

My mom was with us too by then. She must have recognized the voice from upstairs, because she was at the top of the basement steps listening in.

"Look," Sista went on, sounding even more earnest through the speakerphone, "it may not be a megastadium or that Too Shy to Cry tour you guys were supposed to do, but it should bring you more exposure, and who knows, you might even get some useful recordings out of it, especially if you have new material. Either way, I promise it'll be good food, great fun and at least a memorable way to end your summer. Think of it as an adventure. So what do you say?"

For a few heartbeats nobody answered. Charlie was saucer-eyed, frozen in the middle of taking a bite from a slice of pizza. Wen and Mo looked like they'd lost the ability to talk.

But it was Olivia who had my attention. When our eyes met, it was as if she was reading my thoughts.

"I have a question," I said into the phone, keeping my voice steady. "How far is Sweetwater from Lubbock?"

"Oh, not so far. A couple hours by car, I guess. Why do you ask?"

Olivia raised an eyebrow at me.

Inside, my emotions were in such a whirl that for a few seconds I could hardly breathe. What seemed to be happening was too incredible to take in. Suddenly all the chaos of our lives, everything that had seemed so random and unfair, was falling smoothly into place, as if all along everything had always been pointing us in this direction.

As if somehow this was meant to be.

I have to admit, my friends, that at that moment I almost found myself believing in Olivia's mysterious conductor. In my mind I could practically hear Lemonade Mouth's train roaring forward, carrying us headlong down the tracks of destiny.

OLIVIA
Praying for a Moment

Dear Naomi,

Lives have a way of taking unexpected turns. Doors close, windows open, and who can predict any of it ahead of time?

I remember the night we all sat around at Stella's trying to figure out how the heck we were going to get to Texas for the first of Sista Slash's three shows, which was only five days away. We'd called another War Room meeting—an emergency gathering of our families and closest friends. It wasn't hard to convince everyone that this was a great opportunity and that we should grab it. The Banerjees, especially, were glad to have an excuse to fly to Texas, where they could also reconnect with Rajeev's family after so many years. But not everybody could fly. Money was an issue, and besides, we needed to get not only ourselves but also our instruments down there. Just shipping Charlie's drums would cost a fortune.

It was Sydney who had the solution. "Wait a minute," she said, "we still have Penelope, and she's in good enough condition to make the trip, right?"

"Well, sure," Wen's dad said, a little surprised. "She could definitely do it, I guess. . . ."

"So there's the answer. We postpone selling her. There's plenty of space. We can just load up the equipment and drive."

Wen's dad stared at her like he wasn't sure she was serious.

"But Sydney," Wen jumped in, "we're not talking about a ride around the block. The trip from here to Texas is . . . I don't know . . . far. It'd be one heck of a long drive."

So we looked it up. The journey would take thirty-two hours—and that was without stopping to eat or sleep. Plus, there was the ride back home to consider. At first I thought the idea was nuts. But I noticed Wen's dad was looking at Sydney again, and a smile was starting to spread across his lips.

"You know," he said, "in my twenties I drove across the country with my buddies a couple of times. I like road trips. If we split up the driving we could make it to Sweetwater in just a couple of days. They'd be long days but fun. An adventure."

"And on the way back," Sydney added, "we could take our time and see part of the country. A mini-vacation."

Wen's dad reached for her hand. "I like the sound of that."

"Me too," Sydney said softly. For a weird second it seemed like maybe they were going to kiss. Wen must have thought so too, because he suddenly looked uncomfortable.

But they didn't. Not just then, anyway.

After that the momentum started to build. First they asked who else wanted to come along. "With all the seats in, the van fits up to fifteen. If we rent a trailer for the luggage and equipment, then we'll have space to reinstall however many seats we need. Who's in? It'll be an end-of-summer road trip to remember!"

Next thing I knew, Brenda was accepting the invitation (which meant I was doing it too), saying she thought it could be fun. I had to admit that as crazy as it seemed at first, traveling in the van did solve a lot of problems. Then Charlie announced that he wanted to come, and his mother said she did too, and offered to share in the driving. Stella was in on it next. As each of my friends agreed to this, I was actually getting more excited about the idea.

Mo was the last to say yes. "All that time on the highway?" she said. "I don't think so. What on earth are we going to do for thirty-two whole hours?"

But Stella already had the answer. "Didn't you hear what Sista told us? She said we ought to have some new material to record down there. Well, we don't—not yet, anyway. But answer me this, guys—how many new songs do you think the five of us can come up with in two days?"

We looked around at each other.

And that's how it happened.

In retrospect, it's amazing how quickly everyone pulled their plans together. It felt like a dream, as if we were all swept up in the excitement of a crazy idea. But when I later wrote to my father about it, his take was that sometimes the biggest and best ideas arrive that way, from quick decisions made on the spur of the moment—even when meaningless choices, like what to eat for lunch, might take us ages to decide.

So there we were on a Tuesday morning with our bags packed and Penelope all ready to go. On such short notice Wen's dad had managed to find an enclosed trailer just big enough to fit Charlie's drums and most of the luggage, but not everything. A few items still had to be strapped on top of the van. A cooler. Tents and sleeping bags, in case we wanted to camp. Some other odds and ends. We wrapped it all in weatherproof tarps, strapping the bundles to the giant plastic hot dog, which helped to secure it all and would also give some added protection from any bad weather. Wen and I stood on the sidewalk gaping at the sight. We were going to make quite an impression traveling down the highway, all nine of us in an ancient yellow bomber complete with a trailer, a bundled roof and the ends of an enormous plastic bun sticking out at either end.

The morning was unseasonably cool. It felt like an early taste of fall. Even though we were setting out just after dawn, a small crowd came to see us off, including many of the same people who were going to fly down a day later to meet us in Texas: the Banerjees, Stella's mother, Mrs. Reznik, Mr. Hirsh—and of course you and Lyle too. Scott and Liz brought bagels for everyone, which was nice of them. They'd also offered to stop by our house every day to check in on the cats. By then Daisy, our wild, troubled child, had taken to burying herself in a shady spot so only her head would show. At least she was leaving the other cats alone. Plus, she seemed content, so who was I to judge?

As for my mother, I was already planning to send her a postcard from Memphis, where, according to her, she'd spent the happiest days of her life. A day or two earlier I'd received a note from her. She was doing better, she wrote, and she wanted me to know I had an open invitation to visit any time I liked.

Ours was never going to be a perfect relationship. I realized that now. But at least she was trying.

And so was I.

Wen's dad started the engine. He rang the bell and everybody waved and called out to each other as we pulled away. The next thing we knew, Stella was leaning back in her seat, her new cowboy hat (which had hardly left her head since it'd arrived) pulled forward so it partially covered her grinning face. She was already improvising a new uke riff, a progression with a vaguely country feel. Soon Charlie picked out a rhythm on a set of lap bongos. Mo joined in. Since there were only nine of us in the van (including Wen's little brother, George), there was just enough extra space in the empty back row for her bass, as long as she played it at an angle. Wen added a melody. He'd brought along his trumpet mute, which was his idea, but no one objected since in that small space the volume might otherwise have driven us all nuts before we even reached Connecticut.

In hindsight, of course, everyone knows that the music we created during that long, wild ride to Texas would end up being the key that opened the floodgates for us. Fate had more in store for my friends and me in Texas than anyone suspected, and our self-released "Sweetwater Unplugged" album would later become our first big international hit. I couldn't have known that then, but I already sensed that this new music was different from anything we'd created before. Something about it felt like uncharted territory. A new and unexpected direction for us.

And already my pulse was racing.

Before joining in with vocals, I decided to let this sound, so familiar and yet unfamiliar, play out a while, allowing it space to explore possibilities and discover its own mysterious equilibrium. Wen gave me a look that said he understood. I put my hand on his shoulder. Outside the window, the world whizzed past, but my thoughts were focused on this giant new phase of my life that had just begun and was happening all around me. Even in the middle of a grand adventure it's the little things that ground you to the moment and make you feel the most alive. For a long time I sat there taking it all in: The low rumble of the engine under the pulsing music. The glow of the rising sun against the glass. The smell of Mrs. Hirsh's coffee. The softness of Wen's shirt against my fingers. These were the things that mattered, the important details that pass you by if you don't take the time to notice them. But I never wanted to lose this feeling. I wanted to keep it with me.

I held my breath, closed my eyes, and prayed that this moment would never end.✸

ACKNOWLEDGMENTS

Much help goes into the creation of a book. I'm grateful to the many people who gave me their support along the way, including Dr. Jean Brown, The Commando Writers (Michael A. Di Battista, Peter DiIanni, Scott Fitts, Geoffrey H. Goodwin and David A. Kelly), Susan Green, Shauna Leggat, Andy McNicol, Barbara O'Connor, Bhavini and Hemant Patel, Jenny Silberman, John Taxiarchis, Lauren Whitney and Janet Zade.

Stephanie Lane Elliott, my editor and friend, deserves a special acknowledgment, as do all the good people at Random House who helped make this book happen, including Krista Vitola, Beverly Horowitz, Trish Parcell, Colleen Fellingham, Elizabeth Krych and others too numerous to list but whose efforts I truly appreciate.

Thanks also go to Debra Martin Chase and Gaylyn Fraiche for leading the charge that brought the Lemonade Mouth revolution to an even wider audience.

Finally, I wish to thank my children, Evan, Lucy and Zoe, for reading the various manuscript drafts and giving me their insights, and my wife, Karen, for her unwavering friendship and love.

MARK PETER HUGHES is the author of such celebrated books as *A Crack in the Sky; I Am the Wallpaper,* a New York Public Library Book for the Teen Age and a Book Sense Children's Pick; and *Lemonade Mouth,* an ASTAL Rhode Island Book of the Year, a Bank Street College of Education Best Children's Book of the Year (Outstanding Merit), and a Boston Authors Club Award Finalist. *Lemonade Mouth* was also adapted into a Disney Channel Original Movie. Mark was born in Liverpool, England, and lives in Massachusetts, where he is currently sipping lemonade, strumming a ukulele, and preparing for the revolution. Join him at markpeterhughes.com.

To My Students
at Williams College
Who, over the Years,
Have Contributed Much
to Our Shared Knowledge
of the USSR

Government in the
SOVIET UNION

Frederick L. Schuman

WILLIAMS COLLEGE

CROWELL COMPARATIVE GOVERNMENT SERIES

Thomas Y. Crowell Company

NEW YORK   ESTABLISHED 1834

Government in the
Soviet Union